A SEASON OF WEDDINGS

For Ivorji

A SEASON OF WEDDINGS

June Levine

Dublin

A Season Of Weddings
is first published by
New Island Books
2 Brookside,
Dundrum Road,
Dublin 14.

ISBN 1 874597 05 7

A catalogue record for this book is available from the
British Library.

New Island Books receives financial support from The
Arts Council (an Chomhairle Ealaíon), Dublin, Ireland.

Cover Design by Jon Berkeley.
Typesetting by Rapid Production
Printed in Ireland by Colour Books Ltd., Baldoyle,
Dublin.

"It is good to bathe in the waters of tradition,
but to drown in them is suicide."

Mahatma Gandhi

Glossary

Almirah: press
Baraat: bridegroom's procession
Bidi: handrolled cigarette
Burka: Muslim purdah cover
Charpot: rope bed
Chowkidah: caretaker
Dhobi: laundry man
Dhopalta: long scarf, part of Punjabi dress
Gurdwara: Sikh temple
Ji: honorific title, usually used towards one's elder
　　or better i.e. Gandhiji
Khurta: a man's white cotton shirt
Lehnga: Rajasthani dress
Ladoo: Sweets on par with wedding cake
Mataji: mother
Mehndi: adornment of henna dye on woman's hand
　　and feet
Namaste: hello, goodbye, greeting the divine in the other
Pandol: Hindi wedding canopy
Puja: prayer, blessing
Sarees: plural of sari, Indian woman's dress
Tonga: horse-drawn two-wheeled carriage

CHAPTER 1

We're here, Nora thought, Bombay. The light had broken on her side of the aeroplane and she could see small islands off the coast where there were fishing boats and men rowing smaller boats towards the shores.

For the most part, Nora had enjoyed the journey. She had never gone anywhere alone except from Dublin to London, and with a sense of relief she told herself, there was absolutely nothing that she could do about anything up there in the air. She was sick of going over and over things and determined to leave it all behind. Later, whenever panic threatened she refused to entertain it. Repeatedly she reminded herself that problems would wait. No fear of them disappearing. And her confidence grew as she flew to India on her own. She felt interesting. Life had a firsthand feel about it. It was going to be different.

Nora was distracted from the view by a grunt and turned to offer a hand to the old woman who was struggling up off the floor into the seat beside her, but the woman managed without help, acknowledging Nora with the slightest movement of her head.

The Air India hostess had tried to persuade her country woman that she would be more comfortable in her seat, but to no avail. The elder cocooned herself in a blanket on the floor.

The woman was slight as a child, her long white hair plaited against a grey cardigan over a brown Punjabi suit printed with apricot flowers. She rummaged in

9

her handbag until she found her false teeth and was about to settle them in her mouth when Nora looked away. When she glanced back, the woman was still and seemed to be no longer there. The seat might as well have been empty. Nora sensed that the woman had gone ahead to her home in India.

When the woman continued to sit as everyone else crushed past to get off the plane, Nora realised that there was no hurry. She remained in her seat until the way was clear and then as though by special invitation, followed the blanket-wrapped woman up the aisle towards the hostesses who stood by the door with their palms together in salutation: "*Namaste*". Outside, Nora was halted by the wall of heat left by yesterday's sun.

In the queue for immigration, she stood behind a straw-haired young couple who nuzzled and whispered to each other. She wished they would stop. Why should they? They're young, she chided herself. Sadness welled as she tried to ignore them and thought how wonderful it was to be in love and arriving in India. Stop it, she told herself. Here I am and this is the way it is. I should have gone off on my own years ago.

Her hand luggage had grown heavy and she put it down, shoving it with her foot as she shuffled along. She shuffled like that for an hour.

"Purpose of visit?" the immigration officer asked the young couple.

"Spiritual," the young man answered for both, and the stamp came down on their passports.

"Mrs Ryan? Mrs Nora Shee – ob – Si – ... Ah, your other good name Madam?"

"Nora Shiv – aun Mary," she said.

"Purpose of visit?"

"Wedding guest," she replied and was passed on.

Aunt Flo had warned her the airport would be chaotic. The floor was being washed by a woman with a small bucket, her arms alternating breast strokes with a grey cloth which left the air sharp with carbolic. Nora went with the crowd and as she waited for her cases to arrive on the conveyor belt she winced as parcels marked "fragile" were dropped from a height or thrown from one place to another. Porters were everywhere, grabbing luggage. While she hesitated, the porter who had offered his services latched on to a surer thing, a man who had called "Coollie!" at no one in particular. Nora managed to haul her cases onto a trolley with crooked wheels. She paused to take a breather and sat down.

Opposite, a man in a white shawl and a black skull cap faced the wall, rocking back and forth. A Jew, thought Nora, like at the Wailing Wall. Beside him was a middle-aged Indian in immaculate white who sat on a mat in meditation. Two American children played a board game on the floor while their parents raced about with papers, returning to search in a denim travel bag. A woman, with a green sari tied up between her legs, fed a baby. He staggered around her, steadying himself with his fat hand flat between her eyes, as she managed to scoop the mush into his mouth with her fingers. Back-packers slept on tatty bed-rolls next to the mother and baby.

Nora thought that every returning Indian had tried to take as much of the West home as could be packed in boxes and amazingly awkward parcels.

She was coming out of the airport, thinking about a taxi when her view was blocked by an enormous, loosely shaped cardboard box. She watched it wobble precariously as its buried bearer steadied himself. "Mrs Ryan, is it?" A voice came from behind the box as a tall black-clad nun appeared. "Mrs Ryan?" she repeated, "Nora Ryan? I am Mother Bridgid. Welcome to Bombay." She joined her palms briefly: "*Namaste*, I am the friend of your aunt, Mrs Johnston, Florence Johnston. She stayed at the convent with us last year and I had a letter from your aunt to say you were coming."

11

Mother Bridgid was breathless: "Your Aunt Florence's description was perfect. She even guessed you might wear this," she said delighted, while Nora felt a conflict of relief and independence.

It had been Flo who advised a few days in Bombay before arriving in New Delhi."On one's own, to deal with the culture shock, don't you know. The guest is a god in India and whatever else you think about Indians, you'll never say they are inhospitable. The stranger is always welcome. It can have its disadvantages though. You must start on the right foot. If you agree to go to Delhi first and have this Das man pick you up from the plane, then you will never be left alone again. They'll mind you like a child. You won't be let go anywhere on your own, so if I were you I'd arrive in India under my own steam. That way they'll see you're independent. Have a hotel booked from here, not too posh. You don't want to be the rich foreigner. That way by the time you meet them you'll have travelled on your own in India."

And then, thought Nora, she set me up with Mother Bridgid. She had heard much of Bridgid whose mother had gone to the Loretto Convent in Dublin with Aunt Flo. "She looks like the actress, Claire Bloom," Aunt Flo had told her. And far too imposing to ever have been a mere sister, Nora thought.

"Leo," Mother Bridgid said to the young man who had taken Nora's bags: "I found her, this is Mrs Nora Ryan. And this Leopold Sebastian Thomas," she said, "he has promised me to look after you in every way."

Leo picked up the bags and swayed a pattern of head movements which Nora would learn to imitate, but only sometimes understand. He could be a New Yorker, she thought, the blue jeans, crisp white sleeved shirt. And a tiny gold cross on a chain around his neck. He had an air of deliberate nonchalance which obviously impressed Mother Bridgid. A nuns' man. Nora saw, a Reverend Mother's man, a dependable link with the world.

12

Sternly, Leo dismissed a begging child who carried a smaller child in her arms, and carefully settled the women in the back of the car. When he was settled behind the wheel he said: "Welcome to Bombay," and Nora felt that he had rehearsed their opening conversation: Had Mrs Ryan had a good journey? How long would she stay in India? He hoped that her visit would be a good experience, wasn't that how she would say it?

He thinks I'm an American, Nora thought, but seeing that Mother Bridgid was pleased with Leo she said nothing and was soon engrossed in what she saw through the window.

"I hear your daughter just got married," asked Mother Bridgid.

"Yes," Nora replied, "she is still on honeymoon," but not even the mention of Ciara could distract her from the window. She half heard Mother Bridgid talking about weddings and daughters and asking if Nora had other children.

"Just the one," Nora replied. She was aware that Leo and Mother Bridgid were covering her silence, chatting in Hindi and English. Leo hummed cheerily and commented on the massive hoardings which advertised movies and fabrics. "You can purchase such silk at a place I will take you," he offered.

"What is that woman doing there?" Nora asked, amazed by a mother and child in a piece of pipe on a building site,"I've never seen such a big pipe, but do they live in it?" Neither answered, but the nun patted Nora's hand.

They had been driving for about an hour when Leo slowed the car. They were by the sea: "Here we will take refreshment," he announced and Nora was glad to stroll in the cool breeze across the almost deserted Juhu Beach. A jogger panted along the shore. The sun glowed pink by the Arabian Sea, Nora was aware of being a world away from the scenes which had distressed her. A lone vendor stood behind a canopied stall piled high with green coconuts. The man was slight and black and held a machete with which he lobbed off the tops of coconuts bought by Leo.

"He comes from Kerala," Leo said, handing her the coconut in which he'd stuck a straw and a wooden spoon. "That's in Southern India, the home of coconuts."

Nora felt her mouth parched by the smell of India, and would always remember that first sip of coconut milk so naturally cool and more refreshing than anything iced. Traffic whizzed by in the distance, poverty smouldered behind and the city teemed ahead, but here was peace and beauty. Mother Bridgid's neck stretched as she surveyed the beach, looked out to sea. She's proud of her India, Nora thought gliding her spoon through the creamy pulp of the coconut.

The jogger pounded his return along the sand, past the man in white who strolled by the water's edge without raising his eyes from his book, khurta fluttering in the wind. Nearby a woman picked over the scant rubbish on the beach, dragging a sack after her.

Reluctantly, Nora got back into the car. They passed high rise apartments which looked shabby to Nora, but Leo assured her that film stars paid "lakhs of key money" for them and they passed pictures of the stars themselves, high on the hoardings, grotesque from enlargement. The traffic increased until Nora realised that for some time she had not noticed any buildings at all. Even at such an early hour the traffic was heavy and crowds of people got off buses to become part of the crowds on their way to work.

She recalled reading that eighty per cent of Indians lived in villages. Were all of these people only twenty per cent? She had seen such scenes of exotic colour on television, but now she felt that she was watching the reel speeded up. Her eyes tried to keep pace. Leo swayed his head: "This is nothing. Later, will be crowds."

Every few yards the car halted in traffic, and now a beggar appeared from nowhere. A handless man with a tray hanging from his shoulders stuck his head through the window and begged incessantly, his pleading eyes on Nora. The tray was covered with tiny clay pots in which loose wicks bobbed in oil. Only one was lit.

"Offerings for the Friday god," Leo explained, "today is Friday."

"What is the Friday god called?" Nora asked.

"There's no such god," Mother Bridgid chuckled. "Tomorrow he will sell lamps for the Saturday god, and so on. Most enterprising. Also, without hands this fellow could be having an accident." He moved towards the car behind them even before they moved on.

The area they were in now was quieter. "We will stroll around the gateway to India," Leo said and although Nora would have preferred to postpone the sight-seeing, she was delighted when she got out of the car and looked around. To her right she saw a palatial hotel with its liveried men busy with arriving guests, flowers and palms to her left and a magnificent statue of a man on horseback. Open carriages and plumed horses waited, and she could smell the sea beneath the blue sky through the great Arch of Triumph, the Gateway of India. Birds sang, khurtas flashed white and here and there a sari fluttered in the breeze.

"It's so beautiful," Nora murmured and her heart chose this moment to record her arrival in India.

Leo nodded: "This is the foreigners' part of Bombay. They are liking here. Over there behind the Taj, that is the Taj Mahal Hotel, are all the shops you people are liking, restaurants and hotels. And this," he turned towards the statue of the horseman "is the great leader Shivaji on his horse and that is Swami Vivekananda."

"And the Gateway," added Mother Bridgid, "when people used to come by sea to Bombay, it really was the gateway to India. Now, it is a landmark only, a meeting place."

As they moved towards the arch, Leo said: "You see all along there by the sea ...?"

Mother Bridgid interrupted him: "Later in the day it is a promenade, and at night when the lights are on it is called the Queen's Necklace. You know that Bombay was given to the British as a wedding dowry?"

"That was a long time ago," said Leo, almost impatiently.

There were launches by the quayside: "I can take you across to Elephanta Island to see the caves," Leo offered, and Nora thought how wonderful it must have been to arrive in Bombay by sea and cross the road to the hotel, but was distracted by an elephant padding along midst the traffic.

When they reached her own hotel it was a disappointment. She had told the travel agent that something modest would be fine, just clean and simple. It was neither. Nora followed the porter through the hotel, across the roof, and re-entered the building by a ship's staircase a few yards away from her room. The room was a depressing combination of dirty colours and two lumpy beds, a rusty shower cubicle, a mottled mirror. I could not possibly hang anything in that wardrobe she thought, and noticed with relief that the dull clacking noise was coming from an air conditioner fixed in the window ledge. She would not have stayed, but Mother Bridgid had given the place her approval: "Good, it is a middle-class hotel, not too much and not too little money, excellent." And so Nora decided to make do for now and followed Leo and the porter back via the stairs, out the door, over the roof, and at last out of the lift to Mother Bridgid who was waiting to take Nora to breakfast in her convent.

The door-man stood in Moghul regalia on the steps of the hotel: jewelled turban, gleaming brass and white gloves belying the state of the place, but as short a time as she had been in India, Nora appreciated that at least the man had a job.

Mother Bridgid decided that they would walk to the convent and Nora found herself transported by the energy of Bombay. A street away from the hotel, a woman carried water on her head as from a village pump, tiny mirrors glittering around her skirt. Behind her, a tall, fuzzy-haired blonde in a bright pink wraparound skirt and white vest was being pulled along by an Alsatian on a lead. Hitched up on one side, her skirt revealed a mile of tanned leg. As she spoke in Hindi to Leo, Mother Bridgid looked alarmed and slowed down but did not stop.

"See you around," he called nonchalantly.

"A visitor?" Nora asked.

"She is here for six years. She is living near here."

"Can she work in Bombay?" Nora was curious.

"In Bombay anyone can work," Leo said giving her a funny look. She would have enquired further, but her attention was caught by the Mercedes which had purred to the kerb of a hotel. The driver stood by the open door of the car as women and children got out after an Arab in cream robes. The women were veiled in black and left French perfume in the air.

Nora and Leo followed Mother Bridgid into a quiet street of large houses and shady trees. On the pavement in front of the house, a young woman cooked on a fire surrounded by three small children. One child slept on the pavement as the woman fried food in a little pan. Enormous eyes stared at Nora. She could not pass the family of match stick limbs and bent to give a ten rupee note, the smallest she had, but which she knew was well less than a pound. The woman's eyes widened and she left the pan in the burning sticks and fell sideways to touch Nora's feet in gratitude.

Mother Bridgid pulled at Nora's arm: "There are millions of such women in Bombay," she said.

17

"You have many rupees to throw away? You had better give them to me," Leo said lazily.

The morning had jolted Nora and left her confused. She was aware of having lost her independence and felt surrounded by disapproval as she walked between Leo and Mother Bridgid until they arrived at the convent.

CHAPTER 2

Mother Bridgid drew them into the airiness of her office: "You are most welcome," she said as nuns fluttered in with tea and trays of food. And Nora realised that this was her official welcome to India. "That would be Florence," Mother Bridgid said affectionately when told of Aunt Flo's engagement "and you, I know, are her favourite niece. We must take good care of you. Call our Irish friends to tea ..."

It was with dismay that Nora heard the nun's plans for her. There was even a certain guide to Elephanta to whom Leo would mention Mother Bridgid's name. There would be shopping and sight-seeing expeditions, and no need to worry about airline tickets to New Delhi. Mother Bridgid would telephone. Nora began to feel the claustrophobia of her teen years surrounded by nuns, pinned in by the security of their arrangements. It was all too familiar. Now the nun was pooh-poohing the idea of travelling by train when one could fly. "Leo will pick you up for Mass with us on Sunday," Mother Bridgid decided. The assumption alarmed Nora and she determined not to allow herself be taken over. After breakfast Leo walked her back to the hotel. As he slowed down in the thronged street so that Nora could catch up, she realised how easily she could slip into the drawing-room of India and never get to know anything about it at all. She could travel from convent to convent, nuns' man after nuns' man smoothing her way. Like a husband, she thought. And again she was aware of

19

how different this would all be if Dennis were along.

"You would like to see silks, jewellery, batiks?" Leo asked.

"Yes, but another day. I'm a bit weary," she said, longing to be alone for a while and recover from the sights and smells, the crowded experience of her morning.

Outside the hotel, Leo gave her his telephone number: "I will take you where you wish to go," he said, "just call me. If I am not at this place you can leave a message."

Nora lay down on the lumpy bed. She could not talk herself out of the raw, anxious feeling in her chest and she was going to take a pill when she thought that this wasn't exactly an emergency. The doctor had told her: "You can be quite liberal with them on the flight from Heathrow, but go easy after that. Try to save them for emergencies. You can manage without them, I know you can." Probably, the first morning in Bombay was enough to make anyone jiggy, Nora thought and left the unopened pill box beside her bed.

When she woke, the perspiration on her forehead was chilled from the cold air blower. The machine clacked away. Her head ached. She showered and dressed and went down to the restaurant, unexpectedly pleasant compared with the rest of the hotel, and had some coffee and yoghurt.

The afternoon sun was hot, but standing on the hotel steps, Nora decided it worth the effort to get to the sea wall and followed it to the Gateway of India where the boats were now busy taking people out to Elephanta. She watched children diving into the harbour for coins thrown by the passengers on the boat, and was suddenly surrounded by children.

At first there were a few, then many more small hands clutched at her and prodded with bony fingers. She stood panicked, mentally counting heads against her small change. And then she began, from left to right of the children, doling out coins. She was pleased with her organisation, when a hand that had been one of the first to grasp a coin, grabbed again, and attempted another. She held the coin tightly, but it was twisted from her fingers even as another brown arm shot out and grabbed the grabber by the wrist, and then there was just a tangle of children fighting against her skirt. She was struggling to escape when a voice snapped sharply in Hindi, and then: "Scram, scat, that's it," and the leggy blonde of the morning stood beside her. The dog, on a short leash, growled at the urchins and in seconds they had swarmed around other tourists.

"I'm Parvati," the blonde said, "and this is Dog."

"Nora Ryan is my name," Nora said, "Nora, from Dublin. Thank you, I ..."

"We'll go for a drink," Parvati said and walked off, confident that Nora followed. Soon, she stepped into the traffic to cross the road. "C'mmon," she said over her shoulder.

Nora squeezed herself small and wanted to close her eyes as she stepped off the kerb. She thought that they walked a long way in the melting heat before Parvati turned into a narrow door-way. Nora followed her into a maze of metal chairs and tables and when her eyes became accustomed to the dark, saw that the other customers were all young men, smoking, dozing, drinking coffee and that Parvati's hair was neglected rather than styled that way as she had thought when she first saw her. Also, the young woman's skin was the worse for sun, her cheeks red smudges, her arms and neck spotted with insect bites.

"Got any scent?" she asked Nora, and then stood up and yelled towards a counter at the other side of the room. "Two Limcas! From the ice! Got any scent?" she asked Nora again.

Pleased by the familiarity of Parvati's cockney accent, Nora searched in her bag for the toilette water she had decided would suit the Indian climate. Parvati sprayed it all over herself before squinting at the label: *Woods of Windsor.*

"Wild Rose. Woods of Windsor! Oh no. Too much, I don't believe this." She dropped it in the hessian bag hanging from her shoulder. "How did you get here? You're like from another world."

Nora let the perfume go.

"I came for a wedding in Delhi," she said,"I'm going there in a few days and thought I'd like to see Bombay."

"I thought I'd like to see Bombay," Parvati mimicked Nora's soft speech and asked: "Alone? Just like that. You look, er, sorta mislaid. Like in British Rail, left on the tube. Husband with you?"

"No, I saw you this morning with Leo and Mother Bridgid. Down near the Sands Hotel, didn't you see me?" Nora asked.

"Wasn't meant to see you 'til the Gateway of India was I? Parvati said mysteriously.

That irritated Nora.

"A - mazing," pronounced Parvati drawing on the cigarette Nora had watched her roll. Now, she offered it to Nora. Nora shook her head.

"How long have you been in India?".

"Don't know exactly. I've spent a couple of lives here and it looks as if I'll be here this time round too."

Two young men had slouched into the seats beside them, racketing the tin chairs on the floor.

"Hi, Parvati," said the bearded American, "how's business?"

"Great Raju, this is Nora, Mrs Ryan who thought she'd have a look at Bombay."

Raju sat down and peered at Nora: "Beautiful!" he pronounced and Nora knew he was not referring to her looks. Then he introduced his friend, but Nora did not catch his name. "Call him Monty for short," he offered. "He was a German and I was a Jew and now here we are. Another life. Brothers."

"What kind of work do you do?" Nora asked Parvati.

22

"Oh, Gawd," Parvati groaned, "Mrs Ryan wants to know how I am employed."

The men laughed.

"Well actually," Parvati continued in a tight, posh voice, "actually I work at paying my way. I was a temple prostitute and I got greedy and went into business for myself didn't I? So now I've got to spend time correcting the impression that left. I give everything I make to the Ashram until the day I won't wish I could keep it all. And then, and then we'll see. Then," she said in a startlingly loud voice, "then," she repeated dropping her voice to just above a whisper, "if I'm still living this life, beautiful."

Nora thought about getting away, but she could see the crowds beyond the door and not feeling able to face back into the heat of the street, she felt trapped. This isn't exactly what Mother Bridgid would have planned for me, she thought. One day in India and I fall among beggars to be rescued by a prostitute. So much for independence. And they think I'm an eejit. Or a dinosaur, definitely a dinosaur, she decided.

"Where are you all from?" Nora asked, more out of discomfort than interest.

Raju concentrated on eating something from a newspaper cone and Monty also ignored her.

Surprisingly, Parvati sat up straight: "Well, since you ask so politely, I was from Ealing," she giggled, "and came to India on my honeymoon. We went to Pune to meet Bhagwan, our guru and found out who we were."

She caught Nora glance at Raju and laughed. "Hey Raju, she thinks you're my husband."

Everybody laughed as though at a private joke, but Nora knew that it was at her expense and was suddenly uncomfortably aware of herself, of being so obviously middle-class. Her face flamed as their sarcastic banter made her cringe and in her humiliation and anger, she barely grasped that Parvati's husband had returned to England without her, and they had all been informed about their past lives by their guru so that they could work their way through this life to insure a better one next time around. Monty made a speculative remark about Nora's karma and their assumption that she knew nothing about reincarnation annoyed her.

"If you want to meet Bhagwan all you have to do is say the word," Parvati offered. "You could find out where to go from here, find out where you've been in other lives so you can stop fighting against your karma. Start taking control. No more stumbling about in the dark."

"I'll think about it," Nora said and the young men pretended to cringe in pain. She felt thoroughly put down, but her temper was rising. Who did they think they were to treat anyone like this? How dare they despise her?

"That's why we met today," Parvati said. "Don't you see? Now, don't say that's coincidental. That's what you were thinking, wasn't it? But it was no accident. Come alive Mrs Ryan. It's beautiful."

"Save your breath," Raju muttered.

"I've got to go now," Nora said.

"So go," replied the American.

"I gotta go to work, don't I" Parvati said to Nora. "Come on boy," and she dragged Dog after her.

"Is she really what she said?" Nora asked.

"You mean a prostitute?" asked the American, "sure."

Nora let out a sigh.

"Look Ma'am," Raju said, "you don't interfere with a person's rightful track. That's brutality. She knows what she's got to do. Who she is. Why she's here. She knows."

Tired and irritable, Nora started back to the hotel and, because browsing always had a calming effect on her, went into the jewellery shop she had noticed while trying to keep up with Parvati. Inside was cool spaciousness. Sighing with relief, she wandered around the show cases behind which salesmen kept a discreet vigil and sat down in front of a display of amethysts. Ciara's birth stone. And the ache in her throat began again. Ciara would not be there when she returned to Ireland, nor would Dennis. Empty house. She tried to concentrate on the stones.

She could mail one to Ciara. Close by, a stoutly handsome woman inspected a necklace, balancing it through coral finger tips to catch the light from the chandelier. Nora tried not to stare, but her eyes kept going back to the woman's champagne silk sari with its magnificently embroidered border. A boy brought the woman iced tea and putting the necklace down to take the glass she caught Nora staring. Apologetically Nora said: "Excuse me, I couldn't help admiring your sari. It's so lovely, I'm still not used to them ..."

"A gift from my sister-in-law," the woman smiled. "I'm Sophie Rosen. This is my daughter's jewellery. She is getting married on Sunday and here I am. For months and months they are making it and still at the eleventh hour it is not correct. These last minute things! Here please, you have this," and she held the glass out to Nora, "it's nice and cold."

"Oh no," Nora said, "I couldn't really... "

"Of course you must," said Sophie, "the boy will bring another," and even as she spoke Nora saw the saleman's nod send the lad hurrying off.

"You're visiting Bombay?" asked Sophie.

"Yes," replied Nora. She sipped the tea: "I only arrived this morning and it feels like a week ago. I'm not sure I can find my hotel again."

"Just this morning?" Sophie's voice rose, "you must be exhausted. Are you normally so pale?" Nora glanced at herself in the mirror behind the counter, aware that she must look like death to Sophie, but Sophie went on: "Not to worry, no problem, we'll find your way for you. You're English, American?"

"No," Nora said realising that she had not introduced herself, "my name is Nora Ryan. I'm Irish from Dublin, and I'm going to New Delhi for a wedding."

"A wedding? This is the best reason to visit India."

Nora found herself wincing at the energy in the

other woman's voice, as in three minutes Sophie had told Nora her husband was in furniture, their daughter was marrying a doctor at the synagogue on Sunday and she had opted to wear a sari for the event so that there wouldn't be any seams to let out at the last minute. She had tried a diet for the wedding, but her weight just kept increasing because the pills the doctor gave her had only made her chew faster.

When Nora had admired every piece of the wedding jewellery, Sophie said: "and of course you must come. You are so welcome. I absolutely insist."

Nora was suddenly wary. Her first impressions of Sophie were good but she found her a bit over-whelming. Besides, she couldn't keep going off with strangers, Sophie was the second person she'd picked up on her first day. Confused by the way that Sophie acted as though they had known each other all their lives, Nora tried to make excuses, but Sophie would not accept them and Nora was reminded of what Aunt Flo had said: "You won't believe how friendly they are, the women especially." Sophie was actually pleading with her: "I cannot go home and tell my family that I met a visitor from Ireland on her first day in the country, but she is not coming to the wedding. You will be guest of honour and you will see a happy occasion. Auspicious. You'll come?" There was to be a family dinner that night, and a luncheon after Saturday prayers at the synagogue and Nora was welcome to them all.

"I've made arrangements, people to see," Nora said, suddenly glad of Mother Bridgid's existence, but eventually she heard herself say: "Yes, of course I could manage Sunday. For the wedding itself."

Nora thought that even the salesman was glad she had agreed to go to the wedding as he escorted the women to Sophie's car. "Let my driver worry about finding your hotel," Sophie said over her shoulder, "it's no problem to him."

26

When the car drew up outside the door of the Sands Hotel, Sophie asked: "This is your hotel?" and quickly covered her surprise. She gave Nora her telephone number and told her she would pick her up on Sunday: "but before that if you have a change of plans, telephone and we will come and get you."

It was five o'clock when Nora reluctantly entered her room. Even as she thought that she could not sleep with the noise from the air conditioner, she dropped off and did not wake until after eight o'clock. She dressed and made her way back towards the Gateway of India en route from which she had seen several good looking hotels.

In the Taj Mahal Hotel Nora browsed in the shops, strolled around the gardens, watched a group of Indian dancers in one of the restaurants where she ate her first thali, surprised by the variety of food which came in seven tiny bowls. Later, she sipped a drink by the window of the roof-top bar which overlooked the Queen's Necklace of lights along the coast. Someone bent over her.

"You are alone?" asked an impeccably dressed and handsome Arab.

"I am waiting for my husband," Nora said, and the man withdrew. She wanted to smile, but people might have noticed the man trying to pick her up. The encounter gave her confidence. She decided not to move into the Taj after all. She could always come to have her hair done or even just for a cup of tea, but suddenly its sophisticated atmosphere was too separate, too cocooned.

It was getting late, but Nora continued her search for a better hotel, thinking as she walked along that it was the number of people, not merely the weather that made Bombay hot. Many of the hotels were full and could not give her a room within the coming weekend. At least she was holding her own with beggars, vendors, would-be guides and shopkeepers who, from their doorways, offered her cold drinks or a chair to

27

entice her among their goods. And her heart was warmed by the boy who winked at her. About ten years old, his right arm ended in a stump at the elbow and he had only a thumb on his left hand.

When Nora gave him two rupees, he smoothed it tenderly against his chest with his stump, folded it with his left thumb, and carefully put it into his shirt pocket. Then he looked at Nora and winked. Both his wink and his handicap stayed with her through the chaos of the Bombay night until weary she found that she had stumbled into a street at the side of the Sands Hotel. Home.

The air conditioner rattled and Nora turned it off. She was so relieved to be rid of the noise that she decided that by the time the room grew hot she would be asleep, and the heat would not matter. She woke next morning to an all pervading smell of fried onions. The fumes rose through the floor and from the fireplace to fill the room when the air conditioner was off. She switched it on again and showered without washing her hair because she could not bear to stay a minute longer than necessary in that room.

At the Pyramids Hotel she caught the puzzled look on the face of the receptionist who sniffed discreetly. Nora blushed as she saw the woman realise where the smell of fried onions was coming from before she turned away to get a room key. "Yes," she said, "this morning I can give you a room."

CHAPTER 3

The Ryans had been on their way to bed two weeks before their daughter's wedding, Nora was sitting at her dressing table making a list, her slim gold pen a present from Dennis who was removing his cuff-links when he asked: " Nora, how long would you like me to stay after the wedding?"

Nora stifled a sigh of exasperation: "Dennis, for heaven's sake. Don't even think about anything else for that night. We'll be up until all hours."

This latest list was headed: "Food for after:" She hadn't thought about people landing back at the house after the wedding until the surprise gift of champagne had arrived that morning from her sister: "For the party after the party". She looked up at Dennis standing in the mirror and picked up some tissues to dust the glass as though to wipe her husband away.

"I didn't mean the wedding," Dennis said, "I mean us. How long will I stay when the wedding's over? Are we going to sell the house? We ought to talk about it."

"Sell the house? Who said anything about selling the house?" Nora's voice rose. "Why on earth ... In the middle of a wedding, selling the house, what a ..."

"I just wondered," Dennis interrupted, "I just thought you'd find it too big. Ciara's gone, will be in two weeks. Can't say I expected her to go as far as Canada. The years have flown. Anyway, we can do what we agreed, and I wouldn't mind working the

29

London gallery for a bit. And a flat's not a problem ..."
Dennis had stopped, startled.

Nora stared into the mirror aware that her face was
bloodless, her green eyes dark. My hair's too red, she
thought, I'll have to ask Ron to tone it down ...

"Nora?" Dennis asked, "why are you looking like
that? What's the matter? Should I have waited? I
suppose all this fuss and Ciara going off. But...it's
been on my mind." His voice trailed off. Nora did not
answer and Dennis sensed a scene brewing. He stood
there for as long as he could and then went to get
himself a drink.

Even in her shock, Nora was surprised at herself for
being surprised. Her thirtieth birthday. How could she
have forgotten? She had managed to fade that night
away, to smooth over it with years. Day piled upon day.
That night when they had agreed to part whenever Ciara
left home or got married. And he had never forgotten,
Nora thought. All that time: days, months, years,
birthdays, anniversaries, funerals, everything has just
been the surface. The incidentals. For the time being.
He'd been content that an agreement was made and
there was no need to go on about it, just wait thirteen
years. Nora stood up and was unsteady as she passed
Dennis on her way to the bathroom.

She sheltered under the shower, her hair unprotected,
feeling the water on her body, splashing around her
feet, soaping, rinsing, unable to think. Sudden needles
of scalding water stabbed at her. She tried to adjust
the tap, but could not. Enraged, she made her escape.
"Jesus God, damn you Dennis Ryan," she swore. Her
heart pounded as she dragged on her robe and
managed to turn off the water.

Livid, Nora stood at the bottom of their bed, her
body prickly, sweat on her face. "Right," she exploded,
"OK. I want you to leave immediately after the
wedding. That's your answer. The morning after. No,
the same night. That's it. Now, would you please move
into the other room?"

"Ah now Nora, we can talk," Dennis sounded wounded. "What's this about? We agreed ..."

"There's nothing to talk about," Nora interrupted, pausing between each word. "We agreed," she mimicked, "Thirteen years ago, we agreed. And you, you've never let go of it. Full marks. That's it Dennis. Done. Now you've only two more weeks to wait. And I've got to get to sleep. There's a wedding, we're in the middle of a wedding. And this time you can have the other room."

She watched Dennis make heavy weather about gathering his book, his watch and his drink before he said: "I don't see why you want to go on like this. We said we weren't going to get into that kind of thing. Is the bed on?"

"No," Nora raged, still scalded, "the bed isn't on. What bed was ever on that had us in it? Is that all you can think of now, a bloody electric blanket."

"I don't suppose it matters if I catch my death going from a warm bed to a cold one? You could be a bit more reasonable," Dennis said, "All this insane fuss with the wed ..."

"Shut up. Shut up. Stop. I can't bear it. Stay here then. What in Christ's difference does it make?" She charged from the room.

On the landing Nora felt dizzy, stopped and turned left downstairs. In the kitchen, she collapsed onto a chair and thought about having a drink, but instead made a mug of cocoa and devoured chocolate biscuits for the first time since she began the wedding diet months ago. She scraped the brown sludge off the bottom of the mug with her finger and sucked it clean. She was exhausted, thought about cancelling the next day's appointments and panicked.

Best thing is not to think about it. There's plenty of time for thinking later. Keep things normal. That's important. Nothing is going to spoil Ciara's wedding. I won't say a word. Maybe Derry, she's supposed to come with me for the fitting. I could tell Derry. It will be a relief to tell someone. The fitting. I'm inches

31

smaller than I was last month. Nearer a ten.

In America you'd have to make a rumpus, call in lawyers and start divorce proceedings and all that. In England too. Most countries allow divorce. Another chance. Thank heavens it's Ireland. We can just let things be, fade away in their own time. Bleed dry.

She started to cry. Nora had often wondered why couples got so involved with solicitors when there was no divorce. In the worst times of their marriage she had always known that they would have got a divorce had it been available in Ireland. Now, they could manage without lawyers. There was nothing to disagree about.

They had it all worked out. The house was her's even though it had belonged to his mother. Only fair, he'd said, you put all the work into it. And the money from the sale of the shop. Some of the gallery money was her's too. The ideal operation. Bloodless. No mess. No arguments.

But how am I going to get everything done for Ciara's wedding? Nora fretted. What about the invitations on the mantlepiece? Would she go to the McMahon's party on her own, the affair at the Canadian Embassy? What would she say to people? Not that these things mattered, she reminded herself. Still, what was she going to do? And the Coleman's wedding. What about that? And what am I going to do when it's all over and Ciara and Dennis are gone? Just me left. I'll need a rest, maybe a holiday with Derry. Then what? Ann and Kevin play bridge four nights a week. I could learn. Oh God, bridge. What'll I tell people? I can't very well place an announcement in *The Irish Times.* Why not? Get it over in one go.

Nora was agonising over how to break the news when Ciara came noisily through the Georgian hall door, and called out to the street: "Bye, Bewley's lunch-time, bye." The chain fell heavily against the wood as she closed the door and pounded upstairs. Nora followed and stopped at her daughter's room on the next floor: "Hi Ciara," she said carefully, "how was the play?" Ciara had thrown her jacket on a chair, and was seated on the end of her bed undoing her bracelet.

"Oh, you're up?" Her dark hair was shoulder length and her model's make-up made her look like a child. Her smile faded. "Mam, have you been crying?"

"Maybe just a drop or two," Nora said, "it's nothing."

"You're not one to cry for nothing. What's happened? Has something ... Are you absolutely shagged?"

Nora smiled at the word: "Not exactly, Angel. I'm a bit over-tired." She sat down.

"That's what shagged means," Ciara said, "a small wedding would have been just as happy as a big one. Well, maybe it wouldn't be so exciting and glam and all that. It's going to be perfect, isn't it? Dan got the honeymoon tickets. London and Paris before we go to Canada. Oh, is that it?"

Nora's eyes were wet. Ciara knelt beside her on the floor: "Oh Mam, I know it's going to be hard at first. This beautiful house with just you and Dad in it. I was thinking maybe you'd get something smaller, but Dan said it's a work of art what you've done with it. Like something you'd see in a magazine. It's a pity Gran can't see it. It was so different when she was alive, wasn't it? Dan says you'd be mad to sell it. Dan says ... " Nora blew her nose and smoothed Ciara's hair with the other hand. "My bladder seems a bit near my eyes these days," she said, then "Dan says".

Ciara made a face. "Aunt Derry says I'll have to watch it or I'll be an echo of Dan's. I'm not really, am I? Not actually. She thinks it's all about battling for your rights with fellas. You don't think about stuff like that when you're in love. I just happen to think the same way he does about everything. I think we're going to be just like you and Dad. When we get older, I mean, well, you don't start out like that. Some day we'll be like you and Dad and Dan says ... oops, there I go again."

Nora blew her nose: "It's fine Angel. I'm going to get some sleep." She stood at the door, looking at Ciara.

"Night, and don't forget your fitting tomorrow."

"Night," said Ciara and jumped up to hug her.

Nora went back upstairs and looked into the bedroom. Dennis was asleep on his back, snoring. She put off the light on her side of the bed and closed the door quietly. Then she went into the Other Room.

The Other Room had never been known as anything else in the Ryan household. Nobody ever used it except herself or Dennis. On rare occasions when the house was overcrowded, the Other Room was not offered to anyone.

Nora had never put her mark on the room. It was more like a shop window display of furniture than a bedroom. The drawers and wardrobe were empty, smelled of wood. In the bookcase were two books: *At Swim Two Birds* by Flann O'Brien and *My Mother, Myself* by Nancy Friday. Nora had managed to wade through the latter with the assistance of the former. Flann O'Brien's collected clichés had become a family game so that now Nora picked up the book, saying to herself: "and with what could you have knocked over Mrs Ryan when her husband asked how long he would stay after their daughter's wedding?"

"With a feather," she answered herself aloud. And then repeated it grimly: "With a feather". She climbed between the cold sheets, bending to turn on the electric under-blanket as the August wind rattled the windows.

Nora was weary but could not sleep. The joy was gone from her wedding preparations. It was going to be all uphill now. My own fault, she thought. Coming up to her thirtieth birthday she had felt that some things needed sorting. One was her sex life. She had felt so cheated. Theirs was not a real marriage, she told Dennis and as the discussion degenerated, Nora asked: "Am I an alibi? Are you interested in women at all? Celibacy suits you fine, but then why didn't you stay single?"

"Perhaps we'd better call it a day," Dennis offered.

Two nights later, talking until dawn they had agreed on the plan. It wasn't as if they did not get along together. Day by day. They weren't bad friends, were they? Shared interests. They could be responsible, remain together until their only child was married or left home, whichever happened first. After all, neither had anyone else. Then, still young they would go their separate ways. And now she was forty-three.

It was near dawn before Nora fell asleep, over-heated by the electric blanket. She dreamed that Dennis had told her he was leaving, woke to the relief that it was only a dream, and then realised that it was real. Could there be someone else for Dennis, Nora wondered again. Hardly. And yet he was going. To what? He must have something planned.

Theirs had been the wedding of the year. Aunts beamed at the thought of Nora and Dennis. Lovely couple. Nora was steeped in luck to come home from London for a rest and land a catch like Dennis Ryan. No one knew about Nora's life in London or why she had needed a rest, nor did she tell anyone.

Heavy with weariness, Nora listened to the sounds of Dennis rise and leave for work. She dozed off and was awakened by Mrs Byrne: "Would you like a cup of tea? I thought you'd gone out, then I thought maybe she's in the Other Room."

Mrs Byrne brought the tea and waited until Nora had a few sips before she blurted: "Himself is after coming back. After four years, could you credit it? The twins were three months when he went."

"But how can he come back? Wasn't there a court order against him? Wasn't ..." Nora was incredulous. Mary Byrne had had to flee into the refuge for battered wives while she was expecting the twins, the youngest of nine children.

"Fat lot of good the barring order was with the kitchen window open," said Mrs Byrne. "He climbed through the window. Came back from England last night on

35

the boat. Spent the evening with his mates the way it'd be dark before he came and there he was in bed beside me this morning. I never even felt him getting in."

Nora waited, unsure of what to say. Mary Byrne flushed. "He's nowhere to go. The kids are pleased to see him. He was playing with the younger ones when I left. He seems better in himself. Handed me a wad of notes. And he's got the line on a job. I didn't think I'd ever dream of having him back but finding him there, beside me like, well, I was thinking I might give it another chance ... see how it goes. A married woman on her own has no life ..."

Nora was alarmed by her own apathy. How would she get everything done, feeling like this? Each day to the wedding was mapped out with things to be done. And she didn't want to get out of bed. Mrs Byrne's news had added to the sense of losing control. Two women at the mercy of whim. She sighed over the timing. Mary Byrne was doing fine and back he had to come and here she was in the middle of the wedding.

Maybe if she'd accepted the way things were, Dennis wouldn't have ... maybe if she hadn't said it all. The doctors and the text books, the coaxing and complaints ... perhaps? If only.

But it's all so long ago, she argued with herself and wondered why she was not falling apart. Didn't women usually get hysterical? Perhaps it hadn't sunk in yet. Perhaps she would suddenly collapse. It didn't feel like that, it felt flat and heavy. Empty. The waste of it all. The waste. She was reminded of her late mother's attitude to left-overs. "So many people would be glad of it," the woman said, "perfectly good."

"Yes, someone would be glad of it," Nora thought of her marriage.

Dennis Ryan had not expected things to take such a bad turn. After all the ground work. Still, it was one thing to decide, make plans, natural to feel a jolt now

36

it was here. And if she was surprised then why hadn't she asked him to stay?

Last time they'd talked about it ... when was that? Couldn't have been long. That's when he decided to try London. It was when she was selling the antique shop and he told her to hold out for a better price. "You'll be needing the money," he said. And she smiled and agreed that he was right. It did not occur to him that she had only been referring to holding out for a better price.

Dennis parked the car on St Stephen's Green. Bewley's for coffee, he thought, an almond bun and a read of the paper. Methodically, he read his way through *The Irish Times*, glancing up to find the first breakfast crowd thinning. He had not taken in much of what he read. His head crowded with images of Nora. He saw her run into the water in front of him on the beach in Donegal. That was their honeymoon. He saw her in that kaftan thing in Sanary five years ago. Great time in California. They'd always loved the caravan at Brittas Bay. It had been good. Most of it. Even after that night.

He wondered about Nora's plans. Could be a grandmother soon enough. Looked remarkably well lately, taken years off herself in preparation for the wedding. You'd think she was the one getting married. Not likely she'd find the missing link now, a woman with a married daughter. Pity the way things had turned out; she deserved to be happy. Suppose they had been OK in that department, would there have been something else? Probably not, he decided. They'd had the stuff of marriage, companionship. Too much fuss made about the other. He hadn't thought of marriage until he met Nora. Quite the reverse really, he could not recall ever going in pursuit. He had felt bound to go to the hops before he met Nora but that, he realised now, was because it was the thing to do.

"Fresh coffee?" the waitress asked.

"Thank you," Dennis smiled at her.

He could see that the waitress was eager to chat and normally he would have done so. He knew that women liked him, especially women of a certain age. Appreciated his old world manners. And he got on with women. He didn't care for pubs, drinking with the lads. He preferred chatting to women. Women relaxed with him. He was comfortable with them. Nora was sarcastic about that, that was the trouble, she said. Women, what did they want?

He took another almond bun. Women go looking for a fellow, he told himself, and if you're not what they think they want then you're in trouble. That row, God. And her revelations. He pulled himself together. Poor Nora, but when she got into that mood ... She had gone beserk that time, quite mad. Like last night. Like that night.

CHAPTER 4

Nora picked up the two airmail letters from the hall and went into the kitchen. One was was from Aunt Flo in New Zealand and the Indian letter was from R.D. Das in New Delhi. She put the kettle on, setting aside Aunt Flo's letter, the better to be tackled after a cup of tea.

The Indian letter contained a wedding invitation:

Mr and Mrs Rajendra D. Das solicit your blessings and request the pleasure of your company at the wedding of their daughter Nina with Arun, son of Mr and Mrs Deepak Singh, November 4th, 1984 ...

Nora read. She had never known him to call himself anything but "R.D." and had forgotten that his name was Rajendra. She had not often heard from R.D. since London, although there had been one or two Christmas cards since Dennis was introduced to him by another art dealer in Paris. Nora had sent R.D. and his wife an invitation to Ciara's wedding. We'll only have one wedding, she told herself, better sure than sorry. And she wondered again what his wife was like, the girl his father had hauled him back to New Delhi to marry in 1962.

R.D.'s letter had taken two months to arrive:

... so we are come to the time of life for getting our children settled. The time has passed too quickly and we are both losing our daughters. My wife and I are honoured by your kind invitation, but regret that it is

impossible to come. We are hoping that you will like the gift which is sent with our friend, Dr Tobai, who will visit England and post the parcel from there.

I regret that we cannot come to Ireland. Some time, I intend to visit your country. I am so touched that you thought of us but, please, it would be such an honour if you would come to our daughter's wedding. We are expecting many guests and I'm sure that you would enjoy yourselves. It is an ideal time of year ...

The formality of the letter sparked Nora's interest. Had R.D. told his wife about London? It is our season of weddings, the letter said. A season of weddings, she thought as she picked up Aunt Flo's letter.

She sighed wearily as she read that the old woman was returning for the wedding, and wondered would Nora pick her up at the airport? Nobody had wanted Florrie to travel at her age, although she was amazingly sprightly. At seventy-six she insisted on going alone to New Zealand to visit her son, Paul. The family flapped. Or rather, the women did. Who could accompany Aunt Flo? Why couldn't damned Paul or his wife come and get her and bring her back if they were so anxious to have her? It was all very well inviting people of that age ...

"Oh Mam," Ciara had said, dressed that day in a black patent jump-suit that reminded Nora of a refuse sack, "suppose she doesn't make it? What a way to go. Tough on the air hostesses if she konks out in flight, but the old dear is great. Have to hand it to her. Live till you die. No geriatric scenes for Aunt Flo." She had giggled, her jump-suit crackling. "She can't make the journey any younger."

Florrie was furious at the suggestion that she needed someone to go with her: "I'm not a child or an idiot." Then, when she arrived in New Zealand, everyone started wondering would she want to come back? Would she make it back? If she did, surely she couldn't go on living alone? She really was getting past that.

40

Agnes, Florrie's daughter-in-law, had made enquiries at St Brendan's by the sea.

By that afternoon, Nora had resigned herself to having Aunt Flo move into the house with her: "Poor old thing," she thought, "now I'm going to be alone, I'm the obvious one to give her a home. I suppose I'll be glad of her company sometimes."

"So that's that," Nora told Derry when she arrived from Cork on the day after Aunt Flo's letter. "Things work out," she said. Her throat ached.

"That's not working things out," said Derry, incredulous, "that's crazy. You can't see Aunt Flo as a solution to anything. You're only forty-three. Her life is over. Anyway, much as I'm fond of her, Aunt Flo is as mad as a hare. Manic. Always was. Even if she wasn't ... "

"Aunt Flo could teach us all how to live," Nora interrupted. "There's more spunk in her than the rest of us put together. Imagine her landing in the mess I'm in? I suppose it is a mess. Have you ever noticed how tired everyone else seems compared to Aunt Flo?" She sagged in her seat. "Have you?"

"You're surely not going to let Dennis away with this?" Derry raged. "I mean, he can't be allowed to just hop off with himself as if he's gone for a newspaper. And the timing. Jesus!" Her eyes reddened and she mashed recklessly at her chocolate éclair, "I'd like to kill the sod. If I were you I'd kill him before I'd let him do this to me. Honest to God Nora, the bloody cheek of him."

"Derry stop," Nora said, "It's not like that. Try to see, Dennis and I agreed. We said we'd go our own ways. It's silly to work it up into a row. I don't even know how I feel. I mean apart from the timing, maybe ... I dunno. Wait until after the wedding. I'll need all your energy if I come unstuck."

"Oh Nora, it's not right. He must be mad."

Nora sipped her tea. Her sister, ten years older and unmarried, ordered a gin and tonic, and as they drove back to Nora's house, Derry said: "I don't know that

41

I'm able to be in the same house with the man. I really
don't ..."

"Shut up, Derry. If you really care about what I
want, then behave. Don't let on you know anything.
Be civilised. First let's get on with Ciara's wedding.
Quietly. At least I've been able to tell you. I think I feel
better for that. Honestly, if you can, act normal for me.
That's what I really want, for now."

As it happened, Derry didn't have to be in the same
house with Dennis that night. There was a message
that he wouldn't be home for dinner. He had gone to
see some paintings in Galway.

Derry drank a bottle of wine while Nora took a token
sip or two. Derry, went on to brandy. She sat opposite
Nora, her pink hands warming the glass, wearing blue
jeans and an Aran sweater, her crown of bright red
curls around her freckled face, green eyes under heavy
eyebrows. Yet again, Nora wondered what her sister
would look like if she bothered with her appearance,
wore make-up and fashionable clothes.

Even as a girl, long before she got involved in the
Women's Movement, Derry had been different. Their
elegant mother despaired of a daughter who preferred
second-hand clothes – shopped at Designs On You the
first swop shop in Dublin – in the hope of finding
something as old as her black winter cloak of the kind
once worn by West of Ireland women. "Makes me feel
like Grannuaille," she told Ciara. "New clothes are OK
sometimes, like new friends," Derry said, "but you're
never alone in clothes like these. They have a feel.
Cosy. I love myself in a pirate's cloak, feel powerful.
Wish I had a cutlass."

Derry, Nora thought, could never have lived a life of
polite compromise. She's always demanded her own
kind of life. She wondered what made her so different,
who she had taken after? University lecturer in Cork,
psychology, single life, women's groups. She wouldn't
even come to our parties, and yet she cared enough to
send champagne. Nora watched fascinated as Derry

42

rolled the brandy around in her mouth. What's happening to her now, this minute, is what matters, Nora thought. That's why she gets so much enjoyment out of the brandy.

When Nora woke the next morning, the house was empty. Ciara was gone. It was five minutes to noon and there was no sign of Mary Byrne. By the time she'd tidied up a bit it was nearly one o'clock and there was the sound of Derry tapping on the ceiling, inviting her to come down. The thump thump of Derry's broom handle seemed to strike the soles of Nora's feet as she stood in her kitchen.

Derry had occupied the basement flat for three years. It had been guest accommodation, but she was writing a book and wanted a hide-away in Dublin.

Putting on her coat, Nora realised that they hadn't mentioned the last time Derry had come to dinner and driven Dennis into his study. Derry rarely bothered to hide her amusement of Dennis whom she grudgingly liked, and Dennis insisted on calling her Deirdre, her full name.

That evening when Dennis was carving the roast, Derry had asked: "Do you know why men carve at table in middle-class families and working-class women dish up in the kitchen ?"

Dennis had sighed heavily.

"Because," explained Derry triumphantly, "when there's plenty, it's OK to let everyone see how it's shared out. In a poor house the woman can go without, pile her plate with cabbage and nobody's supposed to know there's nothing underneath."

Dennis set his jaw and Nora could imagine him thinking: Why couldn't Nora leave Deirdre in her basement? After dinner and a few glasses of wine Derry had referred to Dennis as "Big Daddy". And then added alarmingly: "... not your typical male chauvinist, our Big Daddy, but he gets his patriarchal goodies just the same."

43

Ciara always described Derry's flat as "Aunt Derry's world, down under," and Nora was delighted by the way Derry stamped her personality on the flat and made it her own. There were political posters, slogans, plants, throw rugs and foreign pottery everywhere and although she had not redecorated, the place was full of colour.

Now, when Nora went down there was a smell of brewing coffee. Derry had set the table to one side of her "jungle", a patio inside sliding glass doors. A profusion of plants and flowers grew from the walls and clustered on the floor. The glass doors framed the old garden. The garden walls were covered with dark ivy and fuchsia bushes heavy with pink and purple ballerina blooms. All looked a bit bedraggled on this windy August day.

The sun was trying to shine through the rustling copper beeches, the tall palm between them almost crowded out of sight. Beyond the copper beeches were the apple trees which Nora and Dennis argued about every year. Dennis wanted to cut them down. They were safe now, she thought sadly.

Derry came in with more food, home-made brown bread. "Pâté," she said, "aubergine, liver and trout from the man in Patrick Street. Ciara popped in, asked if I'd keep an eye after the wedding. She seemed a bit worried about you."

"You didn't say?" Nora started.

"No, of course not."

Nora was surprised by her own tears.

"Here have a fistful of these." Derry passed a box of tissues." And we'll have our coffee."

"I'll miss Ciara ..."

"Remember that time I nearly got married?"

"How could I forget," Nora said, "the year before I went to London. Poor Mother, she kept asking me what were we going to do with my bridesmaid's dress."

"Sorry about that. I never told you what happened?"

Nora looked up.

"I was pregnant and two weeks before the wedding I

44

woke up definitely not pregnant. Best thing I ever did. Marriage would have done for me."

"What about Eamonn? He must have been staggered?"

"He's married now, got two kids. We met six months later and took up where we left off. It ran its course, he met someone else and he married the one after her. Marriage was not the trade I had in mind for myself. D'you know, fifty years ago, marriage was the most dangerous trade a woman could choose, and still is in most parts of the world?"

"Don't talk like that in front of Ciara?"

"How could I? Dan says ..."

"You know I'd have thought that if anyone walked out it would have been you, not Dennis, I mean..."

There was a thumping on the hall door. "Ciara," they said together. They helped her get the box through the basement door. "The wedding dress," Ciara announced, imitating a drum roll with her tongue. She put it on and waltzed, singing with joy, around the flat. As she swirled midst froths of lace and tulle, her veil like ocean spray on a spring day, both women had tears in their eyes. *Peace on Earth, Good will to All People*, proclaimed the Christmas poster which Derry had made permanent.

Nora set out for Dublin Airport after Aunt Flo telephoned from Heathrow.

"I'm in London, Nora. Will you pick me up at Busarus?"

"Oh no, Aunt Flo," Nora replied, knowing her aunt would not think twice about struggling onto the airport coach to get into the city centre bus station. "I'll be there when your plane comes in."

So that's that, Nora thought and her throat ached. From wife and mother to devoted niece and as she drove along the Coast Road she thought of Aunt Flo. "Crazy woman," the adults said, but as a child Nora longed to be invited on Aunt Flo's lone picnics or days at the Zoo.

"Poor Grant," the other aunts agreed, "Flo just

disappears and leaves the household to fend for itself. With three children and that half-wit of a maid, you wouldn't blame Grant." For being cranky, they meant.

Grant was a good man, Florrie often explained, but he did not know how to enjoy himself. After all, she was not playing cards or doing any other wicked thing. It was just a few hours of fresh air in her own company or the odd jaunt to Bray for a go in the dodgem cars.

Through the glass doors in the Arrivals Lounge, Nora saw Aunt Flo pushing a trolley heaped with luggage and packages, her old face flushed, excited. She wore a purple felt hat, dimpled on one side with a feather, and one of those suits she was forever knitting, green. She was straight and agile, carried her years with amazing ease, although when she stooped to pick up a package that slipped from the trolley Nora noticed Aunt Flo's legs were quite bandy, and glimpsed pink bloomer above her knee.

She spied Nora and began talking as the doors slid back. "Nora. Nora. I am so glad to see you. Thought we'd never get here with all the delays. It's lovely being met."

She struggled with the trolley, but would not let go of it as Nora tried to take it from her feeling bombarded by her aunt's questions about Dennis, Ciara and the weather.

"It seems a bit grey," she panted just as Nora managed to get hold of the trolley. "What's the news? Did you make the cake yourself? No? Oh, you should have. I could have iced it for you. Wait until you hear my news. Everyone sends love and I have piles of photographs."

Aunt Flo was talking more loudly than usual. She had kissed Nora, but then as though forgetting she'd done it, kissed her again on both cheeks and squeezed her hand. As they drove out of the car park, Aunt Flo announced that she'd stay with Nora until the wedding "if you like," but then she was going back to her own flat. All arranged from Wellington.

46

At home, Nora made tea while Florrie freshened up and came from the bathroom with her eyelids glistening with vaseline, talc on her nose and wafting *lily-of-the-valley*. She sat beside the tea tray, took a folder of photographs from one of the many compartments in her handbag, crossed her ankles with knees apart and back straight, and handed Nora the first polarised snap. An attractive man stood beside the rail of a ship.

"This is Peter," said aunt Flo, "my sweatheart. We met on that boat. It was a day trip. That's my news. He's my fiancé. You didn't notice my ring." She held out her heavily veined hand. "He's only sixty-seven, much younger than me, but love overcomes these things. Nora, it was love at first sight. As soon as we met each other we knew. Can't life take a wonderful turn?"

The old woman hummed as she shuffled through her deck of photographs and then grinning broadly, burst into song: "... ding dong the bells are going to chime".

CHAPTER 5

The night before Ciara's wedding, Nora dreamed she was getting married. She was on a journey towards her bridegroom, through tunnels in the sea which led her to the beach, but Dennis, whom she was dressed to marry, was not there. Shivering, she struggled ashore to look for him and found only his bridegroom's outfit lying on pale sand.

There was a white flower in the buttonhole of the white suit which lay as if Dennis had evaporated out of it, shirt buttons done up, tie in place. The shoes and socks lay beneath the trouser cuffs. She saw that the socks were uncrumpled.

Nora woke thinking she understood the reason for the dream. Today was her wedding day. Startled when she realised that it was not, she heard Ciara moving through the house, pounding stairs, banging doors, calling to Dennis and Aunt Flo. The bridesmaids had arrived, so it must be eight-thirty. Derry had stayed over.

The day dragged until it gathered speed with hairdressing and last minute well-wishers, the florist's delivery, photographs and a general happy expansion of activities to fill the hours. Nora might have told them about her nightmare but for the presence of Dennis. Nora watched him being attentive: pouring champagne, helpfully running messages, locking Ciara's suitcases, being the perfect father of the bride, even though his own bags were packed, ready for him to leave home after twenty-one years. He's always looked so right, Nora thought, he's always looked so bloody right.

The more Nora tried to enter into the spirit of the day, the more distracted she became. She was aware of being only partly present, re-living her own wedding day. And she was also aware of her daughter acting the bride and that made her uneasy, even though Ciara was smiling and glowing. Warily, Nora watched, recalling her own doubts on the eve of her wedding. Did Ciara have fears, doubts?

"Are you OK?" Derry asked quietly.

"Yes, of course," Nora replied, confident that she looked the perfect mother-of-the-bride. Only a sister would have asked.

Nora's own wedding day seemed more vivid than what was happening around her. Her's had been an unusual wedding, the island event to which every bit of clothing, morsel of food and most of the guests had to be brought from the mainland on a Galway hooker. There was no harbour and the men had to go out in currachs to fetch both guests and food.

She and Dennis had gone down to the beach on the day before that May morning. Her dress had been hung on the back of the door of Aunt Ellen's room for the best part of a month, the date set, the cake ready, awaiting all being well. "All" was the sea and the mood it might take in spite of it being May. The boats were not able to get out for three days before the eve of the wedding.

Finally, Father Flaherty had said it would be as well if they got married on schedule. They could have the party when the guests got there, but the sea obliged and thrashed the boat across the waves. The catering containers were dumped on the beach and those who could not make it on their own were lifted high in the air by the boatmen from currach to sand. There were cheers as each one landed. Aunt Flo in her wellies and oil skins ploughed through the waves while Uncle Grant allowed himself to be carried. "Careful Flo, don't fall," Nora remembered him calling.

"Ah, it's only salty water," came Flo's voice across the years.

Nora's wedding arrangements were only a mild surprise. Even her mother had accepted it not being in Cork. Nora had always returned to the island whenever she could. She was twelve when her family left and had declared that she would go back there to live when she grew up. She spent six months there after she came home bruised from London.

And when she and Dennis got engaged she had told him it was totally unspoiled. "Not even a restaurant, only a Church and a pub. Aunt Ellen's lived there all her married life, since Uncle Tim gave up teaching in Dublin. She complains about it, but she wouldn't leave. Mostly, you have to eat tinned veg but it doesn't matter. There's eating and drinking in the air itself. It's such a different place."

"You mean after London?" Dennis asked.

"After anywhere," she said, "I wish we could live there. You wouldn't fancy a bit of a farm?"

"Not even a bit of a one," Dennis said.

Nora sighed, remembering as she poured herself more tea. Ciara, dazed with excitement, went off to dress. A walk to the church would do her a world of good, Nora thought.

On her island, Nora had waited in Aunt Ellen's parlour with the women. From the window she could see as far as the hump in the road. The music was heard before there was sight of Dennis, himself in front, with the pipes, tin whistles, fiddles and bodhráns filling the air above the happy sound of the wind-blown crowd.

The women had drawn Nora away from the window and adjusted the lace curtains. It took half an hour for the procession to reach the house, and the groom's formal knock on the door. The women preserved modesty. "Hush, hush," they stilled the urge to rush to the door so that there was a modest pause before Dennis and Nora faced each other across Aunt Ellen's threshold.

Sitting now in Ciara's wedding car, Nora could feel herself trotting along arm in arm with Dennis, wedding shoes picking up sand, and the breeze lifting her veil. As they walked, the currachs went out to fetch the last of the guests from the steamer, and the boatmen came across the beach. The wedding walk was the best part of Nora's day, capturing the island so that forever after she could escape to it in her mind. Now, as she drove towards the church in the greyness, she recalled that magical light and felt the island breeze on her face.

Danny's car was parked outside the church and one of the ushers waited. "Everything's cool," he said. Ciara stepped onto the red carpet and Nora felt herself passing into church through the islanders and their music, and the whispered *Dia Dhuit* – God be with you – from along the aisle.

A lone piper played the wedding march and after the service the school children's choir and the tin whistles played them back again.

Now, outside another Church by the sea, the confetti and rice fluttered thickly upon the bridal party, and Nora found that she had somehow missed her daughter's wedding ceremony.

It was a perfect day, past in a flash like a meal that takes ages to prepare, and there was the usual mild relief when the young couple left for the airport. It was at this point that Derry and Nora sat together. "How's it going?" Derry asked.

"Gone," Nora answered, surprising herself, "all over now." Her voice was flat. Derry winced.

"It'll look better tomorrow when it really is all over and you've had a rest. Where is Dennis staying tonight?"

"He isn't," Nora said, "not at home."

"It certainly was a performance, Dennis as father of the bride."

"Well, he is the father of the bride."

"Oh, you know what I mean. 'Her mother and I,' "

51

Derry mimicked Dennis, "and he knows she's going to be 'as good a wife as her mother ...'"

"A bonsai woman," Nora said.

"A what woman?"

"Bonsai. You know, the little Japanese trees. They only grow as much as they're let. Stunted."

"Oh Nora, for heaven's sake. You're just feeling sorry for yourself. Not that I blame you, but there's nothing stunted about you. I'd say Dennis is stunted ..."

"No, he's his own size. He's himself. I'm the bonsai."

"I think you've had too much champagne or not enough. Here you are. Let's drink to Ciara. Everything went beautifully for her. It was all perfect. Everything was so normal. Who'd have thought ..." Derry was stuttering.

"It was. It was normal as usual," Nora interrupted, "geraniums in the greenhouse, sherry on the sideboard, lots of tripe with the onions. That's the way normal has always been for us. Normal. Never mind the cloth, feel the width ..." Nora stopped, surprised at the phrase. "What I mean is that behaving normally isn't good enough. The truth has won out after all."

They drank more champagne and Nora proposed a toast: "To bonsai women." Everyone drank, not listening, not caring what they toasted. Seated near Nora, Aunt Flo left her glass bubbling on the table, finger and thumb upon the stem. "I won't drink to that," she told Nora firmly. "I could never drink to a bonsai woman, but here's to the sunflower."

"Right on, Florrie," Derry said," 'atta girl sunflower."

Only a few people knew Aunt Flo's news. "Mustn't steal the bride's thunder," she'd said, "it's only fair to let Ciara have her lovely day and I wouldn't spoil it for the world. Dennis can announce my engagement when the couple leave."

Aunt Flo had caught the bride's bouquet. Standing near a group of girls at whom it was aimed, she leapt off the ground at the same time as the flowers arrived through the air. She clutched them to her nose, blushing and delighted. "Throw it again, Florrie," someone called. She ignored that.

The party had got its second wind and Dennis called order for a toast. Florrie, sprite and light, was beside him in a flash, arthritic fingers on his sleeve. "God, look at her," Nora said to Derry and they watched the old woman in her navy dress awash with cabbage roses. Mists of grey hair flattered her face, her cheeks flushed, her large nose was pale with talc, and her eyes were bright with happiness.

"Raise your glasses for a toast," said Dennis, "I have an engagement to announce. It concerns our young Florrie. As you know she has been away in New Zealand visiting her son, Paul, for some months. And she is back. Back with a flurry, one might say. Dear me, Florrie in a flurry?"

There was a titter.

"In any case," continued Dennis, "it is my proud task to announce Florrie's engagement. I ask you to raise your glasses and drink a toast to Florrie Johnston and Mr Peter Boles of Wellington. Mr Boles," Dennis said, smiling, "is a lucky fellow who has, I know, our warmest congratulations. The toast ladies and gentlemen is Florrie and Peter ..."

There was silence before Nora called "Florrie and Peter," and then commotion.

The evening of Ciara's day became Aunt Flo's engagement party. She fluttered about collecting a posy of congratulations. News of the shipboard romance kept coming back to Nora: "Love at first sight, she says it was," and "they met on a boat on a day trip, imagine!" Bonnie, Ciara's friend, voiced the main curiosity of the young: "Do people do it at that age?"

The men quickly lost interest in the topic, but the women wallowed, many driven inwards by the news even though as a group they were generous.

"She says she couldn't just stay there and get

married", Derry said, "that engagements have their purposes ... did you ever?"

"The bridegroom is only sixty-seven," someone was saying. Florrie's younger, though dedicatedly geriatric sister, Kate, was clearly irritated.

"One man was enough for me," Kate said, "I don't know what she's thinking of. What use is she to anyone at her age? Anyway, it's in God's hands. We'll see if it's His will that she gets married. It's in God's hands."

"She seems pretty sure God will put a stop to Aunt Flo's gallop," murmured Derry.

The younger the people, the less they went on about Aunt Flo's engagement, and Florrie was quite aware that the news made some uneasy. She was used to affecting people. And she also knew that her time was running out. All the more reason to make the best of what was left. She would not have much longer, but please God, not yet?

"Live until you die," she said aloud and chuckled. "Besides, if the good Lord has seen fit to send me Peter at my age, He must intend to give us a bit of time together."

With the last guest gone and Aunt Florrie in bed, Dennis hung around. He did not know how to leave to drive across the city to the Airport Hotel where a room was booked. Nora had avoided him all day. Now he felt a hollowness. Things were unfinished, so much unsaid. He could not leave like this and at such an hour. He had never seen Nora look so exhausted, the glamorous clothes seemed to emphasise her weariness. He went into the kitchen and put on the kettle.

The normality of the sounds annoyed Nora. Making tea as if ... She went slowly upstairs, heavy with disappointment. She felt the day frittered, lost. For months she had lived for this wedding and somehow it had just happened without her. She had not been present, had not been at Ciara's wedding after all.

Still, Ciara had thought the day perfect, that was the main thing. Nora was in bed when Dennis arrived.

"I thought you'd like this," he said.

She took the cup from him and sipped.

"So," Dennis said, "that's that."

"Yes," Nora said.

"Think it went well?"

She did not want to talk to him. There was a long pause before she said: "They seemed to enjoy themselves."

"Nora," Dennis said, "it hasn't been all disappointment, you know as marriages go ...."

"Dennis please, let's not get into all that again. I'm exhausted. It's settled ..."

"But Nora, there's so much to discuss. It's all so unreal. When can we sit down and talk ....?"

"It seemed pretty real to you two weeks ago, pretty real all those years you were planning to walk out." Her voice had begun to shake: "All too bloody real, and nobody knew what was in your mind ..."

Suddenly, Nora was crying, crying huge sobs that blocked her nose so that she had to breathe through her mouth. She struggled for control, but streaming and gasping she was helpless, hiding her face in the sheet. She was unaware of Dennis's relief when he realised that he could not possibly leave with Nora in such a state, but, weakly, she pushed him away when he put his arms around her. Then, since he did not interfere with her weeping, could not break through her desolate feelings, she let him be. In her misery, she heard him say: "I love you Nora, I always have, in my way." It came from too far away to matter one way or the other.

Nora started awake after nine o'clock. "There now, shush Nora ..." said Dennis. She jumped out of bed and went down to the kitchen. She drank her coffee in the Other Room with the door locked and when Dennis knocked, she did not answer. When she heard him leave she went for more coffee. She drank it as she stared into space and during the next few days she often became aware that she had lapsed into that state.

Almost a week had passed when Nora suddenly erupted in fury. Damn Dennis Ryan. He had ruined Ciara's wedding for her, and after all the planning, the dieting, the lists. He must have known what the wedding meant to her, but it had not stopped him. She'd been a ghost on the day, smiling, sociable, like a ghost. Not there, not at the wedding of her dreams. And now her beloved Ciara was gone. Damn Dennis Ryan, blast him, and she was in this frame of mind when she picked up the Indian letter again. A season of weddings. Weddings. She'd missed the only one that mattered ... Still, why not?

Aunt Flo wrinkled with enthusiasm. "What do I think? I think it's a marvellous idea. At worst you'll see India. And it will give you and Dennis time to sort yourselves out. Just as long as you're back for my wedding! Of course you must go. And October is a lovely time to be in that part of India." And they went together to book Nora's ticket.

It's like one of my binges, Nora thought, I gobbled up Ciara's wedding without tasting it and now I have to have another one.

CHAPTER 6

The sound of water distracted Nora from the window of the cake shop at The Pyramids. It led her to the waterfall which ran down one mossy wall in the garden, cooling the air around the swimming pool which was shaped like a giant lily pad. Forgetting the sugar palace and golden trunk of confectioners' jewels, Nora hurried to get her bathing things.

She chose a chair under an umbrella by the deserted pool from where she could read a sign "AGE," but when she leaned forward she saw it said "Massage". She sat back to relax as a gang of boys burst into the garden. "Look Master," shouted one of the boys and Nora watched him disappear beneath the water.

When the boy surfaced, Nora saw that his "Master" was Leo. "Excellent, now I can see how you are practising," and then spotting Nora, Leo bowed briefly before diving into the water. She watched him swim and instruct the boys, impressed by his skill until she felt the sun bite, and slid off the edge of the pool.

Nora stayed out of the way of boys swimming to practise her back stroke. Leo surfaced beside her.

"Like so, stretch the arm straight, keeping in a circle," he instructed in the same voice he used to the boys. She tried, but could not manage both arms at the same time. "Watch," he said, "watch how I do," and standing straight, he wheeled his arms slowly backwards where he stood, then lay back and rolled away. "See," he called, "the arms are like wheels?" Nora found him an excellent teacher but soon he spied

57

that one of the boys needed attention and swam off.

She practised until she was tired and was sure she had it right when Leo returned: "Like this," he corrected, bringing her arm around in a perfect circle with one hand holding the wrist and the other on her shoulder joint. "Touch the ears barely, like so. Now again. Once more. Ah, here is tight. You should have massage. Massage will loosen this shoulder for swimming. Feel here, it is stiff?"

"Who gives massage?" Nora asked.

"There are three people giving. One lady and a man and me."

"Will you give me a massage," Nora asked. Did she imagine that flicker of surprise?

"OK," he said, swaying his head back and forth, "I will do."

Even as they stepped into the lift, Nora noticed that Leo was different, distant now. Yesterday, with Mother Bridgid, he had been the host: protective, friendly though slightly formal. And the ease of the swimming pool seemed to fade bit by bit as they rose in silence from the ground floor. She fancied that a little more escaped as the door opened on each level and they looked out upon empty spaces of marble and floral arrangements before it closed again.

Nora tried to appear at ease as they walked in silence along the hall to her room, but her face began to twitch and she panicked. What was wrong? Was this a mistake? Was he feeling uncomfortable too? Why was he silent?

Later, Nora would tell herself: "Of course I wouldn't do it here. But you land in situations in a foreign country on your own. You get confused without knowing you are. Everything seemed unreal in any case. Somehow normal behaviour didn't come into it. It wasn't relevant. Anyway, I wasn't sure what normal behaviour was in that situation. And he was an amazing swimming instructor. I really was only thinking of my back stroke. I should have waited until there was a massage room available, but ..."

In the hall on the way to her room Nora battled with the undercurrents. What was happening? She dared not ask in case she was imagining it.

Leo was still silent as they came to her door, but he swayed his head. What did that damn head shaking mean? She could not ask. Why wouldn't he say something? She could not think of anything to say. A stabbing pain in her head made her close one eye as she searched in the depths of her canvas handbag for the key. She searched until the pain passed.

Nora winced at the sight of her room. She had been delighted with it. Now, its luxury embarrassed her. She tightened the sash of her beach robe and tidied the magazines off the bed.

Silently Leo looked around, frankly examining everything, item by item; luggage, silk bed quilt, the flowers, the fruit bowl, her silver backed hair brush and her battery of expensive jars and bottles on the dressing table. She felt decadent, despised. He could think what he liked, contempt for the pampered Irish lady. Alone, so far from home. He probably thinks I'm English anyway. How would she get around the massage? She put herself on trial: Mrs Ryan, you did invite this man to your room?

God, if she got out of this, she'd never tell a soul. She'd been gormless, an eejit. Massage indeed. Will you give me a massage? The voice in her head mimicked. Perhaps massage was all he intended. He seemed well accepted by the people at the hotel desk. She sensed that the joke was on Western women who brought the swimming instructor to their room. He would probably tell them all about it.

The mirror behind Leo's head reflected her sunned pinkness and she panicked. How could she reveal her body's secrets to this perfect stranger? Not perfect, a bit thin, but no scars or signs of aging. Definitely no stretch marks. She could hear her sister's gentle chiding over a drink before she left Dublin:

"You really never looked better. Well, of course, we're not twenty, but you've lost so much weight for the wedding and you have that lovely hair. You dress a bit settled, but forty-three is young these days. Get some jeans. You act settled because of Dennis. Well, now he's gone, you can let bad luck go with him." Derry had been careful not to say anything that sounded like "I told you so", but years ago she had told Nora: "Nature goofed with Dennis, he's a waste of time," and Nora had gone all pink and changed the subject.

"Anyway, you look great. Everyone says you look great," Derry had said, her eyes filling with tears as she threw her arms around Nora and kissed her. "Not every woman gets a complete second chance. Go at it Nora."

If this is it, I'd be better at home, Nora thought.

"Would you like something to drink?" she asked.

"Yes, that would be fine."

"What would you like? I'm having tea." Was he disappointed? "Would you like a beer? Perhaps some lassi?"

"No, no," he said, "tea is good."

She rang room service and ordered. He sat relaxed, still glancing over the room.

"What will I wear for massage?" she asked.

"Whatever you wish," he said, unhelpfully. "This is oil?" he asked, picking up the bottle, "We can use this."

In the bathroom, Nora hung her robe behind the door. She watched herself in the mirror over the sink, and hated the way her body fell into its own shape as she peeled off the well engineered suit of elasticised black. She thought herself horribly white. White and flabby. She could not bear him to look at her. She brushed her hair and thought about putting on make-up, but washed her face instead. Mascara would be a come-on, lipstick worse. Her pink shoulders had grown pinker. She picked up the toilette water and put it down. As she stepped out of the bathroom, the doorbell rang. She opened it and the boy carried the tray past her and placed it on the table in front of the window.

"Sign Madam?"

Would she be asked to sign for the massage? Then she would know. She signed for the tea and was aware that the men avoided each other's eyes.

Nora sat opposite Leo. "Milk?"

"Yes, milk," he said.

"How old are you?" she asked, surprising herself.

"I am thirty years old," he said.

Some day, Nora thought.

Leo took the tea and then with an air of someone learning a new game, asked: "And you, you are how old?"

"Forty-eight," she lied, "how old is your mother?"

He was surprised: "I do not know."

"Is she alive? Where does she live, your mother?"

"My mother is so much alive," said Leo, accepting a coconut pyramid, "she is in my home at my village. She is the grandmother of my twin sons."

He looked straight into her face, aware of having identified himself as a man of consequence, the maker of twin sons. Not a day older than twenty-four, Nora thought.

"My wife, she gave birth to my sons more than one month ago, but she is not strong. She is too weak and my mother is looking after all the things in the home."

"How old is your wife?"

He thought for a moment. "Ah, now she is nineteen years. Last year she has a child, daughter. Before that, a boy died. Now we have twin sons. This will be enough. I am sure. Twin sons," he repeated with the air of someone satisfied at a job done properly at last. Nora almost smiled.

"Do you work all year as a swimming instructor, give massages?" she asked.

"Sometimes I teach. The students you saw with me in the pool. They are going into competitions next

61

month. They come to the hotel to me each day. Sometimes I take the boat out to Elephanta with tourists to the caves. Also I work at my uncle's stall in the market. You will come and see? Many things to buy there. I do many things. Also, at my village." And then, with a hint of a smile he added: "I drive nuns where they must go. Help at the convent."

As Nora put her cup down, Leo suddenly removed his short sleeved shirt and stepped out of the beige trousers. He wore black briefs. Carefully he removed the little cross around his neck and put it on the tea tray.

"Here, place a towel like so," he said, spreading it on the quilt. She took it from him, removed the silk cover and spread the towel before she lay upon it, her cheek pressed into the pillow. She heard him unscrew the top from the bottle of sun lotion, smelled the oil and felt it roll across her shoulders. M-mmm, that was why they were here, her shoulders. The oil was scooped up by Leo's hand as he began to knead and smooth. Nora had quite forgotten her back stroke. She helped him loosen her towel to work on her back.

He had worked for several minutes when she realised he was not a professional, but his hands were firm and sensitive and reminded her that she had not been touched for so long. He knelt astride her hips, working back and forth, and she was aware of an unthreatening softness.

"Tell me," said this man who worked at many things, "if you like something, I will do."

When she did not answer he worked on until she felt his confidence grow and he achieved a rhythm. Gradually, Nora felt the control she had gained by chatting about his family disappear and was conscious only of his hands on her skin. She felt her throat dry and her forehead knot. What would Dennis say if he saw her now?

She was aware of the rhythm and the firming bulge, and her own increasing panic. She must stop the rhythm, but how could she turn on her back and wrap herself in the towel at the same time. She did not want to reveal her breasts. With tugs and difficulty, she managed the switch and Leo, rearranged in the tussle, looked puzzled: "Now the legs, perhaps?" he asked.

"OK," she replied, not without humour. He dribbled oil onto her right foot, rubbing it in all over and working with firm, pressing, soothing movements, reminding her how her feet had suffered since she arrived in Bombay. She thought he had finished with her foot when he began to work on each toe. She did not know her toes could set off such feeling and was relieved when Leo let go of her foot to begin again. Once more, he pressed and continued pressing until he had pressed all memory of pain from her foot before he began on her toes. Nora grew more and more tense as he went from toe to toe, rolled each one between his fingers. Finally, his oily fingers slipped in and out, between all of her toes, massaging.

Nora pressed herself firmly into the bed and sighed with relief when Leo moved back to her ankle. Slowly he worked on her leg. She squeezed her eyes tightly. She should have sent him away after tea. She could see from years ago fat Uncle Eric's face gleaming as he sat at head of table. No wonder he always looked so pleased with life. She bet he didn't screw up his eyes and knot up his insides. He'd been seen more than once with girls so obviously paid. Poor Uncle Eric, how could she have sneered at him? Poor girls.

Nora was aware of shedding years under Leo's hands as feelings surfaced from numbness, feelings never fulfilled, feelings like unexpected but welcome guests. She slipped into a few seconds of pure pleasure when she was unconscious of anything else, but was able to get hold of herself enough to resume resistance. She was thinking that she had forgotten the existence of such feelings when she became aware that Leo's dark eyes were on her face, hesitant. He bent towards her mouth and had barely touched her lips with his when

63

she snapped her head aside: "No," she said, "please let me get up."

He stopped, unsure. Unable to cope, she feigned control: "Enough," she said in a voice trying to be clear and firm but Leo waited. "I have to phone Mother Bridgid," she said and that did it. He moved to let her rise from the bed.

He remained on the bed, sitting cross-legged in his briefs while she went to the bathroom and put on her robe. When she came back and reached for her purse, he shrugged and moved towards his clothes.

"How much do I owe you?" she asked .

He was zipping up his trousers and swayed his head. She handed him some notes. He did not look at them. He was on his way out.

"You are sure I should go? Maybe you call me tomorrow?"

Sensing that anger was surfacing out of his confusion, Nora gently began to close the door.

"Thank you," she said, "I must make that call."

Trembling, Nora marvelled that it had been as she could not have remembered it. Her senses still so enlivened, she lay back on the bed thinking over what had happened. Soon in her mind it was happening again, she should have let him stay, but this time she did not jump up. Presently she fell asleep and when she woke she lay wondering about herself and her awkwardness with Leo. She felt humiliated by her inability to have sex with him. She'd had other massages without getting into a state. Except for the feet, he wasn't that great. Had she really wanted to go through with it? Why couldn't she? Could Derry have done it? If she'd wanted to. She'd been dying to. God, to have let go. Afraid. What was wrong with her? She felt the jeer of Parvati's friends. They were right, she was uptight and middle-class. Pathetic. Still, she wasn't as dead as she had thought. Not at all dead.

Chapter 7

Nora bought a card for Dennis, one of those Moghul harem scenes and wrote: "India is no place for jadedness. More exciting than one could ever imagine. Marvellous weather. Nora." It did not look much on the card, but it took her ages to decide what to say and she could not write "love". Then she realised that she did not have Dennis's address. After a life time, not to even have his address. Ciara must have it. In Canada. Aunt Flo, Aunt Flo would keep in touch with him, so Nora addressed the card to "Aunt Flo and Dennis". Somehow, the message seemed more suitable for both than it would have for either.

Upset, Nora ruminated that night and as the ache in her throat spread into her chest, hurt and anger overcame rest. She saw her life lying behind her in dishes of meat and fish and vegetables, trivia and endless domesticity. So much of her life had revolved around food, no wonder she felt devoured, trapped by diets. Her mind ferried food from the shops to the car to the refrigerator to the table and on to domestic pets, left-overs, garbage, special occasions. There seemed no end to the organising and servicing, her life's work. Ah, but didn't you enjoy it at the time, said a voice in her head. What choice did I have, she answered, brain-washed as I was, what choice? Bitterly, she resented house-wifery as the rat that had gnawed away at her life, day after day, leaving nothing. She wondered why she had never thought like that before.

In her dreams, a convoy of lorries trundled through

65

her head piled high with dirty clothes, laundered clothes, new clothes for everybody and household goods. Years of shopping. She felt robbed, bereft.

What would I have done otherwise? She wondered. If Dennis had been different, they would be going on together ... why had she frittered so many years ... put so little value on her own life, like the money she made at the antique shop. One married because it was expected and then there was all that to do. If she had only thought. If she could have realised. Even the business had not been deliberate. She had drifted into antiques out of her browsing around the shops and love of old things. She had been surprised when she made money buying and selling antiques.

Until Dennis announced his departure, Nora regarded the money she had made from her antique shop as a sort of luxury fund. She had bought some beautiful old things with it: clothes, gifts, and given Ciara a cheque that left the girl amazed.

"It's not a wedding present," Nora had told her, "just for you from your Mam."

And she had never touched the money her mother left. It was understood that Dennis was the bread-winner so that his was the real money. A decrease in that would have alarmed, whereas her money was different, like play money. And now, it made her independent, but like a person who has never suffered a memorable illness she did not appreciate that. She grieved that her life amounted to so little and was ashamed because it was her own fault. She should have faced what was going on and refused to live like that, but as she wondered what she would do if she could start all over again she thought that the mistake had been in marrying Dennis in the first place. Having done that, and there being no question of divorce, she could not think what else she might have done differently. And in most ways, Dennis was easy to live with, she liked him and it hadn't been a bad life. I'm just over-tired, she thought, if I get some sleep it will look

66

different tomorrow. When she thought of Leo's visit on the previous night she squeezed her eyes tight with embarrassment before she remembered that she had not been numb.

In her sleep, Nora thought that she woke because someone had whispered her name. Then she heard the sound of a wave slapping onto the beach. And she knew that it was not the sea outside, nor any wave upon a beach, but the slapping sound made by the enormous snake she would see to the left of her if she turned her head. Staring ahead, for she also knew that she must not look at it, she felt the giant creature raise a coil and slap sluggishly upon the floor. Her head still turned from it, she saw more clearly now, a monster of browns and gold, and piggish bulk. It seemed to Nora that she lay there staring ahead for ages while it squirmed almost unperceptibly within its coils.

Nora's back ached with the creature's effort to rise, so heavy it could hardly move, and she felt nauseated as it finally succeeded in heaving itself up off the ground before it collapsed within its coils. Slowly, intermittently, like the waves breaking on the beach, it rose and slapped. Between each fresh struggle, Nora lay in unbearable fatigue until the awful gasping head of the creature imprinted upon her mind and she slipped into darkness. She woke feeling drugged and looked quickly towards the floor of her room. It was carpeted. The snake had smacked its coil upon marble.

The phone rang. It was Sophie Rosen. Nora had slept until 10a.m. What time would Mrs Ryan like to be picked up? She opted to take a taxi to Sophie's house and was about to go shopping for a wedding present when Leo arrived to take her to Mass. Nora had meant to put Mother Bridgid off but after her bad night was glad to go to the convent. Leo was formal.

By the time Nora had managed to get away from Mother Bridgid's Irish gathering of people to meet her she was in no mood for shopping and decided to give one of her "in case" gifts, a batik of a village by a Cork artist.

It was after two o'clock when Nora reached the elbow of Sophie's cul-de-sac and had to rouse the sleeping man in the gate hut to let her in. The freshly gilded gates were entwined with flowers. Nora rang the bell, startled by the stirring of a servant sleeping on the verandah. Was she waking the whole house, she wondered before the door opened to the refreshing breeze of Sophie's welcome. She wore a cotton kaftan and hair-clips held strategic curls of her hennaed hair.

"Something cold to drink," she said to the air as she led Nora into a cool room of chintz and wicker-work, "I am so glad you are here, I couldn't stop jumping up and down." Sophie poured fresh lime over ice. "Have you ever been at a Jewish wedding before? No? A wedding is a wedding, but it'll be a bit different. You must tell me what you think. Ah, Max," she said, stretching a hand towards the man who had entered. "This is my husband, Max Rosen." She beamed proudly: "And Max, this is Mrs Ryan from Ireland. Nora Ryan, all the way for our daughter's wedding. To bring *mazel.*"

"You're very welcome," Max said to Nora and then to Sophie: "I can't close an eye."

"So don't close an eye." Sophie shrugged. "It's not every day a daughter gets married. Come. Have some lime juice and relax. There's a law that says you must sleep? There's no law."

Max Rosen sat down and Sophie tidied his hair with affectionate brushes of her hand and kissed him noisily on the cheek: "The father of the bride. Look at him. Who would think," Sophie asked proudly, "who would think he was old enough to be the father of a bride?"

Nora was embarrassed by Sophie's adoration of her handsome husband and looked away as Sophie pressed Max's head against her bosom:

"Hey," he yelled, feigning alarm, "I'll smother before the wedding."

"You should be so lucky," Sophie laughed. "Excuse us, Nora" she said, "we're not behaving."

Perhaps someone like Sophie could have handled Dennis, Nora thought and knew immediately that Dennis would have run a mile from someone as earthy as Sophie. She really should write to Dennis, Aunt Flo would forward it. She must write. And say what? She wondered what to say. *Thank you, it was nice being married to you?* And so it was, she flayed herself, nice, ever so nice. Had there ever been a time when she wasn't lonely?

Suddenly the door opened to a commotion in the hall and a woman with her hair in curlers burst into the room.

"Max, Max, come. There is a problem. We have a bridegroom who wants to talk to the bride before the wedding, no less. Come."

In the hall, women argued as they crowded around a slight, balding young man with glasses whom Nora noticed was calm in the middle of all. Everyone stopped talking when Sophie appeared. The young man spoke to her and Sophie answered: "You can't talk to the bride now. You'll see her at five o'clock. You'll see her for the rest of your life. Honestly, Alan, this we don't need. Please now leave. Your mother knew you were coming here?"

Alan stood his ground, calm and ready to take advantage of the slightest gap in the wall of women at the bottom of the stairs.

"Look old man," said Max, "this is no time to upset everybody. You know better. You can't see the bride now."

Alan stretched taller: "Yes, yes, I must. I have to talk to her. Just for a minute?"

Nora winced as everyone talked at once. The argument was going nowhere when suddenly there was silence and Sophie called:

"No, no, Sherna, go back."

Looking up, Nora thought she recognised the girl at the top of the stairs before she realised that the delicate face revealed Sophie's hidden beauty. Sherna waited until Alan broke the silence from the foot of the stairs: "I have to speak to you."

"But Alan, you're not supposed to be here. You know that."

"Superstition. We have to talk. Five minutes Sherna. Five minutes? "

Sherna hesitated before she said: "Let him come up Dad. As a matter of fact it says in the book that the groom is supposed to come and lift the bride's veil off her face before she leaves the house. To make sure he's getting the right bride." "That was the custom," Sophie interrupted, "it's called *decking the challah*, remember Max? Who does it now? Anyway, you're not even dressed."

"Come on Alan." Sherna's voice was tender as she moved back towards her room. There was an exasperated sigh from Sophie: "Alright, but not upstairs. In the study," and she crossed the hall to open the door on the other side of the stairs. Alan followed Sherna into the room and the door closed after them. Everyone waited in the hall while Nora strolled back into the kitchen and stood looking out at the garden until Sophie came.

"He's gone," she reported, "so now we'll dress the bride. Get ready ourselves."

Nora found herself crowded into the bride's room with aunts and cousins who came and went in various stages of their own preparation while the bride dressed. Sophie disappeared and re-appeared in an apple green sari embroidered with silver and tiny stones. She took a bouquet of pink flowers to match her sari blouse from the large box on the bed and fixed them in her hair. Then she handed Nora a yellow sherpa daisy:

"I knew no matter what you wore this would look perfect in your hair," she said.

"She's fasting," Sophie said to Nora. "How are you feeling?" she asked Sherna.

"Hungry," replied Sherna happily. "I think ravenous."

"What was so important Alan had to see you?" Sophie asked, "Oh, and this is Nora I told you about, Mrs Ryan from Dublin."

The bride smiled.

"You're very welcome. He wanted to ask me to marry him," she said. "He wanted me to say I really wanted to marry him and well, other things like that."

"Very romantic at the last minute,"said one of the aunts sarcastically.

Sophie looked down at her smiling daughter. "Now he asks you to marry him? At the last minute he rushes in here like a *meshuganah* and demands to see the bride. Cold feet if you ask me. Definitely cold feet. A bridegroom is entitled to be nervous, but upsetting everybody in two houses? His mother was just on the phone to apologise ..."

"It wasn't nerves," Sherna said. "He couldn't sleep last night thinking that maybe the wedding wasn't our idea. I mean, you and his parents arranged it all, always assumed ..."

Sophie interrupted: "Against your will, we arranged? You didn't go out together? Arranged? You're such strangers. Arranged!"

"Well, it sort of was arranged. I mean, the families brought us together. And we always knew we were getting married, but Alan suddenly thought that he had never asked me to marry him and he had to know if I was just doing what was expected of me."

"So, what if you were?" Sophie asked loudly.

Sherna laid her head against her mother's stomach: "Then we'd have stopped the wedding," she said mischievously, "but it's OK, isn't it? I said yes. After all, it was the only proposal I'll ever get, and it was almost too late to count."

The girl reminded Nora of Ciara and tears came to her eyes.

Sophie sat down. "Too late? All this romance could have been a disaster," she said with mock annoyance.

71

"We're giving our daughter to such a man? At the last minute with the *chuppah* waiting ... and you only know each other all your lives. Romantic? *Meshugah!*"

Sherna smiled at Nora: "It means mad."

The bride was seated on a chair covered with white silk and later her seat in the car was also covered with white.

It's to do with virginity, Nora later wrote Aunt Flo, I thought it was to keep the dress clean. Her dress was white silk with an embroidered hem, fresh water pearls and tiny jewels. I met her mother in a jewellery shop when she was buying a fortune in jewellery for her, but a Jewish bride can't wear any for the ceremony, not even an engagement ring.

They don't stand in front of an altar, although the bride walks up the aisle. They stand under a thing called a chuppah. You make a throat clearing sound to get the "ch". It looks like a four-poster bed with a blue and white silk cover for the canopy part, and the posts were covered with white blossoms of all kinds.

The groom put the ring on the bride's index finger. Then, a blue velvet bag with a Star of David embroidered on it was put on the floor. The groom stamped on it and there was a huge crunching noise. Everybody laughed because there is a glass in the bag and he stamped so hard it must have been powdered. The symbolism is that anyone who wants to separate the pair must put the glass back together. Although Jews can get divorced. It seems everybody can except the Irish."

Writing to Aunt Flo, Nora wished that she could describe the emotion of her "Jewish experience", the enthusiasm. Now and then the excitement had reached a hysterical pitch. "*Mazeltov,*" everybody kept saying to everyone else and Sophie informed them: "She also just got her daughter married." And after that people kept wishing Nora *Mazeltov* too.

Nora did not tell Aunt Flo what happened when she arrived back at the hotel after the wedding. She heard the disturbance when she stepped out of the lift: shouting, furniture falling, glass smashing. She was reluctant to go in the direction of the noise, but when she looked down the hall towards her room, curious guests stood in their door-ways so she continued on.

As she put the key in the lock, the door two rooms down on the other side of the hall was being banged shut each time someone tried to open it. There was fury in the air, men's voices, and when she looked across the hall the door trapped someone's foot. It was a white foot, Nora noticed, scratched and grey with dirt, but definitely white. Suddenly, the owner of the foot broke free of the door and with a yell threw herself into Nora's room, just as Nora's key opened the door.

They were both on the other side of the door with the bolt shot before Nora realised it was Parvati. The younger woman pressed her body against the wall with relief and panted. With the back of her hand she wiped her bleeding nose on the sleeve that hung ripped from the bodice of her wine coloured Afghanistan dress.

Men were outside, shouting. Afraid that the door was going to burst open, Nora pressed her hand over her mouth.

"The phone," Parvati pointed, and Nora ran to her bedside table. "Send some help," Nora told reception. "This minute, please. I need help. Someone is trying to get into my room. They're banging the door down. Please come quickly. Five-O-Seven. Yes, five-zero-seven, hurry ..."

Parvati had staggered after her and collapsed on the carpet, resting her head on the bed.

"Oh God," Nora whimpered, "they'll break the door down ..."

Parvati crawled towards the door. Getting up, she dragged a chair and propped it under the door-handle.

73

"The bathroom," Nora said, "we can lock ourselves in there."

She felt safer in there, sitting on the lavatory seat as Parvati handed her a glass with water. The noise outside stopped and they could hear voices in quiet discussion. The conversation seemed to taper off to a grumble. Then there was a respectable knock on the door.

"Don't open it, it's a trick," said Parvati, as Nora opened the bathroom door. There was another knock, more urgent this time.

"Mrs Nora, it is Thomas."

"Leo?" Nora asked, unsure.

"Yes, yes. Open the door. Only I am here now."

She let him in and he went past her to Parvati who sat on the bed.

"So," Leo said, "This is a fine business. The hotel is entirely disturbed."

Parvati, with her head bent, did not look up.

Leo hesitated before he caught hold of Parvati's hand and dragged her to her feet. "Challah, come. Out of here," he said.

"There's no hurry. Let her catch her breath," Nora pleaded. Parvati was fixing her dress with two small safety-pins she had found on Nora's bedside table.

"Have a shower and take something to wear," Nora urged, "what about some food, tea even?"

"Nothing, no room service," Leo ordered, "she cannot stay in this hotel. I was downstairs or the police would have her by now."

Nora had taken a cotton dress from her wardrobe and handing it to Parvati, asked: "What happened with those men?"

Parvati was indignant: "I agreed fifty rupees with one of those Arabs and all his bleedin' friends wanted a go, didn't they? We jus' got started and suddenly there was five of 'em in 'is room. They wouldn't even listen to givin' me extra money. The one I went wi' sez wot's the different? If he paid for the night he's entitled to treat

74

his friends. I sez the difference was two hundred rupees, that's wot difference. Besides I don't do that stuff. D'you know wot they was on for then?" Parvati was about to tell them, but Leo snapped: "Put the dress on if that is your wish and come with me."

Silently, Parvati took off her torn dress and dropped it on the floor. She stood naked, her milk white body in contrast to her weather-beaten limbs. She concentrated on separating the hem of Nora's dress before she pulled it over her head. Then, she stood straight, dropped her eyelids, and joined her palms with reverence, tinged with the merest hint of mocking, in salutation to Nora.

"Do you need some money?" Nora asked.

Parvati hesitated before she shrugged: "It's been a bad night but naw luv. It probably serves me right for being greedy. I got to pay me way, remember?"

As the pair went down the hall, Nora was held at the door by Parvati's walk. That kind of walk always stirred uncomfortable feelings in her. Mixed feelings. The first time she had seen it was at school, part of an outbreak amongst the girls. The nuns paid no heed. Appeared not to notice. But they had noticed Maisie Daly's walk. Kept on at her about it. Insolent, they had called it. Maisie moved through Nora's head, tormenting the nuns. The way Maisie had said that she could not help the way she walked "anymore than you can, Sister ..." The girl's had been amazed at Mother Veronica's rage in response to that.

Now Nora realised it was the way Maisie had said it, full of her sex: "I can't help it Sister," expressing an awareness of what really bothered Sister Veronica.

Nora felt again the sting of Maisie's brush-off as she watched Parvati, more wondrously "insolent" than anyone she had ever seen. Parvati turned before she stepped into the lift and waved in such a way that Nora thought would have sent the nuns into a fit. She realised with a little sadness that she would probably never see Parvati again.

75

Getting into her cool nightgown, Nora wondered about the Arabs. Such carry-on. Imagine Dennis, but that was too ridiculous. What could a bunch of men want with one woman? She assumed it wasn't taking turns? Or what Clara called a gang bang. It was so unbelievably squalid, and yet wondering about it made her feel cut-off, a sexual outsider.

I must be looking for something to worry about, Nora thought. I wouldn't want any part of that. At least I haven't had to live like Parvati, and then it dawned on her that in a way she had done just that. Dennis did not want sex, so she'd had none. That was selling. To have what she'd had, the safe, sheltered life, she'd been celibate. Danced to someone else's sexual tune. Put like that Nora saw herself in the same boat as Parvati. And Leo.

Lying there, the lonely despair of a night in California leaked from Nora's memory. It was their fifteenth wedding anniversary and they'd gone to visit Dennis's sister, Grace in San Diego and had driven around the Cliff Road. It wasn't until after they had booked in for the night at a motel that Nora realised that the place was full of honeymooners. Young lovers charged the atmosphere. Golden-limbed, they snuggled in nooks midst indoor jungles, beside ponds of tropical fish, or mooned through the air in a two-seater swing. In the bar, young couples sat twinned in corners, or grouped around tables, teeth flashing, tans gleaming, touching, laughing. Their laughter mocked Nora. She eased her hand under Dennis's on the table. He patted it, smiled and passed her the dinner menu.

They ate by moonlight, king crab and steak, listening to the ocean upon the rocks below. Even though she left more than half the food on her plate, Nora always remembered it as a delicious meal. Dennis had given her an anniversary present, a watch with diamonds floating in its face.

Nora made an event of getting ready for bed, chatting, discussing the day, flirting with Dennis. She had not removed her make-up because of the moonlight through the window. She squirmed against Dennis and he said: "If we make an early start we'll get a move on before the day gets hot. Today was a grand day, wasn't it?"

She had felt his lips on her forehead seconds before his snore. Now, she squeezed her eyes tight against the memory as she felt herself move to a space of her own, a space less lonely than Dennis's arms. She was annoyed at having laid a trap for herself. She should have known better than that. All of that was a problem solved, a problem past. Washed blank by time. She sobbed quietly. She had avoided the acid of disappointment for ages before that night.

Preparing for California, Nora realised that she had grown out of touch with her body, lost interest in clothes, put on weight. She'd gone shopping and the sales lady had thrown herself into the task when Nora said she needed clothes for California. Some of the outfits made her feel a fraud. They looked vibrant, sexy. And reminded her that she was not.

The sounds outside the motel had faded away as Nora lay awake and overheard a couple getting ready for bed. Faint voices, a shoe dropped, muffled laughter. Then silence, so that she thought she must be the only one left awake. Until the creaking began. She listened as the creaking overhead settled into a steady, unmistakable rhythm. Unable to distract herself from it, Nora slipped from the bed and went into the bathroom.

She brushed her teeth again, read the blurb sheet in her vitamin pills, rummaged in her bath-bag and removed her nail polish. Unable to stay in the bathroom any longer, she went back to bed and found the creaking had stopped. Maybe now she could sleep. Dennis snored.

The creaking began again. This time the rhythm was slower, the noise clearer. She was drawn into it. She closed her eyes and felt the weight of the man's body on her own, smelled the sunned skin. Her back arched. Her hand slipped between her legs, fingers sliding, taking up the rhythm from overhead, smoothly, relentlessly, until she curled her toes against the desire to clamp her thighs together. Sweating, she counted the creaks, twenty-six, twenty-seven, twenty-eight ... faster, faster, she unclenched her teeth, forcing air out of her lungs. She was afraid that she would wake Dennis, but clutched the hem of her night-dress. Her cry came with the cry above.

CHAPTER 8

Mother Bridgid sent Leo to put Nora on the train for New Delhi even though she had told the nun that she could manage perfectly well.

"Is Parvati alright?" Nora asked.

"Who knows?" he replied. "Probably she is fine," and there was no further reference to the night before. He was silent and detached as he drove.

"You work hard." Nora attempted conversation.

He shrugged his shoulders. "It is necessary." That was that.

When she followed him into the vastness of Victoria Terminus with its crowds and bewildering number of ticket windows, Nora understood Mother Bridgid's insistence on sending Leo. And as the reservations clerk gave them his special attention, she hid her amusement at Leo's pride in the nun's power to smooth the way.

On the platform, the tension between them eased for the first time since the massage as Leo brought cold drinks and they sat to wait for the train ... He asked her about Ireland, talked about survival in Bombay, rail travel, warned her to keep watch on her luggage and told her what to tip the porters.

Nora dared to ask him about his twin babies.

"They are growing bigger," he said. "Come," and he stepped aside to allow a porter to pile Nora's luggage on his head, "there is your train."

They struggled through the crowds as he searched for her name on the lists stuck to first class coaches, and helped her to board.

"You are a kind, but not wise lady," he said before he left, "I wish you to have a pleasant journey to Delhi."

She watched him walk away. Leopold Sebastian Thomas, she thought sadly. He did not look back.

Watching from the window Nora was glad to have escaped the platform and thought that she must be the only lone traveller. There were so many groups in the throngs: families, pairs. Three men chatted in the other seats and she fancied that she saw herself through their eyes, an oddity, a woman alone, obviously far from where she belonged.

She opened her book, but was soon distracted by life outside as the train sped from the city. There were so many people, and such struggle in circumstances so different from anything she knew in Ireland. She focused on individuals, in awe of their battles for survival, watching this one or that one for as long as the train would allow. Her eyes twisted after a hugely pregnant child trying to walk in a sari that was too long for her. Another world, thought Nora, I'm in another world. And then a sudden dread raised goose-pimples on her skin. She could die in India. She could die on this very train, from a heart attack or something. People did die suddenly. Her throat ached and her mind chanted the childhood prayer: "If I should die before I wake ..." If she died in the night they would find her in the morning. She tried to imagine the scene and became uneasy at the thought that her body would be a nuisance to strangers.

There was no nuns' man to pave Nora's way in New Delhi, but a porter came on board the train and without a word carried off her luggage. Twice, she lost him in the crowds and she was trembling with exertion by the time he handed her over to a taxi driver.

The man silently packed her into his yellow and black taxi and waited. "Any place in particular?" he asked.

"Can you take me to a nice hotel, please?" Nora said.

He took off like a dodgem car through the Delhi traffic while he swayed his turban: "How nice?" he asked bluntly, "two hundred rupees? One hundred or five hundred rupees? Fifty rupees? Which nice?"

Nora feared she had underestimated her required degree of niceness as they approached the hotel through gates surrounded by the canvas shacks and string beds of a settled community of street dwellers leading on to a market for as far as she could see, but when the car moved into the driveway there was the surprise of beautiful grounds and leafy shade and she was soon established in old world colonial style.

Her room was Georgian, with a white marble fireplace and boards that creaked under the old carpet. That evening she wrote Derry:

Shades of the Raj, a bit worn in the centre rather than around the edges which are the new bits but the original building reminds me of our Shelbourne, you know comfortable without being flash. Naturally, I don't have a view of Stephen's Green but there's marvellous gardens and I eat out there. The waiters wear high turbans and you should see the sarees of the guests. I'm a bit guilty about staying in a hotel called The Imperial, and us supposed to be republicans, but I love it.

In the next couple of days, before she phoned R.D. the hotel became a haven into which she gratefully scurried after her trips out. She never tired of the bazaar outside the gate where scruffy young Westerners hung around, wearing clothes like those in the stalls. She stopped smiling at them when their glances slid off her and made her feel as she had with Parvati's pals. She bought, without bargaining, a couple of loose dresses. Wearing one of them did not make the slightest difference to how she was treated by anyone.

The young beggar near the brass stall lit upon her

yet again: "Memsahib" he whined, his almond shaped eyes pleading as his fingers made feeding movements to his mouth, "chappati, chappati, Memsahib, very hungry".

"I gave you money an hour ago," Nora said, "and twice this morning," but now the boy was going to kiss her feet.

"Don't do that. Stop. I'll kiss your feet." And laughing, she bent toward his feet. Somehow, he fell on his backside grinning, but startled Nora with a loud whinge just as she noticed an elderly American couple nearby.

"What gives here?" asked the man and the boy whimpered, his face distorted in pain. "She pushed me. Memsahib hit me to the ground. I am very hungry."

"That's not what ..." she began, but her voice trailed off as the pair fussed over the "victim". The American rooted in his pocket while his wife helped the boy to his feet and cooed: "Don't cry sonny".

Nora's face flamed as she moved through the crowd on Janpath, wooed by merchants and beggars, and jostled by the crowd until she was crowded off the pavement into a sort of clearing.

Shock brought her to a standstill. Scattered in the dirt were people like the torn and ragged play-things of a terrible child. Missing bits of limbs were bandaged, faces distorted, patches of hair missing. The awful tableau stirred towards Nora. A hand rattled a tin mug. The man closest to her grinned from a noseless face and held out the oozing stump of a forearm, while a small child, appearing whole, crawled over a blind old woman in a box cart. Frantically, Nora dug into her purse and dropped money into the mug.

The lepers clutched at her core and flooded her with remorse. Human beings lived like this, while she ... Her fare to India would be a fortune to these people. Her throat ached with pity as a blonde back-packer strolled up and asked the noseless one: "How's it been going?"

Shaken, Nora moved on. She felt suddenly silly in her bazaar dress. So much for the disguise, she thought. The leper scene kept coming back to mind as she strolled around, but as she got hold of herself again, she thought why be ashamed of being a tourist? They bloody well needed tourists. She had come here as a tourist, not to integrate with lepers. Silly to think she could be part of India.

Later on she was sipping a cocktail by the pool in the garden of the hotel when she heard music approaching. When it came close she followed other guests through a back gate to see what was happening.

A procession was coming with deafening drums and fireworks, streamers, bells and garlands, flares and huge pictures of movie stars hoisted on high. As it came closer, Nora thought that although the musicians marched as a band, each did his own thing.

Surrounded by revelling young men was one young man whom Nora imagined must be royalty of some sort. He rode a white horse which was as ornately dressed as himself and he sat under an umbrella of fresh flowers with a garland of flowers around his neck. Even as she struggled in the crush Nora was surprised by the face of the horseman. It was vainly coy, his eyes edged with khol. There was wild cheering as flower petals showered upon him. "What is happening," she asked the young woman beside her who had steadied her when she was jostled and had almost fallen as the celebrators parted the crowd.

"Some poor girl's knight on a white charger" was the accentless reply. Catching Nora's reaction the Indian girl explained, "He is a bridegroom on the way to his wedding. What we are witnessing is part of the myth and camouflage of weddings. 'Every culture has its own'." It was the sort of thing that Derry might have said and Nora said nothing in the same way she often avoided tangling with her sister.

The young woman was stretching her neck, looking

for her friends. She was in her late twenties. Her large eyes were hazel, short curly hair brushed back off the wide brow of a creamy face and her body slight and free. She smiled and waved as one of her friends called and turning to Nora asked: "Are you in India on holiday?"

"I was invited to a wedding here in Delhi," Nora replied.

"All this way for a wedding? By the way, I am Arpita Jaganathan. Do you have relatives here?"

"I'm Nora Ryan from Ireland and no, I don't have relatives here, just an invitation from someone I went to college with. My daughter just got married. The invitation was a good excuse for a trip to India, I suppose. I'm glad I came."

Nora felt a subtle change in Arpita, a drawing back.

"Ah," said Arpita, "so you are, as they say 'into weddings'. So are most people."

They stood, no longer jostled by the crowd. "I refuse to attend such a wedding."

She nodded in the direction of the merry-making. "I haven't attended one for three years now. It is the traditional dowry type wedding. Here, I will give you this."

She pulled a folded paper from her handbag. *Brides are not for burning.* Nora read, *Boycott Dowry Weddings. Stop atrocities against women by refusing to give or take dowries. Do not attend dowry weddings ...*

Arpita's friend was back: "We must go," she said.

"Yes, we are already late," Arpita said turning to Nora, "we are a women's group trying to fight against this evil. Dowry weddings must be stopped. There is a law prohibiting dowry, but ..." she searched for a phrase and her friend supplied it "attitude maintains the practice".

"Yes," said Arpita, "and tradition. All the myth and camouflage." She waved her hand towards the departing crowd, "so colourful. What is underneath? What happens if the dowry is not paid or the in-laws are not satisfied? And how does the bride's family gather a dowry? Ask your host these questions. All this fuss is part of the camouflage, just as in the West, romance is camouflage. We must go. Enjoy your visit. Even the wedding, but remember ..."

As she walked back to the hotel the words: *Brides are not for burning* echoed in Nora's head. How could she ask R.D. such questions, much less refuse to attend the wedding if he was giving the girl a dowry?

She telephoned R.D. Das. He answered the call himself and she said: "R.D. Hello, it's Nora Ryan ... Boylan?"

"Yes, yes," was the calm reply, "welcome. So you are finally in New Delhi," and suddenly she was back in London with him remembering his words:

"Visit only, see for yourself before you decide ..."

R.D. insisted on coming to the hotel immediately, and Nora rushed to the dressing table to dab at the years before changing her dress again. Then she called reception and asked them to ring her room when Mr Das arrived. She had barely put down the phone when there was a knock on the door and there he was, in a tunic of raw silk, surrounded by sarees.

"Nora ...," there was rustle and titter as he held her hands and looked into her face. "They all came to meet you," R.D. said, stepping aside: "Come in, come inside," he instructed the women with the confidence of a host in his own country. Nora thought maturity had improved his looks. She was uneasy with his nonchalance. Still, how else could he behave, she asked herself, struggling to appear relaxed ...

"This is my daughter, Nina, the bride, of course," R.D. said. "And this is my son's wife, Bindia. Kumari, my cousin who is also going to be a bride and her mother who is my first cousin from Agra, Maya. Maya, this is Mrs Nora Ryan. Nora, Maya, Mrs Ravi Basai. I have chosen Maya to take care of you while we are busy with the wedding. I think you will become friends. She will be an excellent guide, and she is herself soon to be a mother of the bride."

The other women had impressed Nora as might a clump of flowers, collectively lovely in their colourful sarees and she did not remember their names, but Maya was different.

Nora knew those brown eyes. Maya's face was round, the colour of wheat, her lips full. Her hair was drawn back and coiled at the nape of her neck and a head shorter than Nora, her figure was round as a puppy's. Tiny, ruby ear-rings reflected the silk of her sari blouse.

Again, Nora found herself staring at a sari. This one was silver-grey with a border hem of elephants, hand embroidered in the jewel colours of ceremonial dress.

Maya was smiling: "Ah," she said, "you are counting the elephants parading across my bosom? They are so heavy. I am also admiring this dress you are wearing."

It was the first time that Nora had been offered a handshake in India, and she was touched by how carefully Maya did it, gently up and down in a childlike grasp. A little more? Was it right? Enough yet? Sensing her uncertainty, Nora joined her hands to enclose Maya's hand, and they laughed as she held it still.

CHAPTER 9

After tea, Nora expected the visitors to leave, but they had come to take her with them. "A room is waiting for you at home," R.D. said, "I expected to hear from you after your arrival, instead you came here." He looked around as though they had found her destitute. The wedding celebrations were well underway, many of the out-of-town guests had arrived and Nora must not miss any of the "programme". Maya helped her pack. There was something of a rescue party about the group as R.D. waved Nora aside and settled the bill.

The five squeezed into the back of the white Ambassador with R.D. beside the driver. Nora was aware of the scented warmth of Maya's body as she tried to give her space, but Maya, oblivious of discomfort, pointed out bits of Delhi as though they rode in an open coach. Now Nora realised that what she had taken to be central New Delhi was merely a strip, not the best of it at all. She had spent most of her time around Connaught Place, with its conglomerate of shops and shabby lock-ups squeezed between government emporiums, international businesses, banks and airlines, its pillared arcades sheltering the book stalls and pavement vendors and the touts and pimps working in the crowd. She had held herself on a leash that kept her within a safe distance of her hotel and yet a sense of freedom had risen in Nora every time she passed the doorman on the way out, unaware of how she had settled into a safe bit of the world, as she had always done.

Nora's neck cramped as Maya encouraged her to look through the window. They travelled as a bird might, around and about, spotting this landmark or that monument, past sparkling fountains, the majestic complex of red sandstone government buildings over which wild monkeys scrambled, while red channa lilies stood sentry. They drove through spaciousness, past parks where children played and blossoms fluttered to the grass and each time they came again into crowded settlements. And still the city sprawled, streets running like spokes off grassy circles.

"I had no idea New Delhi was such a lovely city," Nora said. Maya smiled as though personally responsible: "Old Delhi is more fascinating. It is from Moghul times, not Victorian, like this. I will show you all, old and new. And the Red Fort. Whatever is your wish."

The girls chatted in Hindu, laughing. Maya's daughter, Kumari, was the liveliest. She was petite, the features of her oval face were fine upon a delicate neck. Her skin was darker than her mother's and her hair fell below her waist. She wore a yellow tunic suit under a chiffon stole. She was a law student and the girls giggled when R.D. said: "Soon Kumari will be married and we will all go to Agra for the wedding."

Nina, R.D.'s daughter, was the quietest, but Nora's eyes were drawn to her. She was so like R.D., the same colour, features and long leggedness. They both had moles on their right cheeks and smiles made rakish by slightly crowded front teeth. Not that Nina smiled easily, and Nora was reminded of how R.D. had often seemed serious in the midst of light-hearted conversation. She had put it down to his being from a different culture than their friends in London.

Nora's eyes went from the back of R.D.'s head to Nina's unsmiling profile and thoughts, so long forbidden, surfaced. Tears came to her eyes. Why hadn't she had the sense to leave London in the past? And this man, for if it hadn't been for him, who knew what course her life might have taken? What was she doing here? Crazy. In India of all places, much less in a car with R.D. Das. She was unaware of what was going on around her as she realised that she had brought this upon herself. Even if she had insisted on staying in the hotel, but she was going to his home. He must have been shocked when she accepted the wedding invitation, especially on her own. Was he sorry that he had invited her? In spite of its formality, the letter had been warm. But it was different for him. London must seem so far in his past. A lifetime ago. Suppose I had said yes and married him? Marriage was such a random thing. What had they known about each other? How much could they have understood, strangers even then? Much more so now. The vulnerable curve of Nina's long neck merged the past into the present, and made Nora bite her lip. It was astonishing the effect that strangers had on each other's lives. It occurred to Nora that she was about to meet the girl R.D. had been hauled back to India to marry and her curiosity about his home life, heightened now that she was so close to it and helped her to compose herself and control forbidden memories. She was relieved that she was able to do that, for looking at Nina there had been a moment when she thought it was all going to burst inside her. That would have been dreadful. And awkward if R.D. thought that she was getting emotional over seeing him again.

The car edged along. A rush of people poured from a building and merged in the throng, their brown eyes catching Nora as she passed. Fascinated, she stared back over the pyramids of golden sweets, sizzling vessels of buttery nuts and banks of fruit.

"This market is like a honey pot," said Maya, opening the window, and Nora sniffed syrup in the air. The car stalled beside a woman buying toffee from a pile of golden slabs. She broke off a piece, turned it over and scraped at the black grave of flies on the other side before giving it to her child. An older boy sat cross-legged on the stall stirring a pan of bubbling toffee balanced on a little stove.

A family had been knocked off their bicycle in front of the car and Nora was shocked that R.D.'s driver sounded his horn at them. The young man got back on his saddle and helped his wife and son up on to the cross-bar holding the bicycle steady as an old woman settled onto his back seat, with a tiny girl on her lap. The driver still held his hand on the horn, as did others.

The noise pitiless. The woman on the cross-bar held on to a rickshaw as the cyclist moved off under his load, and only then did R.D.'s driver take his hand off the horn.

Eventually, they again entered the calm and space of suburbia where the evening was cool and smells became separate and recognisable as mown grass, a waft of spice and the scent of burning wood. The houses stood behind locked gates, each different and all shaded by verandahs and mature, freshly watered gardens. Cars were parked three deep on the pavement.

Nora's attention was caught by R.D.'s house before they came to it. The gates stood open behind a ten foot high arch of white silk, held apart with ropes, and in the dark now, they drove under a darn of branches twinkling with fairy lights. Scented blossoms and flickering wicks floated in vessels on the steps to the hall door. The house, splashed with scarlet creeper, shone light from every window.

Nora had barely stepped onto the black and white flagstoned verandah, when R.D.'s father appeared. "Welcome to my house," he told her with hearty enthusiasm and she felt a sting from the pronoun. Mr Das was a short, slight man with white hair above bushy white brows and thick spectacles. He looked spruce in navy silk: "I will take you to see my wife," he said and R.D. and the young people melted away.

Nora declined the platters of spicy morsels offered by servants as she and Maya followed the old man past tables lost under food, Nora would have preferred to freshen up first, but she accepted a glass of iced juice.

Off the Persian carpet and across a black marble hall-way Mr Das led them to the family dining-room which was cosy compared to the grand scale of the reception rooms. He stood in front of an old carved sideboard on top of which a wick flickered in front of a shrine where the photograph of a girl was garlanded with flowers.

"This is my wife, the most beautiful flower of India. Here she is fifteen-years-old, and here too," he added, tapping his chest.

Nora hid her surprise by studying the photograph. She was touched by the innocence of the raven-haired girl in the old-fashioned print, her lips and cheeks tinted pink by the photographer's brush.

"We were married when she was eleven," he said and, anticipating reaction from Nora, added: "It is the best way. Then the girl learns to think of nothing else. From then, her whole mind is on her husband only. She waits for his visit. You understand she did not come to live here until she was fifteen. Yes, she waits for his visit and he too is excited to catch a glimpse of her."

Nora was confused. The girl would be old now; why was he showing her this picture? She had never enjoyed looking at photographs of old people when they were young. She could hear her grandmother reciting: "As you are now, so once was I, as I am now, so will you be."

The old man's voice was quite drowsy with romance, "My God, we were in love".

"Ah yes," Maya murmured, not meeting Nora's eyes.

"And when she died," said the old man, "I could not believe it. Our third child died with her. She left me two sons. My parents chose well a bride for me. She is the mistress of my house. She did not come to me for four years after our marriage and she died when she was twenty-one years. My Karminia."

With relief Nora saw R.D. approach:

"This is my wife, Sarla," he told Nora, "and you wished to speak to the musicians," he said to his father, "they are waiting."

The old man swayed his head about and followed R.D.

"Welcome to our daughter's wedding," Sarla said to Nora, "it is too good of you to come so far ..."

Nora hardly heard her as smiling, she winced at the fleeting expression of disapproval she caught on Sarla's face and recognised her air of oppressive competence. A no-nonsense woman, Nora saw. About a woman's business. She was tall, not bad looking. That sari, Nora thought, how could she think ... but it's magnificent she realised, silver on purple. Yet it does nothing for her, just looks expensive. Doesn't she ever look in a mirror? And she decided that Sarla must do something to get that dot spot-on in the middle of her forehead. So this was the girl R.D. was called home to marry. The bride his father chose ... and again Nora was reminded of passing time and the fact that Sarla had probably changed with the years.

Nora was exactly as Sarla had feared, even though she could not have said what that was. This is not what any mother of the bride needs at such a time, she thought, a butterfly woman to charm the men folk and put nonsense in their heads.

Maya had whispered that the lady from Ireland was charming, but Maya was a fool, she thought. If this lady is so fine, Sarla asked herself, then where is her husband? How can she come alone to strangers? So much paint on her face. Gold in her hair? Already the old fellow is making a fool of himself. And she is surprised I am not a beauty. She thinks my husband could have got a wife like her. Probably in a public drinking place. Sarla read *Eve's Weekly* and knew that Western women were even worse these days with their ideas of liberation. Talking against husbands. If a woman could not serve her husband, then ...

"What protection will men give women like that?"

she had once asked R.D.. He did not answer. Usually, she discouraged talk about his days in London, viewing that time in his life as a secret pocket in which were things fearful and foreign. Now Nora had got out of that pocket and Sarla was wary. But she is my husband's guest, she chided herself, my guest. The poor lady is far from home.

"What you will have?" she asked suddenly, her voice sugary with effort, "or perhaps first I will show you your room?"

"This, I can do," Maya said hurriedly, "you are busy with many things ..." But Sarla insisted. They passed bedrooms packed with people's belongings, and there were several bedrolls on the verandahs.

Nora thought that the room she had been given was obviously the best in the house, overlooking the front gardens, with a patchwork quilt of silk and heavily carved furniture. Perhaps it was R.D.'s and Sarla's?

"This room is next to my daughter's, the bride, of course," Sarla said, "and no one is coming in here with you."

"Oh, but I can share," Nora volunteered, "it is such a big room. What about you, Maya?"

A glance passed between Sarla and Maya. They had assumed that foreigners needed a room to themselves. "Yes, I can share," Maya smiled, ignoring Sarla's disapproval. "Why not?"

And Nora asked: "Or perhaps you have a room with your daughter?"

"Kumari is preferring to have fun with the other girls," Maya replied. "It will be nice sharing. I will move in here."

After Sarla left, Maya sat yoga style on the bed watching Nora unpack. "She is not entirely fierce," she said, "marrying the children is a difficult time for womans."

CHAPTER 10

Nora woke and lay wondering how everyone else seemed to manage without sleep. She had heard Maja moving about at dawn. Last night it had been the musicians from Rajasthan who journeyed from their villages by camel to Jaipur before coming by train to New Delhi. The night before there was a singer. Nora enjoyed the evening until midnight when the woman stopped, but soon she began again and went on and on.

Maya and herself were going back to Old Delhi today to visit the Sikh temple and Jami Masjid, the great mosque. Nora looked forward to it, but as she got out of bed, she recalled the depth of steps over which the mosque towered and wondered where she would get the energy to cope with it and face the festivities at the other end of the day.

Yesterday, they had arrived by scooter in Chandni Chowk, near a row of motorcycle repair shops and with deafening noise. "It stains," Maya warned as she bought wine-red pomegranate seeds on shiny green leaves and handed one to Nora. They picked their way through the crowds careful to keep the juice from their clothes. "Don't lose me," Nora said as she would have told Dennis. Maya laughed. "I will not lose. Our Prime Minister was only a girl when Mahatma Gandhi sent her here to quell riots. That was after Independence. And we are not girls."

Nora tried to imagine there being room to riot in Chandni Chowk. She stood still to finish her pomegranate seeds before stumbling after Maya who seemed unaware of the state of the pavements.

"These shoes of yours are useless," Maya said, "come, we will purchase chappels."

Sandal after sandal was placed on Nora's foot. They were thrown with alarming accuracy by someone in a loft overhead answering to the shouts of the salesman. "Each foot a different size," he decided, "you will take for this foot a size five and a six for the right one, isn't it? Stand. Ah, it is comfortable. Yes, I can see ..."

In one of the gullies off the main street, Nora could see a woman covered in black burka and two small girls sewing sequins on cloth. She recognised the glitter of the cocktail wear sold in the tourist shops. And above her was another crowded layer of life, with "windows" of rags or sheets of paper. Nearby, a skinny cow relentlessly chewed vegetabes while the stall-holders pleaded and shooed.

They passed a man cleaning ears, his equipment a prong, a chair, some cotton wool and grubby bottles of liquid spread out on a newspaper over a box on the kerb. Beside him was a shop filled with bicycle saddles. Hills of hard-boiled eggs balanced on the next stall. A young man handed out newspaper twists of salt as customers helped themselves to eggs and threw their money in a blue plastic basin.

As Nora and Maya pressed through the crowd, a small girl stood and stared, clutching two skinny, struggling hens in her arms. The birds slipped a bit and the child squeezed them tighter, going down on her haunches and opening her eyes wider to take in the sight of Nora. Nora smiled at her but the child did not even blink and ignored the struggle of the birds.

Nora followed Maya into a large air-conditioned sari shop. A merchant in crisp white ushered them to chairs, sent a boy running for cool drinks and settled himself cross-legged on a white mattress. The walls of the shop were lined with shelves of sarees. Two boys kept the merchant supplied with these, and good-humouredly he threw them about in rivers of silk for

95

their appraisal. Maya concentrated, only occasionally raising a finger to consign a particular piece of silk to a pile for later consideration. After an hour, the merchant was buried to the waist in a rainbow pool and still the sarees came.

Maya rose to her feet, fixed her sari on her shoulder.

"Sit, have tea," the merchant coaxed, "what is the hurry to go out in the sun."

He remained seated midst the silk. Nora paused, then followed Maya.

"This man is trying too much to tempt us," Maya said without bothering to lower her voice, "I am not in the mood today."

"Perhaps tomorrow?" the merchant asked pleasantly.

"Yes," Nora said, mortified, "yes, we'll come back."

"Perhaps," Maya said over her shoulder, "perhaps."

It was almost noon when Nora made her way downstairs, aware that most of the women would have already spent a few hours in beautifying the bride who spent her day like a beloved house in preparation for new ownership. Nora had offered to paint butterflies of silver on Nina's cheek-bones. Yesterday morning, they'd had a trial run, before Nina's face was immersed in yet another purifying concoction. And Nora had felt more accepted by the women since she had a part in the bridal preparations.

As Nora passed R.D.'s study he was putting down the telephone. "Come," he invited, his arms outstretched as he came to greet her as though for the first time since her arrival in India. He embraced her. Surprised by the feeling this stirred in him, he drew back.

"Outside you haven't changed at all," he said, and she was conscious of him being close enough to see the scratches of time on her face, just as she noticed that he dyed his hair.

"We must all be different, London seems centuries away. Our children, after all, are as old as we were then," Nora said. "A lifetime ago, surely?"

"A lifetime, yes. A different world. Youth, as your Bernard Shaw said, wasted on the young, isn't it?"

"Not wasted, just gone and now it is someone else's turn."

"That is why I am so glad you are here for the wedding, to see for yourself," he said, looking at Nora steadily, "I did not forget."

"See for myself?"

"I have not given all for tradition. I fixed this marriage with a boy Nina liked, even though he is a Sikh, not a Hindu like us, and she will not be walking around the holy fire. My daughter is a mysterious girl. She wished to study in London. How could I permit such a thing? I saw how she liked this boy and I arranged with my old friend Singh." He looked pleased with himself and said slowly: "Perhaps, all that was for a purpose after all."

Startled, Nora heard her own words across the years: "But if your father can call you home to marry, what was the purpose of all this?"

"Education," he replied.

"What good is education if you cannot even choose a wife for yourself?" she had asked. "What's the purpose?" she repeated.

"I have chosen and she rejected me, so perhaps you can understand that I am not impressed with this method of gaining a wife? To be rejected once is sufficient."

Not even then had she realised all he had been prepared to brave to have her as his wife.

"Oh God, I was awful," Nora recalled, "I couldn't even accept the way things were done in England, a spit across the water, much less India. Have you been happily married?"

He almost smiled.

"I believe, more than ever, in traditional marriages," he told her, "with modification perhaps. And I will ask you the same question."

"We have parted," Nora said, "Dennis and I have separated."

R.D. sighed.

"I wanted to take care of you for all of your life."

"I know," she said softly and felt an urge to tell him what had happened after he left London but R.D. was drawing her close again when they heard : "Mr Das, Panditji would like to see you." It was Sarla.

Nora felt her face flame as she met the stunned look on the other woman's face. "Excuse me," she said and left the room. She felt the study door close quietly after her.

Maya concentrated on placing the red dot between her eyes. "What is the matter?" she asked through the mirror.

"Nothing," Nora said, but Maya turned around. "You are not feeling well? You are upset?"

"It's nothing really, something happened in the study. R.D. and I were standing talking, close together I'm afraid, and Sarla walked in ..."

"Ah," said Maya, "close together." Then she remembered that Rajendra and Nora had known each other in London. "That is not nothing. How you were close?"

"It was nothing," Nora repeated. "He just put his arms around me; it was harmless. It was the first time we were alone after all these years, we were just talking, and Sarla came in."

"That was Rajendra's foolishness," Maya said, "Sarla will be fierce. Oh dear."

There was silence until Maya said: "My sister is not well at all. My brother-in-law sent message and I promised to go to his village and return on thirty-first."

"May I come with you?" Nora asked, and realised that even if nothing had happened she would prefer to go with Maya. "I would enjoy the journey," she added.

"But the wedding celebrations, you will miss ..." Maya stopped as she realised that after what had happened it was a good idea to take Nora with her.

"We'll be back in plenty of time for the wedding, unless you think I should stay?" Nora said.

"No," Maya said, "we will be good companions. It is on the way to Bombay is the only thing and you are just coming from there."

She was warmed by the relief on Nora's face as she added: "since we are decided, let us make haste."

They were met at the station by Shashi, Maya's brother-in-law, who joined his hands in salutation to Nora and told Maya: "Vimla has had a miscarriage, but my mother says she will recover now."

Maya was quiet during the two mile drive to the village and when they arrived at the big old house she hurried inside to her sister, leaving Shashi to arrange for Nora's comfort. When Maya returned she took Nora to meet Vimla and even in the dim light Nora could see that she was red eyed. She was too thin and wore a scarf around her head to protect her from getting a chill. Her bed was on the floor even though the room was comfortable with other furniture and mats. Vimla whispered something. Maya's voice was hoarse as she drew her sister's head on to her bosom and answered in Hindi.

"She says," Maya said "that she cannot face her mother-in-law. This is the second miscarriage. I am telling her to have courage, that these times pass and when she has a son all will be forgiven. Even forgotten," Maya said.

While Vimla slept, Maya walked with Nora around the village, sheltered from the sun by a black umbrella. Shashi's was the landlord's house, the largest within sight.

It stood on untidy grass, inside a wall which sprouted yellow weeds. Beyond, the village houses huddled together on mud lanes. The fields in the distance were lush for as far as the eye could see, woods to one side, and in the crowded village Nora coughed against the scent of hot jasmine which did not quite overpower earthier smells.

A camel pulled a plough in one of the fields while

99

nearer-by men, women and children sat on the ground and chopped up sugar cane for replanting. In the dusty lanes of the village, people worked at grinding, husking, pounding, making bidis. They passed a temple, busy with worshippers.

To Nora the whole village seemed calcified with ritual. She saw no shops except for the butcher's, a stinking place of flies and congealed blood. A dark café sold packets of glucose biscuits and cups of tea to old men who smoked the day away.

In the afternoon, the school children in their smart blue and white uniforms came to look at Nora and she knew that she had become part of their education. People crushed into the house to stare while she and Maya ate the meal presented by women who did not eat with them. "They will eat later," Maya explained.

That night they slept on a mattress in Vimla's room. Nora was wakeful, remembering the scene in R.D.'s study, and wondered how Sarla would act towards her when they returned to the wedding house. She felt humiliated by the incident, as though she had been caught red-handed. She knew how it must have looked to Sarla and felt that the loss of status she had feared in Ireland had become a reality here. She wished that she did not have to return to the wedding house. A woman alone. It was not fair, she thought. The scene could just as easily have happened if Dennis had been with her.

Resentful thoughts kept her awake and when at last she slept, she dreamed that she and Vimla were drowning because they dare not show their heads above the water. Next morning, Shashi's mother, a large, slow-moving woman with splayed feet, served Nora and Maya breakfast, delicate whorls of fried rice with honey, puries, spicy biscuits and milky coffee. She smiled and gestured to Nora to eat more while chatting to Maya who sometimes translated. "She says, Vimla's temperature is gone and soon she will take her on a pilgrimage to ward off the evil eye," Maya told her.

100

"Third time will be auspicious." Maya's acceptance of this gave Nora a jolt as they set out on their return journey.

At the station, she was still thinking about this when she was distracted by the family who carried a bier onto the platform. Other travellers had cleared a space for them, and the three men of the family watched as the women ministered to the man. The older woman tenderly massaged his feet, lost in concentration. The two young women tended on either side, a third lovingly wiped his brow and massaged his temples. The youngest of the women had poured something from a flask onto her fingers and dripped it into the old man's mouth until he turned his head away.

Nora was still captured by the scene when one of the men came and spoke to Shashi.

"They are wanting you to help," he said, nodding towards the group.

"Me help, but ...?" Nora had not felt herself noticed.

"Perhaps you will speak to them?" he asked. "It is their father. They are village people and they believe you know something, how to cure."

"I don't know anything," Nora looked at Maya.

"Perhaps you could comfort?" Maya said, "Give some advice from your place?"

Nora was alarmed by palpable hope as she approached the family.

"She speaks English," Shashi said of the woman who looked at Nora from over her joined palms.

"My father was in the hospital many days," she said, "we are taking him so far because his cousin is doctor there. His lungs are sick and the coughing and spitting. He coughs out blood. Uncle says we must take him home to die ..."

Her eyes were terrified. "Please, you will look at him? Tell me please, what you people do about this sickness? What we can do for him?"

"I'm sorry, but ..." Nora was about to confess her

101

ignorance when she recognised the look on the woman's face. That look of Ciara's childhood, the belief that Nora could fix anything. I'm a stranger from the great West, wealth and miracles, Nora thought, they believe I must have some magic.

"How old is he?" she asked. He could be Aunt Flo's father. "Only fifty-one," his daughter-in-law said. "He is not old," she added unconvinced.

"That is young," Nora said, "but it's not a matter of age, is it?" She knelt beside the white bearded man. His huge eyes were glazed, but he came out of himself as she searched for his pulse. She felt the group take heart in the pseudo-professional way she held his wrist and studied her watch.

Their father lay like a cradled infant, a large black umbrella shading his head. His carefully oiled skin was lifeless with that last pallor common to all races. Slightly built, his face was wet with perspiration and Nora thought he would be more comfortable without the turban, but she had read about Sikhs in her guidebook. The turban must not be removed. It was one of their five "things".

The old man's breathing was gurgling and congested as the women tenderly massaged his limbs. Nora had seen this death come to her father, and had often heard it described during her island days. TB. Even if she was wrong, she knew the man was dying, and she felt that he knew.

Anxious not to intrude upon him, she sat on her hunkers, silently holding his hand for several minutes. At last, she whispered: "God be with you," and went to speak to the woman at his feet.

"You are doing right to take him home," Nora said, surprised by her own words. "My own father died in hospital with every modern aid, but alone among strangers. He was so full of medicines that he did not know us when we visited, and there were tubes hanging out of him. They did not call us until it was too late. I'm sorry I cannot help, but there is no magic.

102

We must all die. You have done the best you can, the best that can be done. You are right to take your father home. He will be at peace there."

The young woman's eyes were grief-filled, but Nora sensed her relief. She reached for her overnight bag and searched until she found her scented cushion.

"Put this by his head," she told the woman. "It's filled with flowers that grow near my home .... the scent is soothing ..."

Gratefully, the woman took the pillow of dried flowers that Aunt Flo had given Nora for her trip to India, and turned away.

Maya's eyes filled with tears. "You are generous as well as wise," she said, "I know you are resting with that little cushion."

Shashi helped them board the train. "You are sharing a coach with Sikhs, a wedding party, ladies and men," he said.

CHAPTER 11

When Nora came back from the lavatory on the train the man in the blue turban was sitting in her seat. He made to rise. "No, please don't bother," Nora said, slipping into the seat he had vacated on the other side of the aisle. Then she realised that he had not imagined she could do otherwise. That irritated her even though she was relieved to sit with the women. Maya had also moved to a seat among the women.

All four women knitted with dark wool: navy, wine and green on thin needles. And spoke a little English. "She is coming from?" one woman asked Maya. "And she is going to?" asked another. Maya answered on her behalf until unnerved, Nora cut in. "I met the father of the bride when we were both at art college in London." From then on they addressed her directly, except for when they spoke to Maya in Hindi.

"A long way you come for a wedding," said the eldest woman smiling, as though personally complimented by Nora's visit to her country. "Your husband is also here?" With elaborate nonchalance the woman accepted that Dennis was not. They were also on their way to a wedding, said her daughter, so many weddings in the season this year.

Nora was fascinated by the Sikhs. There had been so much on television about them and their Golden Temple in Amritsar before she left Dublin. The temple had looked so beautiful, surrounded by water through which people entered in their bare feet, that Nora had wanted to visit it, but there was fighting there and the

Indian Embassy had said tourists were not allowed in Amritsar until things settled. She thought that the fighting seemed something like the trouble in the North of Ireland, with Sikhs demanding their own state. The guidebook described them as "proud defenders, entrepreneurs". She knew they had long hair fixed with a comb under the turban and wore a dagger, a copper bracelet and underwear. However, when she asked a question about the fighting at the Golden Temple, Maya nudged her and nobody seemed to have heard her question. The women talked about their knitting, so Nora picked up her book.

The women contentedly clicked away the stitches of the journey. Nora could not remember their names, but knew which husband belonged to which wife by the way a woman expressed her pride when her man said something that was informed or witty. She ground her buttocks into the seat, arranged her sari in position over her left shoulder, bangles clinking as she pulled a fresh length of wool from her knitting bag and threw a glance of admiration at her husband. And he sat up straighter, his turban seeming more splendid.

Eventually, the women put away the knitting and went in convoy to wash their hands before unpacking food. She was enjoying the meal when she realised that the women were not eating. Maya also had a tiffin carrier in her hold-all, but did not unpack it until the women began their own meal and Nora felt that she should have declined the food she was offered with the men.

Nora believed she could pin-point the moment the news had come on board the train and crept through the coaches. She had sensed something in the air even before everybody stopped speaking English. And Maya remembered that Nora could not understand what was happening.

"Ah," Maya said, her voice hoarse, "at a time like this the mother tongue comes from the heart and you are not understanding. A terrible thing has happened. Our Prime Minister of India is shot and she is in hospital. Her condition is most serious. What we will do if Mahataji dies? Before he got on the train a man down there spoke on the phone to his brother in New Delhi and he said this news."

"Mrs Gandhi must be alright," one of the women said in a self-assuring voice, "The All India Medical Institute is having the best doctors, only the best. They can save Indira Gandhi, certainly they will save, of course. They must."

"Shssh," her husband urged and there was silence, except for a shattering blare of film music as someone tried to get news on a transistor.

Maya was squeezed in her seat beside Nora. Someone took out a flask and began to pass around cups so that soon there was only the slurping sound of hot tea. Cutting her way through stillness, Nora went to the lavatory. She passed a screaming infant as its mother quietly rocked it in her arms, comforting herself. She noticed that the women in the ladies' coach sat in silence as she passed their open door. She returned to silence.

Maya had drawn her feet up on the seat, crossed at the ankles, her sandals on the floor. "Who knows how much is rumour?" she asked Nora.

The man that Nora remembered as Mr Siddhu came back to his seat. "Film makers from your country were waiting to see Mrs Gandhi," he told her, "Peter Ustinov was waiting to see her with your Mr Smith from Irish television. Do you know Mr Seamus Smith?" he asked distractedly.

Nora shook her head.

The Sikh continued: "She was walking from her home to meet them outside the office. That is just a garden path and everyone heard the shots ring out and the guards told them it was fireworks, but your Mr Smith was in Cyprus and he said he recognised it was bullet shots. She was shot many times in the

106

stomach ... this is the darkest day for India."

One by one, the men left their seats and went to the back of the train. As each returned, he reported a similar story and everyone listened as though for the first time. Then another went to find out for himself. Maya translated for Nora who wanted to go and find out for herself, but something held her among the women.

At 6.30 in the evening the radio brought the first official announcement. Indira Gandhi was dead. The women cried but were hushed by their husbands.

"It is a great shock to us, you understand. Mrs Gandhi is slain by Sikh guards, her own bodyguards," explained Mr Malik. "They are extremists, but still they are Sikhs like us and we all feel shame."

"Ah yes," Maya said, and Nora sensed that Maya was glad she was not a Sikh.

It was too early, but everyone started to prepare for sleep, anxious to put the day behind them. Maya tucked herself and Nora tightly under one blanket and by way of good-night said: "A black cloud is over Nina's wedding," and promptly dropped off to sleep. Exhausted, Nora slept.

Nora woke and rubbed at the anxiety in her throat as she remembered her dream of Indira Gandhi being murdered. No, it wasn't a dream. She turned to find Maya gone. Pained eyes around her confirmed disaster. The carriage was in mourning. There was the smell of burning sandalwood, some were praying, others sat in meditation. A few rows up she could see rosary beads slipping through brown fingers, and she sat back in her seat and prayed for the soul of Indira Gandhi. God be good to her, she prayed and when the tears rose and she had to get out her handkerchief she wondered if prayer, like grief, was contagious.

She had never given Indira Gandhi a thought and now the woman's face with its streak of white hair at the temple, was vivid in her mind. Her own bodyguards.

A sob escaped Nora. She wondered if she would have been so affected if the IRA had got Mrs Thatcher with their bomb in Brighton a few weeks previously and recalled that watching the news she had been outraged and sympathetic when Mrs Norman Tebbit, the politician's wife was carried out of the debris. She had not cried though. She must not let herself become so emotional.

As she queued for her turn in the bathroom, Nora remembered Aunt Flo's words: "Something unexpected always happens to people visiting India," and supposed that this was her unexpected thing. She looked at her watch, November first, three days to the wedding. She wondered about cancelling a wedding. It would not be all that difficult to postpone an Irish wedding, although bad enough, but how would one halt an Indian wedding? It seemed to gather speed. A fortune had already been spent what with entertainment and hotel bills for guests. Hundreds of guests were still to come, and her mind filled with musicians on camels and bridegrooms on elephants, the daily caterers at the house. At last she was through the door marked "latrine".

As she got back to her seat the porter arrived with "boiled eggs" and coffee she had ordered. The coffee was awful, but washed down the egg and chappati which Maya produced with satsumas.

"Less than two hours to Delhi," Maya said and Nora thought how the time would drag in this sad silence. She had reconciled herself to this when she heard the noise, far off. As it drew nearer, she puzzled over it. A parade? What? Nora had just seen the alarm on Maya's face when the chanting emerged from the blur of roars. Everybody was on their feet now, one of the women whimpered. The train was slowing down, moving towards something frightening. Nora could feel the fear. Angry voices. Was the train so late that people were furious?

"Please," someone urged, tugging at the back of

Nora's blouse, "close the inside window, pull down the blind!"

"Jesus, Mary and Joseph," Nora said, and sat down. Shocked by the scene on the platform she still held the end of the blind. We're going into that she thought. God Almighty what's going to happen? What am I doing here?

In the seconds before she covered the window, Nora had seen men shrieking in rage as they pushed towards the train, brandishing flaring torches, knives and anything that served as a weapon. There was blood everywhere and attackers further back in the crowd flayed about them even as they battled to the front where mad men lined the edge of the platform ready to jump on the in-coming train. Nora had seen a group of people who looked scalded, an infant's face like a skinned tomato. People were being knocked down and trampled under foot. All around were tangled clothes, ripped baggage and smashed stalls. Where a cooking stove had overturned a man was beating at a patch of flames with an overnight bag.

Don't stop, keep going, Nora's mind urged, don't stop or we're done for. She felt the train drag to a halt. A terrible cheer went up. Maya buried her face in her hands, the other women clutched at their husbands and when she looked up one of the men held a dagger, his eyes staring.

Leela, the only woman who had not called herself "missus" was whimpering: "They are killing Sikhs isn't it? We all must pay ..." The hellish noise came closer. Leela's husband broke away from her and Nora watched with relief as he secured the door while he shouted for someone to fix the one at the other end. Just then the window-blind snapped up beside Nora and she saw a body land in a heap on the platform. It was the sick man to whom she had given the cushion. Liquid hurled upon him and a youth touched the old Sikh's turban with a torch. Someone pulled down the blind, but not before Nora saw the old man's head engulfed in flames. "Sacred heart of God," she groaned, and overtaken by a spasm of shaking, she hugged herself around the chest and rocked back and forth. "Holy Mary, Mother of God," she implored.

"Stop," Maya's soft voice was strong with urgency, "we must be brave. They are shouting only women will be saved," she told Nora, "they are saying all Sikhs will pay for our Prime Minister's death. At Partition men hid in the compartment for ladies in burka my father told me, but ..."

"But what?" Nora asked, realising that the women she had seen wearing black tent-like garments would be safe in their special compartment.

"These are Sikhs," Maya whispered behind her hand, "brave men, specially proud. We cannot ask them to hide behind burka ..."

"Nonsense," Nora snapped, aware that her sister Derry's voice had come out of her mouth: "they must go in there."

The Sikhs hung back, embarrassed as their wives pleaded with them until in desperation, Nora herded them towards the burka carriage. "Please, move quickly, it is only common-sense. Come on, please. It's better than being dead. Better than being butchered, you cannot stand up to a mob, go in, it's the only sensible thing ..." She barely noticed the shock of the older man as she pulled at him.

As the last Sikh went into the ladies' carriage the cry, "*Koi sardar hai? Goli se mar daleige,*" came from the platform.

"They demand to know if Sikhs are here," Maya said, "they want us to hand them over to them."

Nora and Maya squeezed into the burka compartment with the Sikhs. Nora bolted the door and Maya tried to reassure the women who huddled together in terror under their black.

Snatches of what was happening in the coach outside could be heard. The pounding on the heavy metal of a door was accompanied by threatening

110

shrieks. "They are saying they will set fire to the train," said Maya, her bangles jingling as she bit her nails. Suddenly the pounding stopped and the shouting broke through. The mob was in the train, further down, but coming closer. They heard shrieks of terror, roars and wailing, and an infant screaming with the relentlessness of an alarm clock.

Inside the burka carriage everybody stood looking at the door until the two women, knees trembling, sat down with their backs against the door and covered their ears against the noise.

And then came the pounding on the door and a roar: "*Koi sardar hai?*" They could hear a woman's voice: "Only ladies in there, only ladies." Maya and Nora clutched each other. Malik drew his dagger again, his eyes on the door. The other Sikhs simply stood, and Nora realised that they were unarmed. Sikhs are supposed to be armed, she thought frantically. A scream rose, terrible, above the noise of the train. They'll be butchered, thought Nora, and us too for hiding them.

"They are asking if those women out there are travelling alone," Maya said miserably. "They know, they know," and she prayed aloud.

Nora screamed. It just came out of her and deliberately she screamed again and nodded at Maya to do the same. They screamed and screamed, drowning the noise outside, until one of the Sikhs stepped towards the door as if to open it. Nora stopped screaming and jumped to stand in front of him.

Maya put her head on the seat, and sobbed. Why had they got involved with these people she asked herself. What happened to Sikhs was not her concern. What were they to her, a Hindu mother with children waiting at home?

Nora was talking to the men on the other side of the door. Maya thought she sounded like a real English Memsahib. She raised her head to listen.

"Please leave us alone," Nora ordered. "We are ladies

only in here. I am a visitor to your country and I was having tea with these ladies. You have upset them terribly. Are you interested in entering the ladies' compartment?" she asked hoping to God that she was going to get away with this, but the noise had stopped and a man's voice asked: "Who is this speaking?"

"It is I," Nora said, trying to sound terribly English, "Mrs Nora Ryan from Ireland and I have come to attend the wedding of my friend's daughter in New Delhi. Why are you attacking the train? Are you robbers? I am a tourist travelling light." There was murmured argument and then: "Ladies will be spared. We will punish Sardars only for the murder of our Prime Minister. Her death will not go unavenged. Are there men in there with you, madam?"

"Certainly not," replied Nora, hoping that no one outside would give them away, and as if on cue, Maya started to scream again. When she returned to sobbing, Nora repeated: "Are you there, are you still there? You are upsetting the ladies. Certainly there are no men in here. This is a ladies' compartment. Men are not allowed."

Nora sensed she was making some progress as the dotty tourist. "Please, please, do leave us alone," she ordered. "We are only women here." And then inspired she added: "We are all mothers." There was mumbling and then suddenly, the men outside the door were gone. The Sikhs sat, their heads in their hands.

At last the train moved into New Delhi station. The door which had been broken and wedged back could not be opened at all now and Nora struggled along the train, looking for an exit. Maya said something about their luggage. Nora thought with relief that she had left her passport and travellers cheques at R.D.'s and pressed on.

They reached a coach door, but it was blocked by the body of a man. His bloodied head was jammed against the door, his beard gouged. His arm was hacked through. People in front of Nora stepped over him towards the next door.

Leela's husband pushed past Nora and Maya and lifted the body out of the way, while Mr Siddhu got the door open. As she moved towards the door, something stuck to the sole of Nora's sandal. She picked off a lump of hair, messy with blood and let out an "ah-a-a-ah" of revulsion when she saw that it was attached to flesh. She felt herself sinking and being lifted, and then she was on the station platform. Everywhere, people cried and moaned, children shrieked, and, close-by, a young woman knelt vomiting into the tracks. Nora held her handkerchief to her nose against the stink of spent rage. Only Maya's eyes showed above the sari she held over her face.

The Sikhs were removing bodies from the train, carrying the injured. Nora squeezed her eyes shut against the sight of dead men and hacked limbs, rivulets of blood running down razed beards. When she opened them again, she swayed back from the blood spouting out of the gouged crotch of blue jeans, a young man's face beneath a raw head. Here and there, yards of fabric straggled in the dirt, and Nora realised that they had been turbans ...

She could see no way through the crowd, as she stepped back against the other women to allow two of the Sikhs to push past, carrying a young man. His leg was gone. "He is not dead," Leela's husband said in response to Nora's gasp, and she closed her scalded eyes. Compulsively, she rubbed her thigh. God, imagine waking up to find your leg had been hacked off. She and Maya were crushed in the crowd. A Sikh's bruising fingers inched them forward until he lost hold, and disappeared. .

Nora wondered vaguely if the uniformed men who made way for them were the police. She did not know what the man who had hold of her was saying.

"Rajendra has sent them. It is alright, we are safe," Maya shouted, just as the force of the crowd broke

Nora free of the man. At the top of the iron station steps, the crowd moved helplessly, tangled and crushing with women clinging to children and each other, while men pushed and shouted instructions. Nora felt the ground go from under her before she realised that she was on the steps and was being carried down with the crowd and struggled to stay on her feet. She thought that this descent was worse than anything so far, but at last her feet were on flat ground.

"There," Maya shouted in front of Nora and pointing with her eyes over the crowd, "there is Rajendra, there beside the ambulance bearers, there is R.D." They pushed on until Nora felt she could not bear a moment longer. As she looked for Maya she breathed relief when she recognised the man who had lost her at the top of the stairs and now gripped her arm so tightly. And then suddenly she was aware of being in different, more gentle hands.

"Nora, it's alright, it will be fine," R.D. said and Nora saw that he had Maya too. "This is bad," he said, "but the army is getting things under control." It seemed an endless struggle before they freed themselves into the sunlight. A soldier held the door open while R.D. helped Nora and Maya into the back of his Ambassador and while the women lay back exhausted, he stood talking to the soldier. Maya sobbed, her head on Nora's shoulder.

Over Maya's head, Nora saw that ambulances and cars came and went. Some people had collapsed outside of the station. She saw two men help a man and woman up off the ground, and the woman became hysterical when she recognised her rescuers. A young woman sat cross-legged in the street, her face distorted with grief, and Nora recognised that it was a bloodied turban which straggled around her, and lay in a heap in her lap.

Shock made Nora silent and Maya thought aloud : "It will be better when we get away from here," but even after they left the area around the railway station

114

where so many Sikh taxis and auto-ricks had been burned, hooligans still ruled and trouble was not easily avoided. They drove through smoke-filled streets, past burnt out shops and homes. Maya saw a woman stumbling naked out of a blackened doorway, her hair matted with dust, her thighs bloodied, her mouth torn. Maya looked away. Where would she go now, a woman dishonoured for all the world to see? Ashamed, she looked around and was relieved to find that Nora's head was turned towards the other window. Maya had never known a foreigner before, but she knew that it was impossible to explain her country to them because Rajendra had told her so. Nora is a foreigner, Maya thought. How can she understand what is happening here? Even I cannot understand this India.

An iron bar clattered upon the bonnet of the car as R.D. commanded them to keep calm: "We are not Sardars and therefore we are not targets," and the car pushed through the mob, jerking to gain speed, past smouldering skeletons of cars at a taxi rank. They drove through raped and shuttered business streets until they came to deserted, trouble-free Delhi where well-off folk stayed indoors. Amidst the space and trees, they might have been in another country.

"We are coming to a congested area," R.D. said, "there may be disturbance."

"Poor Mrs Gandhi," Maya sighed, "she would not have wanted to be the cause of all this."

"She is not the cause," R.D. said.

"And to die at the hands of one's own Sardarjis, men she trusted. So many bullets, poor lady. She was bleeding too much. One bullet would have been enough."

"One bullet would have been too many," R.D. said, looking straight ahead. "If you murder someone, why count bullets?"

"They said they would celebrate Diwali with the blood of Indira Gandhi," Maya said, sniffing and wiping her eyes in her sari." Diwali is over. It is over and we have lost her ..."

"This is not helpful," R.D. said sternly, "do not talk like that. It is enough!"

Maya sank down, her forehead pressed into Nora's arm: "But they have their celebrations," she murmured, so softly that Nora did not think R.D. heard.

The wedding preparations mocked them as they drove under the archway of gleaming white silk, past the dimmed decorations. Sarla was in the hallway, distracted: "The servants are gone," she said, "they have left me like this with a wedding. Even Darshanker is gone after so many years ..."

"They are safe," R.D. told Sarla gently, "the train was attacked, but they are safe."

"Oh," Sarla said, but she could think of only one thing. "The servants have run off. What we will do?"

R.D. left his wife standing there and walked into the house.

"Tea. Tea is needed," her father-in-law told Sarla, "everyone is requiring tea." Sarla began to trail after him, but someone sat her down.

Miraculously soon, tea began to flow from the kitchen. No one remembered to give Nora light tea with lemon but she was grateful for the sweet milky liquid which spread through her body. For a while, the silence was broken only by slurping and clinking china.

Sarla put her cup down, tea slopping into the saucer in her lap, and stared into it. Her mind panicked around the wedding and the fecklessness of servants. All her plans, made over months down to the last detail, were threatened. She dreaded a débâcle where she had anticipated a triumph. Out loud, she gave herself positive little messages: "So, it won't be a great occasion, just a simple affair. The band is cancelled. We'll pay them, of course, it is not their doing. The baraat must come quietly," and she was off again in a vortex of anxiety.

"The Prime Minister of your country has been assassinated," Mr Das said sternly and Maya, seeing the impact of the remark on Sarla's face, hastened to protect her: "Please," she coaxed the mother of the bride, "please come and lie down and I'll bring you tea."

Other women crowded around, but it was Nina who got her mother's attention when she said: "You haven't touched your tea. Please do as she says."

"Everything will come clearer after a rest," Maya said, "after a while."

Sarla stared at Maya, but got heavily to her feet. Nora was so close that it would have been natural to take Sarla's other arm, but she hesitated, awkward about touching Sarla and Nina stepped in: "Please you bring the tea," she said to Nora. Sarla shuffled along, dazed, and as Nora followed step by step upstairs she felt sympathy for her. The poor woman had been so organised and on top of things, everything going so well and this had to happen. Like me until Dennis made his announcement, Nora thought and decided to give Sarla one of her pills. They had got her through some bad days.

They settled Sarla in her bed, but she would not rest, took only a sip of tea and became so agitated that she wanted to get up.

"I think I have something that might help," Nora said and slipped away.

When she came back, Sarla looked sharply at the Valium on Nora's palm: "That's a tranquilliser," she pronounced, and the sudden calm of her voice held all her darkest suspicion about the Western way of life. "Indian women are not taking such things."

"Well, maybe they should," Nora said, "and you definitely need something, so swallow this. It's not every day of the week that your Prime Minister is assassinated in the middle of your daughter's wedding." Put that in your pipe and unravel it, she thought, and amused by the Irishness of what she had said, her voice softened. "There's a good woman. It'll help you to rest. Wash it down with some tea."

"Please," Nina pleaded, "she is trying to help you," and she took the pill and put it in her mother's mouth.

"How about you?" Nora asked Maya.

Maya took a pill, bit and gave half back to Nora: "I take only half because it is not my daughter's wedding," she said solemnly. Wearily, they sat with Sarla while Nina pressed her mother's limbs with gentle squeezing movements and stroked her hair. At last, drowsiness replaced Sarla's agitation and they stole away.

Nora spent an hour trying to phone Dublin to tell them she was safe. "The lines are impossible," R.D. told her, "take some rest and we'll go to the Sheraton, it will be easier from a five star hotel. Let me try to find out if it is safe to go. First, you rest."

Maya shook her awake with the telephone in her hand: "It is your sister, Nora, your sister is telephoning from Ireland."

"I'm fine," she shouted to Derry, "tell everyone I'm fine."

"I told Dennis you'd be OK," Derry yelled, "he rang from London, he saw the news and he's worried ..."

"No, it's fine," Nora said, "I was just having a rest."

"What's it like where you are?"Derry asked.

"Indescribable" Nora called back, "but I'm safe and I've met a lovely woman, made a friend."

"Write," Derry said, "everyone wants you to write."

Nora had just finished dressing when the phone rang again. It was Dennis. She was pleased to hear his voice: "Nora, are you OK? I'll come and bring you home." That was the last thing she wanted.

"No, no, I want to stay. All Delhi isn't like you see on television, it's perfectly normal where we are ..."

"Let me speak to R.D.," Dennis asked, and he might as well have asked to speak to "someone in authority".

"He's out just now," she lied. She would not be talked

about, treated as a problem, their joint responsibility. "Anyway, I'm safe as houses," she said, her voice steadied, "perfectly able to look after myself. There's nothing to worry about. We're all getting ready for the wedding. Oh, and Dennis? Derry has my address," but they lost the connection and she did not know if he'd heard.

Maya was chewing paan, her mouth a gash of red: "I wish we could leave Delhi now. As soon as the wedding is over, you will come to my place and stay for Kumari's wedding. I am writing a book about the Taj Mahal. You will enjoy so much to see the Taj."

"Will Nina's wedding go ahead now?"

"Of course, the day after tomorrow. Naturally, if there was a close death in the family, the wedding would stop. Then nothing could happen for one whole year.

"While I was in the bathroom" Maya said, sitting down beside Nora, "I thought I would tell you the story Rajendra told me when my father died. He was having cancer. I hid in the garden. I was afraid if I went into the house that it would come true that he was dying. He told me about the warrior, Arjuna. In the Mahabharata it tells how God gave Arjuna the knowledge life and death and explained this mystery to him.

"The Lord drove Arjuna's chariot into battle for him. Arjuna," she said, settling down to her story, "because Arjuna did not wish to lead his brothers in battle against his cousins in the Mahabharata war. It was fought in Delhi. In this very city, I am telling you.R.D., as you call him, could tell you which time that was. So, he told Arjuna, God did, that in fighting he was only the instrument of death at the desire of Almighty. Just like my father's cancer was instrument. But this is good part, the best part," and Maya straightened her body and her voice filled with emotion: "The soul cannot get wet with water nor dry with wind. It cannot burn with fire and you cannot kill it with arms. It is immortal, so do not cry ..."

"This is from our Holy Book, and when Mrs Gandhi is lying in state at Teen Murti House, someone will always be reading the book where her body is. We must not cry, that is what Arjuna was told."

"So you don't blame the guards? They are just instruments?"

"Ah yes," said Maya, "but that is the Holy Book. Who will pay attention? Sikhs have taken revenge because she sent an army into the Golden Temple, the holiest of holy places for them, you see. And they were having it like a fortress, keeping guns inside. You were reading in your country?"

CHAPTER 12

The bridegroom's father, Deepak Singh, was furious when he heard Mrs Gandhi had been assassinated. The sheer stupidity of such a thing. His mood swung from anger to sadness and the sadness confused him because he was no admirer of Indira Gandhi's and had not intended voting for her party again even before she had sent the army into the Golden Temple. And if not for Congress (1) then for whom could he vote?

Deepak Singh was as proudly male as he was proudly Sikh. The Prime Minister was a slight, elderly lady and those fellows had mown her down. He cringed with shame at the betrayal and the brutality. In the eyes of his neighbours and the world, he felt he had lost his Sikh's dignity, and he cared more about his neighbours than the world. Nor was he interested in a Sikh state, a Khalistan. He was an Indian. Unity was essential to India's future, he believed, or else they might as well go back to the principalities.

As Singh drove through the suburb in which he lived, it was deserted. A disastrous business, he told himself for the umpteenth time, and it would have to be a quiet wedding. R.D. will have it in hand. It is up to us to get on with it in spite of all this. The country is in mourning, he reminded himself, but young people easily get over these things. He could vaguely remember such a wedding from his youth although he could not recall why there had been no music or flares, but he

121

could see the bridegroom on his white mare as a ghostly figure moving up the street accompanied by silent relatives and barely enough light.

He was snapped back into the present at the sight of a car in flames on the side of the road and as he drove through the black smoke, past the cheering hooligans, he saw that the newsagent's shop was ablaze.

Young thugs taking advantage of the silent, unpeopled streets he thought, glad of an excuse to lash out. The police would stop that fast, he decided and passed more burning property, and looters actually loading a truck from Sikh shops.

Long before he reached Connaught Place, he could no longer drive the word "riots" from his head. Delhi was burning. There was fire and craziness everywhere, and men in packs brandished makeshift torches and weapons. He watched horrified as a bunch of fellows unloaded containers of kerosene from the back of a truck. As he sped past, a silken tangle of sarees lay in the street, seeming to have flowed from the door of the shop where he and his wife had recently shopped for the wedding. Arm loads of electrical goods were being dumped in a van, scavengers clutching as much as they could carry, and roars of applause rose for the passion of flame which sprang from the kerosene smoke that blackened the pillars of Connaught Place.

This is trouble, he thought. As he bumped and skidded his roundabout way to the hotel, he felt himself a moving target in his navy blue turban. He considered turning back, but decided to press on. His wedding guests, Thakuur and his wife, would be expecting him and he must see R.D.

A stone hit the windshield and with a yell a young man flung himself across the bonnet of the car. Singh swerved around the next corner on stones and rubble, driving for his life, and the fellow fell off and ran towards another looting mob. A lump of wood crashed through the glass beside him and lay smouldering on the seat. As he flung it out through the window, out of the corner of his eye Singh saw two policemen, their behinds propped against a column of Connaught Place, chatting, one twirling his lathi. The hotel was burning, the fire and the mob roaring at each other. Smoke billowed from the bedroom windows and, as Singh swept past, he yelled to an elderly man trying to start his car: "What has happened to the hotel guests?"

The man stuck his head out of the window: "Get away from here, Sadarji," he urged, his eyes fixed on Singh's turban, "the guests are getting out the back. These fellows are making all sadars to blame. They burned the furniture shop next to the hotel and the fire has spread." His car started. "Go Sadarji, get away," he called as he took off.

If he removed his turban, he could cut his hair. He was damned if he'd let them reduce him to that, he thought. He must find his wedding guests. Around the back of the hotel there were no flames, but a crowd caught in chaos and smoke. He recognised the fire-fighter's uniform on a man packing Westerners into a taxi. Others were being herded by hotel staff, pushed into the nearest vehicle and there wasn't a Sikh in sight. Some people clutched hurriedly packed luggage or none at all. Like refugees, Singh thought. As he stepped away from his car, he saw the Thakuurs and shouted to them before he felt himself felled. He yelled with pain as he thought: "The bloody buggers have broken my neck."

A strange, dishevelled woman stood on the Das' doorstep. "Help him, help ..." Surabhi Thakuurs' eyes were wild as she looked from R.D. to her husband who was struggling with someone whose feet were stuck out the back of a car.

At first R.D. did not recognise his friend, Deepak Singh, his suit dirty and splashed with blood. Then he saw that the blood came from the raw patch on the top of the Sikh's head where the comb had held his

123

knotted hair. He had often seen Singh rewind his waist long hair and wrap his turban. Now, his friend's beard was torn from one side of his face, blood ran into his mouth. The Sikh moaned, but could not move and passed out as the two men carried him indoors.

Nora was coming downstairs. "Watch the stairs," R.D. ordered, "we'll get him into the study, but don't let anyone come down. He must not be seen in this state."

"What Happened? Who is he?" asked Nora, staring at the bloodied figure on the floor. Nobody answered. Surabhi Thakuur was unable to speak, but even in her shattered state she was aware of the Western woman's air of belonging in this house. She had never met the bride's family, but she had the wedding invitation in her handbag when her husband said: "He was going to see Das about the wedding plans, he mentioned it when I phoned. We'll take him there." She could not find words to say to this foreigner who seemed so friendly. Her husband panted exhaustedly in a chair.

"This is Deepak Singh," said R.D. to Nora, "my good friend and father of Arun, our bridegroom to be."

Nora watched the door of the study close on the injured man as what was happening dawned upon her. The nightmare of the train had followed them home. She must have been in a fog not to realise that it would. The servants had known ... This was a house with Sikhs in it, a Sikh bridegroom on his way. And it was full of things to loot, jewellery, expensive sarees, wedding gifts. Since their return, Maya did not always translate Hindi for Nora. And even though she was sometimes curious, Nora let it pass, sensing that if they wanted her to know what was being said, Maya would draw her into the conversation. It was like being a guest in someone's house when there was a row in the family. One tried to pass over it, not become involved. Nora felt that some people found her presence embarrassing. She went upstairs to Maya.

"Maya," Nora said, "I've just realised why the servants left."

Maya peeled off the red dot from between her eyebrows, and appeared to concentrate on its replacement as she peered closely into the mirror.

"Who is knowing why servants do anything? It is always at the most inconvenient time they are letting down the housewife. I am sure it is the same at your place."

"There are no servants at home," Nora said absent-mindedly, looking out on the driveway, "well, some people have cleaning ladies, mothers' helpers, but you daren't call them servants."

"Ah yes, I have heard of this state of things," Maya said, "perhaps soon in India also, the situation will be impossible. Then all ladies will be servants."

"Maya, I'm not talking about servants," Nora said, irritated, "You understand what I mean ..."

"Of course this house is safe," Maya said, "who knows what servants think? What crazy thing? They are more foolish than children. R.D. will guard. Nobody will get in, some men will stay watching in the night. They are having guns ..." And hurriedly, she rambled off again, talking breathlessly about servants and the incompetence she'd left at home. "If it was not that my mother-in-law is there to oversee all the things, I could never come out from home," she finished. "I could not research my book on Taj."

She's scared, Nora thought.

Even a foreigner senses danger in such a house as this, Maya thought, so I am not so cowardly.

Nora watched R.D.'s car go out. Probably gone to bring someone else she thought. More people kept arriving, so that now there were beds on the floors of the grand reception rooms. There was no question of space, room was found for everyone and Nora wondered how many more people would squeeze into the house before anyone appeared to notice.

"Come," Maya said, "we will visit Nina."

Next door, the bride was in the hands of her adorners. Propped on a bed against a heap of cushions, her feet seemed tatooed with dark lace. An old woman applied the same pattern to one of Nina's hands with what looked to Nora like melted chocolate. The woman formed a wet needle of paste between her finger and thumb and worked with such concentration that every now and then she had to stop and take a deep breath before going on and it looked as though the sticky stitches of the lace were being bled from the bride's pores. Nina's eyes had a far-off look.

Nora and Maya watched until both hands gleamed with chocolate lace, and Nina was helpless so that one of the other girls held a drink to her lips. "The news, it is nearly time," Maya murmured to Nora at last, "we must go and see."

As they passed the study, Nora noticed that the smell of disinfectant had killed the scents of the bride's preparation which had lingered on the stairs. Nora and Maya left their sandals with all the rest outside the television room before inching inside.

There was no mention of the train, surprisingly little about the riots, although curfew was declared.

"Is the news censored?" Nora whispered to Maya.

"Of course," Maya replied, "if you tell about these things others get the idea to do like this."

The news concentrated on Mrs Gandhi lying in state at Teen Murti House. Garrett Fitzgerald, Nora noted, was expected from Ireland to attend the funeral on November third.

"Ah, they are keeping her a long time. Must be on account of foreign dignitaries," Maya sighed.

Again there was Rajive Gandhi, acting Prime Minister, calling for national unity, and by now he had gone out to troubled areas himself. "He did not wish to go there," said the woman sitting in front of her and Nora nudged Maya.

"Naturally, he did not wish to rush out from his family at this time," Maya whispered, "people dismiss the feelings of a son, but he is no more a son only. Even now he must be a Prime Minister."

After the news, musicians continued their mourning music for the nation. Maya and Nora slipped away and were having tea when Mr Das hurried in, flustered: "Mrs Nora, quickly, if you please. My son wishes to have those emergency pills of yours. My daughter-in-law is in collapse. Where are they? You are having?"

R.D. met Nora and Maya at his bedroom door. A few of Nina's friends stood about on the landing. "Please, it is better that she is kept quiet," he said to everyone and to Nora : "She has found out about Mr Singh, my wife is suffering from shock, also there is worse news." Taking the box of Valium from Nora's hand he quietly closed the door. Commotion spread through the house. Now, everyone knew that the "boy's" father was in the study and an ambulance was coming to take him to hospital. R.D. had been seen helping a devastated Sarla up the stairs. As one, everyone sought Mr Das.

"Come people," he said, "sit please, here near the table." He joined his finger tips, looked around as though searching for someone and said: "It is not good news I am telling". He waited before he said: "This marriage is being stopped. The father of the bridegroom cannot continue with this wedding, cannot bring this baraat," and noticing Nora, he added, "the bridegroom's procession cannot come through these streets."

There was silence. Nobody moved. Nora saw Nina in the doorway, hands held out to dry, a strange look on her face. A smile, of what? Nora watched the girl tidy away all expression until her face, at its most beautiful, seemed to be cast in bronze. Who could guess her thoughts? "A mysterious girl," her father's voice echoed.

Mr Das continued: "Mr Singh must go to hospital, he is being too ill. Relatives and guests have been injured coming to Delhi, the bridegroom and his friends are defending the gurdwara. Mr Singh's house was attacked by hoodlums. All there are being helped by the Hindu neighbours. It is no good to hope for a wedding now. The brother of Deepak Singh will not bring this baraat. India has suffered disaster before," his voice shook. "We will survive." He pushed his chest out and pulled himself up to his full height; his voice was strong again: "Everyone must stay until it is safe to leave. This is my wish."

CHAPTER 13

The men were going to pay their last respects to Indira Gandhi, but it was taken for granted that Sikhs, like the women, would stay at home. Two of the Sikhs appeared with haircuts. "A brave gesture," said Maya, and Nora saw that she doubted their chances of being taken for Hindus.

The day before there had been a stampede outside Teen Murti House, where the Prime Minister lay in state. Some of the people who had queued all night were trampled underfoot. Meanwhile, the caterers had failed to appear at the wedding house, so the women buzzed around the kitchen. They made tea from mineral water because of the rumour that now Delhi's water supply was poisoned and, with the markets closed, there was a shortage of food. Mr Das had ordered all the sweets to be stored away:

"If we cannot buy food then we must eat them, but sweets are for celebration, not this time," he said.

The men left the house in groups to pay respects to Mrs Gandhi. One group returned to let the next group go. They all reported enormous crowds and Bombay film stars driving up to the special entrance for dignitaries. The aged and infirm stood as long as everyone else to see their leader. Others came from the outskirts of the city despite the danger of breaking curfew.

More and more people squeezed into R.D.'s house having fled riot areas or felt insecure in hotels. A few came from the Imperial Hotel on Janpath where Nora had stayed and which was now a stockade guarded by staff, Sikh guests and relatives of the Sikh owners. Nora tried to imagine the busy crowded strip deserted, the settlement outside the gates of the hotel cleared, the market dead.

R.D. saw to it that the house was well guarded, although they were so clear of trouble that one could not even see smoke in the distance. Kumari had moved in with her mother and Nora and there was still ample space for the three of them. Nora missed being alone with Maya and feeling claustrophobic in the crowded house, longed to go beyond the gates. R.D. did not see any reason why she and Maya should not go for a walk. At first Maya was reluctant, but the further they walked from the house the more relaxed she grew. The air was good. There was no traffic.

They were on Kasturba Marg when a procession of people all in white, approached. There were about thirty of them, each garlanded. Some paces ahead of the group a man read aloud from a book held on open palms. Nora was suprised that there were women among them.

"These people are villagers," Maya explained, "probably they have walked for hours to pay respects to Mataji, many will come like that, praying all the way, bringing garlands."

Seeing the women, Nora decided that she wanted to go to the funeral. R.D. said it was impossible, it would be too dangerous and women were not expected to go to cremation grounds: "And I cannot take you there," he said, "I must look after things here. Besides, we will probably have a better view on television."

His father disagreed: "She is not like the other ladies, she has come so far she should see such a historical thing. I will escort her there. She will be safe with me."

R.D. did not argue. The funeral was not his primary concern. He had expected his daughter to be upset when the wedding was cancelled, but was shocked to discover that she actually sympathised with rioting Hindus.

"How can people expect everything to be normal after such a thing? Sikhs have murdered Indira Gandhi," Nina said and R.D. was glad that she was not overheard. "Should Hindus pretend that this is not so?" she asked, "Sikhs should not be punished?"

Her attitude frightened him. Suppose the assassination had happened after the wedding? Would she speak this way in the home of her Sikh in-laws? He had attempted to reason with her, but she had gone to bed; she always slept when she was upset. She had slept that time her mother was in hospital and when she found her dog dead in the garden. More recently, when he had refused to let her go to study in London, she had slept the whole weekend. Now she was sleeping again, with her mother under sedation in another room. He would not risk leaving the house this weekend.

Maya who would gladly have avoided a visit to Shantivana felt she must accompany Nora. They went with Mr Das, setting off shortly after 8a.m.

It was noon, although still cool, when the gun carriage bore Indira Gandhi out through the gates of Teen Murti House. The red saried body lay on a flower covered bier of pink carnations, marigolds and white roses. Strings of white chrysanthemums formed curtains so that Nora thought the hearse looked more like a Cinderella coach.

"She is riddled with bullets, the poor little lady," Maya said, "and she must make her last journey on a gun carriage."

"That is highest honour," said Mr Das and Maya looked away.

As the music struck up, Mr Das said: "The Rajputana Regimental Centre playing the Mrityu March."

There were about two hundred men from the army, navy and air force in the procession, plumed officers on horseback, twenty-four buglers, and all the while

Mr Das kept up a running commentary for Nora's benefit. The carriage that followed Mrs Gandhi carried Hindu and Parsee priests.

"Mrs Gandhi's husband was a Parsee," Mr Das said, "perhaps you are thinking she was Mahatma Gandhi's daughter?" Not waiting for an answer he continued: "They are not related, she is the daughter of Jawharlal Nehru and she married Feroze Gandhi, no relation to the Mahatma."

White cars with Rajive Gandhi and his wife, Sonia, and the Sikh president, Zail Singh followed the body. Nora was surprised to see so many Sikhs among the security forces.

"Ten per cent are Sikh," said Mr Das, and the driver started the car to follow the procession along the twelve kilometre drive to the banks of the Yamuna, a route that shaved away the poverty of the city like a bruise from a mango and showed the best of Delhi.

People lined the way, watched from roof-tops and doorways and spoke their love or anger from slogan boards. Outside of Delhi, trucks and cars smouldered on the highways, smoke rising as far as the eye could see.

"Such a poor crowd," said Mr Das surprising Nora who had not realised that by India's standards the crowd was sparse. Incredibly, Maya was singing softly:

"Wish me luck as you wave me goodbye,
With a cheer, not a tear in your eye.
Give me a smile I can keep all the while,
In my heart while I'm away ... That was a favourite song of hers," she said, her eyes full of tears, "she said it when she was being led away to jail." Mr Das blew his nose.

As the funeral procession turned from the President's place, once the home of Lord Mountbatten and down the long impressive Rajpath with all its bougainvilaea, Maya translated what people shouted: "Indira is India." "While sun and moon remain in heaven, Indira will be remembered."

132

"I brought my wife to say goodbye to Mahatma Gandhi," said Mr Das, "and not an inch of this green could be seen on Rajpath. Everywhere, only people crying, praying. They were old and young. All the family came and the servants. The whole route was like ants, and we all cried without shame. Today all these armed men are here to protect Indira's son."

"It is because the trains are stopped," Maya said, "how can people come from outside Delhi?"

"Delhi must be having more than six million people living here," said Mr Das. "No less. They are not here. Fear of violence is keeping them away."

At the cremation grounds, they met Dr Doshi and two other men. Mr Das had no difficulty in leading the troupe to an enclosure where they stood against a fence near the "chief mourners".

"There's Mother Teresa," Maya said, and Nora saw the Taoiseach, and recognised Yassir Arafat, Imelda Marcos and others from television. Was that Shirley McLaine, she wondered.

She was stunned by her unobstructed view of Mrs Gandhi, so close, the Patrician nose still proud days after death. "Five jewels are in her mouth for the gods," Maya told Nora. The offerings being placed around the pyre were also for the gods. The chanting of prayers rose over the loudspeakers, accompanied by drums as the pageant of the ceremony got underway.

She was not prepared for the reality of the cremation. Shocked, she thought R.D. was right, she should not have come. She shivered and could not stop. She could see the pain on the faces of the Gandhi family, the little clutch of grandchildren, and the bewilderment of the smallest, Feroz Varon, as he stared at his grandmother.

Ghee was being poured on the sandalwood. "You wish to move away?" Maya asked, but Nora was transfixed. The flag which covered the leader had been folded, she lay in the logs, her son with a flaming torch in his hands. Nora watched, her throat aching

133

as Rajive touched his mother's head with flame. The faint scent of burning hair caught Nora's nose as Indira Gandhi's famous white streak disappeared.

As Rajive walked to his mother's feet and touched them with the torch propitious unctions were being poured on the flames. Each child went to the pile of sandalwood and brought a log to stoke the fire, smoke in their faces. They stood back. Rajive Gandhi's hand was on Rahul's shoulder. Sonia wiped her children's tears and they her's. Nora blew her nose and kept the handkerchief to her face. Wails rose from the crowd as the flames engulfed Indira. Nora and Maya stumbled away, supporting each other.

"It is not over," said Mr Das and then on second thoughts, nodded and ushered the women on. As they crossed the grass, Mr Das looked back and said: "There, over there, are many bodies no one can recognise, none can claim." Nora and Maya followed his gaze. Beyond the funeral, across the river, the dark breath of carnage rose in clouds of black smoke.

CHAPTER 14

"Mr Basai is there," Maya said as they crossed the tarmac from the plane, and Kumari waved to her father who acknowledged with a sway of his head and a smile.

"You must take rest," he greeted his wife, and Nora was surprised to see Maya become a woman in need of rest. She appeared fragile as she walked into the tiny airport and sat on a chair while her husband claimed the luggage. And when Mr Basai helped Maya into the back of the car, she lay back with a weary little sigh and closed her eyes.

She's putting it on, Nora thought feeling vaguely abandoned, for Maya had been in high spirits on the short flight to Agra. She had giggled about Nora's tactics over getting tickets midst a crush of fleeing Sikhs in the Indian Airlines office, and she and Kumari had mimicked Nora several times: "We are ladies travelling alone ..." In fact, Nora had mimicked Maya, having realised that a hint of vulnerability in the use of the word "ladies" would get a woman anything in this part of the world.

Having insisted on speaking to the manager, Nora handed him her passport and told him softly: "Our husbands are waiting in Agra, surely you will not detain us?" And Maya added: "Even now, there must be a quota for foreigners?"

Maya had been impatient to get out of Delhi and R.D. had seemed relieved to let them go.

"Can I help by staying?" Nora had asked him.

"Perhaps it is better not," he said, "you are safe

going by air. Most of these people will be here until the trains are running again. Sarla is in such a state and Nina also not so good." He swayed his head. "Perhaps, it would be better for us to meet when things are more normal. There has been no trouble in Agra. I regret only that I cannot help with the tickets. Under the circumstances you may get tickets more easily than I could. I will send the car with you to wait in case you must come back. Be careful."

Nora looked out of the window of Basai's car. It was as grey as a morning at home, misty with rain. The lack of sun left people exposed and Nora felt she ought not be watching them struggle into day. Here and there some still slept under rough blankets, like things dumped. Those with hovels did their morning chores, squatted beside mean threads of smoke, shook out blankets, washed children, suckled infants. Two men stood over an open sewer, their backs to the street. An old woman in white carried an offering in a coconut shell towards the clanging bell of the temple. Women glided along with vessels on their heads, carrying buckets of water.

Vessels waited in a gleaming line while a teenage boy commandeered the pump, soaping his body white with soap. Did he do that every day, Nora wondered, or was today special? A chance of a job, maybe? Nearby, stood a herd of buffaloes, as still as drenched black rocks and Nora wondered why they were there.

She watched Ravi Basai as he chatted in Hindi with his daughter. Kumari was more like Maya, Nora thought, although not at all plump. She had inherited darker skin and a longer neck from her father.

Ravi Basai was handsome, of average height and Nora saw that beneath the air of authority he was a shy man, making an effort for her sake: "The Sardar shops will remain closed," he said as they passed a row of shuttered shops. "There has been no trouble here. Many places, but not Agra. Just the same, the shops have been closed."

"Ah yes." Maya was awake, "Delhi is a different place. There, they have taken advantage of this tragedy."

"Sikhs in London handed out sweets," said twenty-one-year-old Kumari, "these foreign Sikhs have money to send for fighting, but they are safe in England or Canada. Perhaps they will learn from this lesson."

"She was also Prime Minister of the Sardarjis," Mr Basai said, "also of what use is teaching lessons if all India is torn apart? People wish to live their lives only. They are wanting nothing to do with violence, that is most of us Hindus, also most Sikhs do not even think about a Khalistan."

At last they reached Maya's home. Servants came running to open the gates. They stood around in a tattered, cheerful group, delighted to see Maya and Kumari, joining their hands in shy greeting to Nora. They giggled when she said "Hello".

"Take rest," Mr Basai repeated to Maya before he disappeared.

"See," Maya waved her hand as they walked through the cool house, "they have put flowers for your welcome."

"Why do you call your husband 'Mr'?" Nora asked Maya when they were alone.

"It is custom with Indian womans," Maya said.

"Women," Nora corrected absent-mindedly.

"Ah yes," Maya replied, "I am singular woman. The name of the husband is never spoken."

"What do you call him when you are alone?" Nora asked.

"Then there is no need to call, when he is there," Maya said. She sipped her tea and whispered: "Listen! If he is not in the room I call 'Listen' and he knows I am meaning him. It is respect for the husband, Indian woman's husband is god, I tell you."

"In Victorian times, our husbands were also called 'mister' by their wives," Nora said, "and the husbands called their wives 'Mrs'."

"Ah yes," said Maya, "but in India it is also protection from evil eye that we do not say name. Neither he says my name."

A few minutes later, Ravi Basai came into the living-room while Maya was taking a telephone call, and asked: "She is where?" Once directed, he sought his wife in silence.

"Do not forget that as guest you are goddess in Indian home," Maya said later on as she showed Nora the house, "so you must state demands. Just mention to me. Come, I wish to show you special thing," and Nora followed her into the dining-room. "I wish to show you my gods, we are keeping them in this cupboard, specially made." She opened the carved doors, releasing the fragrance of fine sandalwood figures midst a rabble of plastic and papier mâché images.

"This is Lord Shiva," Maya told Nora, "and this is his consort, Parvati." Reverently, Maya touched the blue trunked plastic elephant. "This is Ganesh, god of knowledge, and this is Lakshmi, the goddess of prosperity. In the picture is my mother-in-law's guru, our family guru. She is naturally having gods in her own room, and look what is here." From a corner Maya brought forward a slim porcelain blue-veiled statue of the Virgin Mary. "You are having the Lord Jesus, isn't it, and this is his Mother, but he has not a wife. This is the statue of how you say, Your Lady?" Nora glanced at Maya and saw that she was serious.

"Our Lady," she murmured.

"R.D. brought her from London, very beautiful" Maya said. "Sometimes I ask her for a boon to do with ladies. She is good for these requests. Also, there are a lot of followers of the Lord Jesus, called saints? Would you like to take Your Lady to your room?" Maya asked, lifting the statue.

"No, no," Nora said, returning the statue to the democracy of Maya's god cupboard. "I can always come here."

The stony greeting of Maya's mother-in-law did not spoil Nora's welcome to the house. The old woman was sitting outside her quarters on the other side of the courtyard, her white sari pulled out to a hood shading her eyes. Nora joined her hands in salutation and stood uneasily while Maya stooped and touched the huge pink-soled feet. Her mother-in-law pulled her shawl across her chest and ignored her.

"You are well?" Maya inquired. The hugely fat woman stared ahead. Eventually, she spoke to Maya, who answered her in English.

"It is only Wednesday, he will come again on Friday."

The woman is ancient, Nora thought, and that expression on her face says "damn it, I'm still alive".

Alone, Nora lay awake on that first night in Maya's home. I've spent my loneliest times in bed, she thought. She had forgotten she would be alone again. Naturally, Maya could not sleep with her now, and she was surprised by a twinge of jealousy at the thought of Maya in bed with her husband. She recalled feeling self-conscious when she thought that she and Maya were to share a double bed at R.D.'s, but when the quilt was removed, there were two beds beneath with one head-board.

Now, in the morning while it was still dark, Maya slipped into Nora's bed.

"Could you not sleep?" Nora asked, resting her cheek on Maya's hair.

"Yes, I slept," Maya sighed, "Mr Basai is taking his bath early."

Why was it, Nora thought, that the simplest statement wives made about their husbands always seemed loaded with intimacy? She was relieved that this was the end of the conversation.

When the sound of Ashoke's motor bike was heard on Friday, Nirmal dumped the tea tray on the table so that the cups rattled, and rushed to meet him. The house-boy had been giddy since morning because Ashoke was coming for the weekend, after a couple of weeks at the college hostel, only half an hour away. Ashoke boarded there, Maya explained, because Mr Basai thought it was good for him to be with other boys.

Thangamani, left her cooking, modestly covered her face with her sari and came to chuckle with pleasure at the sight of Ashoke. Uma, the little vessel girl, twisted her body against the door jamb. Kumari who had come running from her room said: "Ah, it is only you, what fuss," but waited with everyone else while Ashoke touched his grandmother's feet. Knees bent, the old woman struggled step by step, her hand on his arm, as he brought her to tea. It was the first time Nora had seen her enter the main part of the house. "Fetch Dadiji's shawl," Ashoke told Nirmal. The boy went running.

"How do you do?" Ashoke asked Nora five minutes after the introductions.

"Very well, thank you."

"That is excellent," said Ashoke. He put Nora in mind of a llama, with his long neck and the way he held his head. She imagined that adoration flowed in his veins, so great was his self-esteem. An esteem, she thought, that stopped well short of arrogance.

During tea, she found herself part of Ashoke's devoted audience. His grandmother's eyes never left his face, though her angry, bitter expression did not change. Nirmal stood in the doorway of the room, anxious for the chance to be of service and Uma crouched on her heels, her eyes never leaving Ashoke. He talked about his medical studies and how he had been able to use the time saved by not having had to go to the wedding with his father after all.

He told them all about the trouble in Delhi as though he had been there. Maya listened as avidly as everyone else without mentioning her own experience of the rioting. Nora took the hint.

140

After tea, Ashoke went off on his motor bike with the bare-footed Nirmal on his back seat. The next day, he slept until two o'clock, the while Nirmal was on the alert for a sound from his room.

Later in the afternoon, Ashoke drove them to the Taj Mahal. Nirmal polished the car for an hour before they left and waved goodbye, his smile huge. Ravi Basai sat beside Ashoke with naked pride in being driven by his nineteen-year-old-son.

"Do not bring directly to Taj, go first by Tajgani," Maya told her son, "that way she is seeing setting for Taj, history of this place." And so they went through the sprawling streets of the village built for the craftsmen who were brought to Agra in the Seventeenth century to build the monument.

Smells and sounds mingled in Nora's senses, the clanking of a bullock cart, cow dung, children at play, spices, charcoal fires, hot dust, perfumed incense, cawing crows, even the heaving breath of labourers and the pungent smell of the bidis. Yesterday's life today's, she thought, except for the sound of a transistor and me in white jeans.

"So much going on," she said.

"Yes, there are still Taj craftsmen here, descendents of the first who came," answered Basai, "they make for the Taj shops and repair the monument itself. Only the finest artists repair the Taj."

"And they are using the same tools as then," Ashoke added.

Outside the village, the sun gilded homes sculpted from mud, red as the earth beyond which dung patty cakes were piled high against a wall, each branded with the hand print of its artist. In front of the wall, a camel lay munching, and women, exhaustion in every line of their bodies, chatted as they lay on a grassy patch propped up on their elbows. Women passed on their way back from the river with water, the pain of burden obscured by their graceful balance. And in the haze beyond all, was the Taj Mahal.

The ticket seller told Maya that Nora was the first foreigner to arrive at the Taj since the assassination. As they passed through the red sandstone gateway of the main entrance to the Taj Mahal they looked up at the doves paired in the eaves of the portal. Their cooing nudged Nora towards the mood of the place even before her first luminous sight of the Taj, perfectly framed by the inner arch of the entrance from the outer grounds. Like most people Nora thought she knew what the monument would look like, had even seen it in the haze of distance. Now, she winced at beauty beyond her imagining. What could have been a cry stirred in her throat at the whiteness of the marble dome against the pink sky, beyond the path of springing water-falls.

Nora walked through the frame, into the presence of the Taj Mahal, its perfect, milky curves floating on a square pond of gleaming marble. So this was Maya's Taj, the inspiration of the "real love story" she was writing. Here was the mystery of beauty. She wanted to see it as clearly as she could, clear of the distraction of the fountain path, but even as she felt the urge to hurry closer, she stopped. She had already stepped through the frame. She should have taken her time and savoured that picture. She must not squander this. She wanted to stay in this moment of anticipation a little longer. Soon I'll be on my way back, she thought. Slowly. This time will pass so quickly, Nora thought, although she already knew that it would never pass from memory.

Maya squeezed her arm, her smile on the monument: *Only let this tear drop, the Taj Mahal glisten spotlessly in the cheek of heaven forever and ever!* she recited, "the cheek of heaven", Maya repeated, "our poet, Tagore, said this. You have heard of Tagore? Come, we will first enjoy the gardens, and make ourselves ready." Seeing the look of enchantment on Maya's face Nora felt herself privileged to have such an introduction to the Taj Mahal.

142

Maya led her about the voluminous hem of the Taj, through its hidden folds, its femininity seeming to scent the air above the roses and exotic bushes, while flash bright green parrots, sang all around them. Over their heads was a white froth of bougainvillaea. They sat silently in a warm nest of sound absorbed in the humming, buzzing, rustling, ticking and throb of hidden life. As the others waited, they stayed as long as they could and often a bird or squirrel, secure in this paradise, came to look at them. A lizard remembered something and hurried off, as, sharing a drugged smile, the women rose at last.

Eventually, they took the path to the left of the fountain path where the men and Kumari were waiting for them. "When water is there, it reflects the Taj," Maya said.

"When water is there," Mr Basai teased.

The bed of the Yamuna was barely covered with water, here and there garlands lay ragged, straggles from the nearby cremation grounds. Two boys attempted to cool buffaloes with water scooped into tin cans, and beyond some men in white stood around a smouldering fire.

Dennis would love this, Nora thought, as she walked around the balcony of the Taj. They could have had such a wonderful life. Dennis had always wanted to see the Taj Mahal. The men hung back chatting as she and Maya rested on the terrace edge, and Maya told the story of Shah Jehan's great love for the favourite wife who bore him fourteen children. "Imagine, if you can, how happy this lady must have been to have her first child. Three wives before her could not produce for the emperor." Kumari giggled at her mother's intensity.

"Inside Taj we still feel this great love, so great that we will not wish to hear words, whispers only. The Mumtaz," Maya said, "is the most loved lady in India's history. The world is knowing about this love. Not every day thing. Such a love and such a husband to

143

keep his word to build for his wife the most beautiful tomb in the world. How many men are doing this, even emperors?"

"He loved her so much that she died in agony having a fourteenth confinement," said Ashoke.

"Ah, you talk like a medical student, but that is to be expected."

"He loved her so much she was pregnant each year. Why did he not consider this lady?" Mr Basai teased Maya. "Ladies are always speaking about consideration. And such family planning."

"Correct," said Ashoke, "India is being destroyed by such love."

Maya's voice shook.

"You cannot understand. His love for Mumtaz was so great. He was not concerned with other ladies. She was knowing this. She died knowing such great love. Forever she will know."

At last the party stepped into the lovers' silence of the Taj Mahal, down the steps to the inner sanctum. "Here, death is defeated by love," Maya whispered in the blissful hush. "You can feel? You can feel love is here?"

Nora smiled and heard Ciara ask: "... is she for real?" And yet she did feel it. Could it possibly be the love of Shah Jehan and Mumtaz? Or had the atmosphere absorbed something from all the people who had come to see this monument to love. This is a tomb, Nora thought, but there is no aura of death. Perhaps what is in the atmosphere is simply a reflection of human longing. Like Maya's. Even as she wondered, she felt herself caressed by the weightless air inside the Taj Mahal.

More than the tombs, or the great soaring dome of the central chamber or even the atmosphere, the finely cut screen around the Mumtaz was to Nora the most perfect symbol of love's mystery, with the light magical through the lace work of marble.

"This light is magic by moonlight," Maya whispered, "we will return by moonlight."

144

"And by dawn and sunset and every hour of the clock," teased Basai, swaying his head.

Nora was engrossed in the fine detail of the semi-precious stones of the building when a guide came to tell them the gate was closing. "The Taj is closing at 6p.m. because of bomb scares," Ashoke said as they prepared to leave.

During the next couple of days, the tales and architecture of Moghul Agra became a muddle in Nora's head. Akbar had a harem of 5,000 women, there was the courtyard "board" upon which he played chess with people as pieces, and there were stables for 10,000 horses. The refuse from the kitchens had saved thousands from starvation.

The ghosts of the wretched crowded Nora as she walked through the ancient magnificence of Fatehpur Sikri, Shah Jehan's fort which became a palace, Agra Fort and Amber Palace. They were outside Fatehpur Sikri, looking at souvenirs when Nora became aware of a weight on her foot. It was a tiny baby. She gave the child's mother two rupees but she begged more, leaving Nora in the crab-like grasp. Nora gave another note and the mother picked up her beggar baby.

Maya chided: "It is foreigners who are not understanding our country. They make these people worse. Give a child money and for life you make it a beggar. Why work if money comes so easily?"

Easily! Nora's throat was tight with frustration. She could not bear the sight of the skinny mother and her scrap of a child. Beggars ignored Maya but they seemed to materialise around Nora and stayed in her mind. Her sleep was haunted by unfortunates. Only within the house and the high walls of the courtyard and gardens, did the never-ending struggle for existence recede.

"Agra has not many beggars," Maya said, "they are controlled here. Anyone can find work if that is their wish."

"How can someone work if he is weak with hunger or has no hands?" Nora asked, irritated.

145

"Sometimes these people are maiming their own children to make them good for begging. Come we will take tea."

"I don't want tea," Nora said through clenched teeth, and there was a shocked silence.

"Mrs Nora," Ashoke said at last, "it is correct that India has too many poor people, but my mother is not responsible. You are not having poor people in your country? No beggars?"

The reminder of children begging in the cold streets of Dublin made Nora blush. She saw them sitting on the pavement with cardboard boxes to catch coins. She put her cheek on Maya's head by way of apology. Maya did not soften: "If we give away to all the poor peoples, soon we will be begging from others. This is hardly solution."

"I am sorry," Nora said, "I find it upsetting and it's so hot."

Maya looked surprised. "No need for sorrow," she said, "my father always said to think of positive things. So, I care for everyone in this house. Also some others. I work with All India Women's Conference to help poor people ..."

Kumari feared a rift was developing between Nora Auntie and her mother. It was not a good time for a guest to be in India. So quiet after the funeral. They should have a welcome party, just a quiet one. After Ashoke went back to college, Kumari dispatched invitations. Two ragged children took the envelopes around a few at a time, returning breathless between deliveries, until lunch time. In the afternoon, Kumari sat cross-legged on the floor shouting Hindi into the telephone. It drove Nora out into the garden.

CHAPTER 15

Startled out of sleep, Nora sat upright in her bed and the roar came again: "Al-l-a-a-ah". She lay down, eyes wide. The sun was rising and Nora listened to the earth stretch and Virgoe, the elephant who lived next door, grumble as she padded about.

Nora had been visited by her snake again, so that her back ached from working with its weight, but she was too restless to stay in bed. She slid back the door of her room and stepped on to the roof as the call from the mosque spread like an umbrella over Agra.

From the verandah Nora could see into a room of the house next door, where an elderly Muslim's pyjama khurta gleamed white as he prepared for prayer, prostrating himself as easily as a boy. His daughter appeared, a dung-coloured blanket wrapped about her, her nose jewel glittering, plait swinging against her bottom, and Nora watched as his wife joined them and knelt down. Before bending forward the woman glanced up and saw her.

Embarrassed, Nora turned away. The sun brightened as she heard the unmistakable voice of age, a weary wail so relentlessly anguished that it could only be Dadiji at prayer. Damn it, I'm still alive, Nora thought.

Maya came and got into bed beside Nora. Again, Nora knew that she had been crying. Her heart thumped. Red eyed, one morning, Maya had murmured something about "no more than wifely duty ..." and Nora was afraid that she would say more.

"The Muslims are God's alarm clock," Maya said, "yours also."

"I wish they would let Him lie in," Nora replied.

After a while, Maya went downstairs and Nora sat in the new light, listening to the birds, before she followed and found her in front of her god cupboard, incense burning, presenting offerings. Maya smiled at her and held out a palmful of rose petals. Nora placed them in front of the Virgin Mary and although she did not feel like praying, she stayed awhile with Maya. Then she went back to bed.

It was after ten when Nora woke again and remembered that today was Kumari's party in her honour. The centre room waited like an old woman in her finery, dressed before everyone else. The huge divan, the marital bed upon which everybody seemed to live by day, shone with gold satin, under multi-coloured cushions heaped against the wall. Garlands of flowers adorned pictures and blossoms floated on a bowl of water on the table.

The Irish crochet mats Nora had brought adorned the wood. Records lay in little piles beside the record player, and worms of smoke scented the air with magnolia.

In the courtyard Nora tensed at having to pass Dadiji's room on her way to wash. The old woman sat in her doorway, snapping instructions at the dhobi's daughter nearby. The tiny woman struggled with an enormous mess of clothes in a tin bath of grey water. Out of the tangle, her tong-like arms dragged the bottoms of coral coloured pyjamas. Squatting, she slapped them against the slab of concrete bridging the steps of the courtyard. With the first wallop, a squirrel raced out from beneath the steps, up the trunk of the pink budded tree which overhung the wall.

Nora had come to respect the anger on Dadiji's face. But for it, she would be just a pathetic old woman. Instead, energy glowered in her eyes and one noticed that those long protruding teeth were her own. Even

148

when Dadiji talked with her grandchildren, her smile barely hovered over her permanently bitter expression without ever lighting it. Nora joined her hands in respectful salutation. The old woman ignored her.

A box of soft drinks stood in the shade. Thangamani and Uma were working in the kitchen. Something sizzled and made the air buttery sweet.

Nora entered the concrete shed that was the bathroom. In the raw little room Nora often thought that if only Dennis could see her now. She took her bath from the two barrels of water, one fed from a geyser, the other cold. She threw the water over herself with a plastic jug, soaped and rinsed again. Dennis would cope very poorly here, Nora thought. There was water everywhere, but it gurgled down the drain in the uneven concrete floor.

When at last she had relaxed with the discomfort, she threw a final bucket of cold water over herself. The tiny clothes line was so slack her towel swept the floor, but she emerged with renewed confidence to return past the furious elder.

Usually, after Nora's bath, Thangamani and Nirmal came with trays for Maya and Nora who sat cross-legged on the bed as they ate breakfast. This morning Nirmal came alone with a tray and simply nodded happily when Nora asked for Maya. "Didi had to go," he said using the Hindi for "older sister" which was all he ever called Maya, just as everyone referred to Basai's mother by the term given the paternal grandmother.

As Nora found herself listening for the clink of Maya's bangles she recalled Aunt Flo's warning about having to assert one's independence in India. She had become quite cocooned here, she thought, and ought to be making more of an effort on her own. So when Maya did not appear, Nora decided to go for a swim at the hotel and have her hair done.

At the gate, Nora felt the heat of the spice grinder's body as the woman squeezed past on her way to

Maya's kitchen. A hairy black pig trotted by as dhobies swerved along the road with the bundles of laundry on their crossbars. Beside the house, on the other side of the wall hung with Maya's jasmine, two men stood urinating into the sewer, while a few doors down builders raised the dust. A woman in a purple sari was making scurried runs into the neighbour's garden with basins of earth on her head while her baby played, bare-bottomed, in the gravel. There was to be a wedding there too and accommodation was being extended for the new couple. To the other side of Nora, the little servant was drawing a rice flour design that Maya had explained was a blessing, on the pavement outside the house. The girl's tongue curled in concentration at the corner of her mouth and she did not look up.

Across the road, two saried women got out of a car and instructed the driver. Nora watched him wait until they were indoors before he ambled along to what she supposed was the equivalent of a pub, a hut around which men gathered, and reddened the ground with spittle. A tiny stall did brisk business with people waiting outside the eye clinic, and as Nora walked on she recognised the car owned by the smuggler who called door-to-door with Western cosmetics and perfumes at crazy prices. The tailor hurried past, too shy to greet her.

Nora had arrived at the rickshaw stand at the corner of the street. The men were asleep, ankles on the handlebars of their bicycles, but as though getting her scent, two sprang awake as she appeared: "No, no," Nora waved them off and ignored the auto-rick that moved along beside her until she was overwhelmed by the traffic on the main street and had to climb into it.

They were soon engulfed in traffic, and Nora was marvelling at the rainbow painted horns of two bullocks pulling a cart load of logs when a bangle seller scuttled through, pushing a precarious cart of glittering glass in rows of colour. He was the cause of even greater chaos as women came from everywhere to surround his bangles.

Stalled in traffic again, Nora watched a family settled by the road. Their rag roof was attached by ropes and nails to a wooden fence, the front peeled back for daytime. The mud floor was wet with newly spread dung. A man and a woman occupied two string beds. The man's face was covered with the back of his hand as he lay stretched. The woman sat, middle-aged and hardy, a tin mug in her hand, her eyes on the traffic as though on a dull television programme. Her arms were sliced with red glass bangles, her sari orange with brown flowers, and vermilion parted her hair.

The woman's house was so obviously in order that Nora wondered if she would sit there for the rest of the day. There was a flat tin trunk under one bed. At the end of the beds, facing the bus, burned a little fire between stones and slates upon which stood a pot. Against one wall was a low bench made of bits of slates and wood, supported by stones. This held the kitchen things, all gleaming. Nora counted four of everything, and at the end of the bench were four neatly folded blankets, near which there was a tiny shrine enclosed in white-washed pebbles, strewn with bits of fruit and petals. A picture of a fat guru with a garland of paper flowers took pride of place. A wick smouldered in a tiny bowl. Everything was obviously the way it was supposed to be, thought Nora. The woman exuded contentment. Nora sighed, remembering that house-wifely feeling of having accomplished all.

In the patch beyond the tent a girl of about ten years squatted in a loose cotton dress. Absorbed, she scooped dung from a wet heap and shaped it into a cake, round and flat, slapping backwards and forwards, before handing it to an old woman with her back to Nora, who slapped it hard, before placing it with others in a row. Glancing up, the girl's eyes lit upon Nora with interest.

"How long has that family been there?" Nora asked

the auto-rick driver, but he only shrugged. How did they come to be there, she wondered, were they squatters or what? Suddenly, the auto-rick man said: "Life is bringing them to this place."

They are probably wondering how I got here, Nora thought. Nobody knew the real reason, except maybe R.D. She must tell Maya. She felt Maya was entitled to know that the unexpected break-up of her marriage was a deciding fact in her coming to India for the wedding season.

A giant "WELCOME" was written in blossoms on the marble floor of the foyer, but the hotel was almost empty since the assassination. Thinking about a wedding gift for Kumari, Nora strolled around the air-conditioned hotel shops, surprised at suddenly feeling herself at home. She had not felt in the slightest bit homesick at Maya's, but now enjoyed the familiarity of the Western atmosphere. She was tempted to speak to one of the tourists and was immediately dismayed with herself for wanting to talk to strangers simply because they were white.

There were some glorious sarees on display, but Nora felt awkward about giving that traditional Indian wedding gift to a couple. She pondered over a set of hand-painted goblets. They reminded her of a gift she had received for her own wedding. And the memory put her off. Anyway, she thought, the Basai's did not use alcohol except for the whiskey drunk by men in Mr Basai's study.

After Nora had her hair done, she sat in the lounge sipping iced tea and overhearing the conversation of the tourists, became aware that living with Maya, she was seeing an India they would never see. They would shop for jewellery, perhaps even for sarees, go on tours. Buy carpets. And they would see the Taj, but not with Maya. She smiled at the thought of Maya's house, of the wedding in Bombay, R.D.'s house, the village and the train. Still, they were obviously enjoying themselves, the Indian tourist trail was not dull. For all she knew they might have run into Leo or Parvati. They all seemed to be in couples, and she felt vaguely sad about that for the first time since she had left New Delhi. The thought reminded her that Maya would be wondering where she had got to.

On the way back the auto-rick battered along with a prayer to St Christopher attached to the dashboard. It was soon stuck in traffic, honking furiously. People stared in so much at Nora that she felt the red of her hair and her eyelids puffy with heat. Alongside her, schoolchildren smiled vividly from their tonga. And to think she had considered riding home on an elephant; what a spectacle that would have been.

A buffalo with a pink trumpet bloom fixed to one horn blocked the way of the auto-rick. Upon her back, awaiting her pleasure, rode a boy. Round and round turned the buffalo, slowly and relentlessly, drawn after her own tail. People shouted advice to the boy as the traffic honked and beeped, whistled and clattered and sometimes managed to squeeze by. There was a palpable bond between the beast of burden and the over-burdened boy who eventually got through to the animal and beamed as the pair moved off at the sullen pace of a buffalo urged to hurry.

As the vehicle rattled on, Nora promised herself that never again would she get into an auto-rick before examining the state of it. It stopped. Now what? She could see that a newly dug trench narrowed the road. Workmen sat under a tree playing cards.

Something glittered from the trench. Nora stretched out of the auto-rick and saw someone out of a children's story-book wielding a pickaxe. The young woman's skirt was embroidered with beads, pinks and silver upon indigo with a cerise sari blouse. The sari shawl of embroidered indigo had slipped from her hair and sparkling fuscia flowers dangled from her ears. She looked up, and her bangles clinked as she raised

153

the pickaxe. The winged, almond of her eyes were shaped with kohl. A jewel glittered at the side of her nose, and when she put her axe down and raised the back of her hand to her forehead, its palm showed mehndi. Her foot jewellery glittered although a film of dust covered her from toe to toe. Nora called into the trench: "May I take a picture of you?" and waved her camera. The woman waved her head with a smile of agreement, and a crowd settled to watch. Nora was focusing her polaroid when with swift anger a young man grabbed the girl's wrist, and dragged her with one pull out of the trench. She lay on the rubble as he shouted at the auto-rick.

"It is her husband," the driver shrugged, "he is not wishing photograph of his wife."

Before Nora could speak, a man in a business suit spoke to the angry husband. He turned to Nora.

"He says you are going to tell in the foreign press how poor we are in India. How bad. He has seen foreigners taking pictures of beggars. He says his wife has not his permission."

"Please tell him I'm not going to do that. I just want to bring back a picture of his wife to my home in Ireland. They will not have seen such a lovely dress," Nora explained. The husband shouted more angrily than ever.

"I think," said the man in the business suit, "best to forget it. He understands what I tell him, but he is not convinced. He is an ignorant fellow." And he walked away.

Nora climbed back in the scooter and as they drove off the driver said:

"She is bride of this fellow. She comes to do the work for her husband. That is against the law. Perhaps he is afraid if you take the picture that he will be caught. And this girl, she should request her husband's permission."

CHAPTER 16

Maya was sitting in the arbour with a tea tray. She often ordered tea to be brought, enjoying the image of herself sitting behind the silver although as a beauty precaution she rarely drank tea claiming that, "Tea and coffee is darkening the complexion."

As Nora approached, Maya looked up from the mistiness of her pink sari: "Ah, you have been doing battle with an angry husband?"

Nora felt watched.

"I was amazed to see the girl in a trench with a pickaxe, and dressed so beautifully, even with jewellery," she said.

"Ah yes," Maya said, "the women of Rajasthan are most beautiful in India. These ladies are known for their physical strength and beauty. Strength is marriage value, and the women are working harder than the men. The men were great, great warriors. We will go to Jaipur. You have heard that the city is all pink? And we will see the City Palace and the beautiful things in there. Also Johari Bazaar is best place to buy jewels in India, even better than Agra they say." She sighed, staring into space, "Jaipur is glowing pink in the moonlight."

"How did you know what happened this morning?" Nora asked, still feeling uncomfortable.

"Ah, that is simple. My neighbour, Mr Kakar told me. He saw his client pleading for you, I think? Poor Mrs Kakar sent for me this morning. She is far from well. Look, tell me your first impression." She handed

155

Nora a snap-shot of a young man. "Handsome," Nora said, and thought, a bit overweight. "Who is he?"

"I had a letter from New York. His parents are looking for a girl from India. What do you think about Archana? Will I give her opportunity?" Archana Rai was Kumari's friend and a neighbour's daughter.

"You mean match her up with this fellow. In America?"

"She is good girl, but she is motherless girl, perhaps these people ..."

"Maya, you're not serious. You wouldn't send a girl off to America to marry a fellow she's never met."

Maya was exasperated: "She will be lucky to be accepted by these people. This boy is having green card. And she will not be sent, he will come here for the wedding. It is not easy to make a match for daughter of widower. Sati Rai is not so wise; he should have remarried before this."

Nora sipped her tea. Sometimes the gap between herself and Maya seemed impossible.

"Dearling?" Maya said, with a hint of pleading in her voice. "Dearling, we have our ways of doing things." Maya had given life to the mispronunciation and Nora softened.

"How did you feel when your marriage was arranged?" she asked. Startled by the question, Maya poured more tea.

"Very well, I will discuss with you. I will say. My heart was broken before that time. I was promised to a fine family. In India we say we rear a daughter to be property of another house. All was arranged. I met the boy when I was twelve and after that I thought only of him. Then he went to college. Still, I dreamed always of him. How romantic I was then." Maya's eyes filled with tears. "And then came the news. It was only one year before we were getting married. He had fallen in love with a girl from his college and a new marriage was arranged between these two. I was dismissed. Nothing was required of me, I thought I would die from the shame in my heart.

156

"From my village I came to stay with my aunt near Agra and I thought my life is finished. I am thrown on the scrap-heap at sixteen years. My aunt said I must go to college and improve my marriage prospects. I was realising that she was only wanting the best for me so I thought I will get this prospect, and I went to college."

"And didn't you meet anyone?"

"I did not think of such a thing to cause my family more trouble. I had such hurt and I worked all the time at my studies. I had one friend only. Then one day a letter came to my hostel. I had to go to my uncle's house. I was already 19 years. I went in a simple sari and I did not adorn myself. The women measured me for my height and that way, you say 'et cetera'. After more months I was called back to my uncle's place, and my husband's family came there. There were so many male persons from his side I did not know which was to be my husband. But he must have known about me and was knowing I am inferior, rejected by that boy."

"Did you fall in love with him?"

"You marry the people you love, we love the people we marry." Maya was pleased with the turn of phrase. "Duty is love, what else? Or perhaps the other way. Who knows? I had two daughters and the first one died at one year. Of fever. In those days Dadiji had the personality of a general. Her furiosity was intolerable. Then at last I produced my son and she has not the heart to be so hard on his mother.

Ashoke's father honours me now. He does not stop me doing writing and poetry, but Dadiji says I should stay home. I am a free soul, I tell you. I come alone and I will go alone. Even if I must obey, always my soul is free ..."

The boy came and took the tray away and Maya moved further into the shade.

"Often when I was too much sad I went to sit in the gardens of the Taj. In that place we sit together. So many people to see Taj, but mostly only to see. You must feel the Taj Mahal inside," Maya touched her breast, "in here is this Taj. Some see only with their eyes."

Her energy restored, Maya said: "I have heard they are making film about the Taj. Twenty-eight millions they have spent, not rupees. I read all about this. All aspects of Taj is in this movie, also gardens, but no lady. No Mumtaz, merely a mention. They say she died in childbirth. Correct. But the Mumtaz was not a child-bearer only. They have made a film about the Taj Mahal without the Mumtaz. Forever, she will laugh at them." Maya sighed, adjusted her sari on her shoulder and said: "Tomorrow we will go again to Taj. We will go early and stay long. We will go alone," she added, her eyes on the man who now waddled across the lawn.

It was the jeweller with one of Kumari's wedding sets and as the work did not please Maya, the discussion developed an edge: "I cannot send my daughter to her in-laws with such an ordinary piece," Maya said, "yes, yes, the rubies are good, but not like this ..."

Nora left them and found three letters on her pillow. One was from Ciara:

... you're staying there a long time, so you must like India, well your letters sound as if you do. Can't say the telly scenes turned me on to it. Now, it's all Rajive Gandhi, Dan says its like the Continent, to think of it as Europe and what happens in France isn't happening in Germany, for instance. Actually, people here are inclined to think that we have British soldiers around the corner in Dublin, and all that doesn't effect our lives much at all in the South, does it? Might be a different country.

I spoke to Dad in London and told him he ought to take a holiday and join you out there, but he says he'll see. He's very busy. It's odd the way we're all somewhere else now, isn't it? I've never known you and Dad to be apart so long.

158

I love it here, but one of these days I'll have to think about work again. I'm sure I won't go back to modelling. It suddenly seems a bit pointless. I might go to university after all. Yes, I know you told me so. Honestly, I'm not that keen to do anything yet. I'm so happy, we're so happy. The house is all fixed up except for the garden, well just for a few things, but I suppose I can't stay on honeymoon forever. Why not?

Derry's letter was written while she was down with flu.

Why didn't we think of my going with you? At least I wouldn't have the flu, but of course I couldn't have gone at this time of year. If we'd planned it I could have gone out to meet you at the end of term.

I was in London for a weekend and came back with this dose. Dropped in on Dennis and he seems to be managing. I spent hours in Foyles and brought back a load of books. I brought a few for you. When I was dipping into one of them I read that Mahatma Gandhi advised anyone wanting to learn about India to study India's villages and her women. It seems as though you have the ideal opportunity for doing that, although I suppose Agra is larger than a village.

That could be an interesting book, Nora thought, smiling because she rarely fancied any of the books Derry pressed upon her with the obvious intention of improving her mind. They were usually about psychology or feminism, or simply impenetrable and Nora had long ago given up trying to struggle through them to please her sister.

Recalling some of the books she had rejected, a dark cover with the title *Surpassing the Love of Men*, in bright pink lettering sprang to Nora's mind. It was about romantic friendship between women.

In the blurb on the back of the book, Nora had read that the author had constructed a cultural history of women's passionate friendships with each other and that in the eighteenth century romantic friendships beween women flourished. They had written each other passionate poetry, fondled and slept together. Two phrases "the near impossible dream of spending their lives together," and the "dignity of love between women" echoed in her mind as she recalled reading how the spread of Freudian ideas had condemned such relationships as deviant, but modern women were reclaiming them.

Nora had not been in the mood to plough through the scholarly book, but wished that she had it to read now. She made a mental note to ask Derry to keep it for her.

It was a shock to realise that you were in India at such a time, wrote Dennis in the letter forwarded from Delhi. *I thought of flying out after I spoke to you even though you'd said not to, but it's impossible to get a ticket and Derry advised against it in any case. She had your number from the wedding invitation.*

I'm getting more settled in the flat. It's strange being on one's own after all the years. Derry was in London and hunted me down. You can imagine my reaction when she landed on the doorstep. Literally. But it was rather decent of her, I admit. She helped me organise the flat a bit, left me a list for the supermarket. I had bought steak and eggs and coffee and so on, but I didn't have salt or a coffee pot or stuff to clean the bath and she sorted it out. She went on about me being conditioned, helpless, but she's not a bad old skin. Anyway, now I have a woman coming in and the place feels more like home .

I had a great letter from Ciara. I'm going to phone her tonight. Have you any idea when you are coming back? R.D. should be able to get you a ticket. Let me know and I'll come and meet you at Heathrow. Take care of yourself. Dennis.

Nora was irritated by the letter, irritated by Dennis and his "woman coming in". And she thought that Derry with all her talk could have let him find his own bloody stuff to clean the bath.

Lying on her bed, Nora felt a bit low. What would Maya think of this letter? Maya and her matchmaking. What sort of husband would Maya have chosen for her? Her parents would have chosen Dennis, and thought of him as such a catch. She dozed off and woke to the sound of female laughter.

Downstairs, she found that girls in Punjabi suits filled the middle room. Kumari was proudly self-conscious in the Western gear Nora had given her; yellow jeans and a tee-shirt, her hair complicated. Some of the girls wore jasmine in their hair. There were no boys. The girls had brought their mothers.

The music started and Nora found herself dancing with Mrs Fernandez, "a Christian lady who is doing fine work for charity." Mrs Fernandez looked about the same age as her daughter and was as energetic, so that soon Nora sat on the edge of the divan exhausted. Maya passed her a drink, and Nora sipped, listening to the words of an Irish rock group:

Baby don't leave 'til I wake up,
Baby don't leave 'til I wake up ...

The words embarrassed her. Did they listen to the words, and if so, what possible relevance could they have for these girls? And yet it was all Western music. To a slow number, the girls mooned in each other's arms. "Ah yes," said Maya who was sitting at her feet. "I am watching Smita over there. She is very happy these days. Always a smile. I hope that she is not in love. Her parents are having big plans for her."

Nora thought that Maya's neighbour Usha Sarnad looked like a priestess in a disco, her classical Indian dance movements keeping the Western beat as her sari became a blur of primrose. Delighted cries came with the end of the record and Usha sank among the women on the satin of the marriage bed.

"Your husband is coming when, Mrs Nora?" a woman who had lived in Leicester asked.

"He isn't coming," Nora said, glad when the woman blinked. Fat busybody. She caught the pained look in Maya's eyes before she turned towards the record player. "Now, we will have something for the mothers."

As Maya spoke Nora was startled by the appearance of an old woman suddenly framed in the doorway. White candy-floss hair clouded about the ancient face. Her stick-thin body was stock still, until suddenly, she sliced her way to the centre of the room, poised with her arms held like a wishbone above her head, her feet planted apart. There were murmurs, a hush. Her sari was of lime-green cotton, her ankles grasped with flowers. Nora winced at the mercilessness of age cruelly exposed by the dance costume. The woman's mouth mocked a pout. She held her position with a tremor, her body flacidly smooth in the wake of an avalanche of flesh which had long since completed its descent from her long neck to just above the folds of her sari. The dried arms looked fixed as though they might never come down, her finger nails clawed.

One of the women called in Hindi to Maya's back, and she turned and smiled in recognition before she changed her selection for the record player. The music began and Nora thought, surely Maya will not allow this? She must stop it. The women were still, waiting. The old woman began jerkily with the first boing of the zitar, her body seeming unable to remember. Unwilling. But gradually, the dancer began to unlock until the music seemed to trickle slowly into her limbs. Her face ceased to mock itself as her body thawed, faltering still, but obeying. Her eyes were closed and her mouth set in an uneven groove of concentration. The women held their breath as she gained control, neck and arms loosening, her fingers twitching as they warmed. The white hair remained a still cloud upon her back. And at last, her movements loosened and became almost smooth. She was

162

dancing for a while when Nora turned away to adjust her cushion and when she looked back the rhythm was gathering in the dancer's belly.

The room relaxed now, enjoying the dance. It went on and on, with slowly increasing power. The woman's thighs had, incredibly, grown strong enough to take her to her knees. There she knelt, her shoulders trembling, head revolving with its unmoving hair. There was hush beyond silence as the dancer finally cast off the old crone's body and danced and danced. Her movements were smooth and supple when a pelvic shiver took her by surprise. She resisted the movement, but nourished by her female audience, she took control and went with it. Age was their common enemy, and Nora felt herself merge into the will which rescued the dancer from its tyranny, bore her to freedom. Maya, her eyes moist, placed a hand over Nora's.

The dancer's face was wet as her lashless eyes opened. She started to relax, but suddenly she froze, aware of something, and her body tumbled back to ruin before she fled, her arms held over the back of her bent head as though to ward off a blow. She passed Ravi Basai in the doorway and vanished into the courtyard. The master of the house, thought Nora. Sarees were tidied, the girls assumed nonchalance. Mr Basai smiled at his friends' wives and daughters as he nodded his way through the room towards his study. Except for tea, the party was over.

At dinner, Ravi Basai concentrated on his thali. And even though Nirmal hovered, Maya kept disappearing into the kitchen to return with special pickles, hotter food, and even his favourite, stuffed paratha, which she made herself.

Nora knew that Maya pleaded with her husband when she spoke to him in Hindi. He replied, and Kumari said: "But Daddy, some Sardarji shops are open, the trains are running perfectly ..."

He swayed his head: "It is a matter of respect only.

163

Dadiji is also not pleased. It is too soon for music and dancing," and then noticing the expression on the face of his guest, he shrugged. "It is done now, past. Eat. Who will share this paratha?"

CHAPTER 17

It was Tuesday, Nora thought, Maya would not slip in beside her this morning and say: "It is the Muslims only, sleep." This was the day when Maya kept Vratas, the Hindu wife's weekly fast-day of prayer for the well-being and long life of her husband. On Tuesday, Maya began with early morning prayers, and clear herbal tea was all she took for breakfast. Later, she brought offerings to the temple and spoke as little as possible throughout the day.

Her tea was brought to the garden and as they sat beside the rope gate, Virgoe pushed her trunk through and delicately nudged towards the sticks of sugar-cane laid in readiness for her. The elephant was a welcome guest who knew exactly how far she could infringe on Maya's hospitality, and Nora noticed how Virgoe did not step through the gap, but daintily toed the line of the carefully tended lawn.

Maya slurped the scalding tea. "I am too upset to be silent today. I must speak. I have heard very bad news."

Nora took Maya's hand and waited.

"It is Ashoke," Maya said, "this girl at college is after Ashoke. She was so bold to ring here more than once. When I spoke to Ashoke he said she is study friend only. They have been seen together. I do not know what to do. A mother's heart is just to be tormented ..."

Nora managed not to smile.

"But surely it is not as serious as all that? College students together ..."

"Of course it is serious, this girl is wanting to get hold of him. How you are not understanding?"

"If you interfere, it will drive them closer together," Nora said.

"I fear they are already too close. It is impossible. This girl is not for him in any way. It is not for them to decide, this family of hers will destroy Ashoke's future." Unable to sit still, she rose and hurried towards the house. Nora was about to follow her, but thought better of it. What could she say now? Leave it a while. In any case, Virgoe's trunk wound around her arm.

Nora often sat alone in the arbour. If the elephant was not at work, she simply stood nearby in silent companionship or fondled Nora's neck with her trunk. Nora saved confectionery and quavas for Virgoe and it saddened her to learn that as hard as the elephant worked she did not earn enough for her keep. "Acchaa," Basai said, "but so, neither do most humans."

In a rush of sympathy, Nora had given Kalu, the mahout, money to buy the elephant a treat. After a day of visitors and matchmaking Nora was often grateful for Virgoe's company. With the elephant she never felt like a foreigner. The mahout was glad to leave Virgoe with Nora.

This morning, after Virgoe nuzzled her hand open with her trunk, Nora noticed that her palm smelled of alcohol. She waited until Maya broke silence again at sundown.

"Is it possible that Kalu is giving the elephant whiskey?" she asked.

"Anything is possible," Maya said, "but where he would get so much whiskey for an elephant? No doubt Westerners at the hotel will give money for elephant treat. Virgoe is not well lately, perhaps meenopausal. The animal is never producing and her mood has disimproved lately."

"But why would Kalu give her whiskey?" Nora asked.

166

"Because he is also liking it too much," Maya said, "without money he cannot purchase. Do not say to anyone about smelling whiskey. A Muslim elephant should not drink alcohol, you understand," she added solemnly.

"What will happen about Ashoke?" Nora asked.

"I will attend to it," Maya said, defensive, "that is my duty."

The word struck Nora. Was she being told that she was a woman without duty? No, Maya would not do that. Funny, the way that word stood out from others, she had always disliked the sound of it. A bullying word, she thought. Duty. It aroused uneasy feelings.

Nora sensed that over the matter of Ashoke there could be no discussion, and strain developed between the women. Maya became too quiet, though polite, and did not come into Nora's room next morning. Nora lay there, aware of Maya's scent on the pillow. Guilty on two counts, she thought: my attitude to Ashoke's love life and Virgoe's whiskey. Maya must have guessed whose money had bought the whiskey for the elephant.

"Are you annoyed with me because of what I said about Ashoke?" Nora asked when Maya's quiet mood continued.

Maya's eyes filled with tears: "I am Indian mother. It is for me to protect my son, who else will do? And you are concerned with Western way only. This too is natural, but ... Come, sit with me and take tea."

But the matter of Ashoke hung between them.

About the time callers came each evening, the television was switched on and everybody listened, as though for the first time, to Rajive Gandhi's talks about national unity and the intentions of Indira's party. Even the servants had begun to refer to him as Mr Clean, and Nora thought that he looked like anyone's favourite brother.

The servants had visitors too and they all huddled on the floor around the door so that Nora wished that

167

they would either come into the room or go away, but they just squatted there in the doorway spellbound by the television playlets depicting tolerance between the different peoples of India as the way to national unity. Barely able to follow the Hindi, Nora found the playlets simplistic.

When Ravi Basai was home he suffered a ration of television with his guests and then glanced at Maya. Simultaneously, he distracted everyone while she waited with her hand on the knob for the speaker in the box to finish before she turned it off.

There were no visitors on the night that the Bolshoi Ballet was broadcast from Delhi, a performance Nora feared would be cancelled because of Mrs Gandhi's death. Mr Basai disappeared when the dance began and the female servants watched for a couple of minutes, then rose as one and scurried off with their sarees drawn across their faces. Nirmal left too, but he kept returning on some pretext or another, shaking his head in disbelief as he left again. Maya fidgeted with embarrassment before eventually settling to watch. She loved the dance, but felt "such clothes, especially on men, are causing offence to simple villagers like these servants."

CHAPTER 18

"India is limping back to normal," Maya told Nora one morning in late November when Indira Gandhi looked down upon them in the main street. A larger than life poster of the leader, above the words *Not a drop of my blood will be wasted*, was balanced by the taintless face of her son, Rajive, on the other end of the banner which overhung the road. Electioneering had spread from down-town Agra, and as the streets became over hung with bunting, the atmosphere of mourning appeared to lift in a city which had not suffered rioting.

Congress (1) youths were everywhere, in auto-ricks, cars and the backs of vans. Young men herded onto cattle lorries, and took turns at a microphone to proclaim how Mrs Gandhi's party could lead India ahead. They were giving out blankets and vessels to the poor. "Because people are poor, they are not stupid," Maya told Nora, "they are entirely capable to take from all the candidates and not bother to vote for anyone. After all, what are they caring about giving politicians a big job on a high chair?"

"Rajive will not survive as long as she did, no chance," Basai said during a ration of television, but the remark had slipped out and he changed the subject.

Nora was increasingly edgy with what she called "the cocktail" hour, those two hours before dinner when callers came. She felt excluded when the men took to Basai's study each evening and irritated by the women

169

who settled into their silk, sipped tea and chatted about nothing until their husbands returned to boom more banalities.

Maya seemed to Nora like a different person when there were visitors. She fussed over the husbands: "So, how was your day? You must not work so hard."

"You have not met my friend from Ireland?" she asked a new arrival. "Her husband holds a high chair as an art dealer, and she is also knowing about antique things. My friend's daughter was married recently, she has made an excellent match into a family in Canada. Such a fine match." Nora was annoyed. She had never commented on what sort of match Ciara had made.

And Maya never introduced a woman by name: "Her husband Mr So and So is an architect," she'd say, "he sits on a very high chair ..."

Nora began to see men sitting in baby high-chairs, bibs under their chins, banging the trays with their spoons. And she was uneasily aware that she might as well be invisible for all the notice they took of her. It was only when Ravi Basai referred to her as "another member of my household" that Nora realised she was being treated as one of his women folk, and with the respect appropriate to a mother who had married off her daughter.

Maya accepted the thumping pride of Indian men: "It is the way it is. Some day I will be mother-in-law and then I too am a general. How can I be father-in-law?"

Even Sati Rai the widowed neighbour who was often a morning caller did not speak to Nora from his place among the men in the evening, although he had brought Nora a grubby copy of Mahatma Gandhi's autobiography: "If she has not read, she will enjoy," he said as he handed the book to Mr Basai. "I have also read about your Mr DeValera," he told Nora, "a fine fellow."

The book validated her criticisms of India, and she fancied herself a Gandhian. She could not imagine

170

him in a high-chair. Through Gandhi, she saw a different view of her own culture, her lazy acceptance of Irish society, and thought about things she had never thought about before. Gandhi would have approved of Derry, she thought. His ideas were more radical than Derry's, she was surprised to learn, especially in the Indian context.

She read bits to Maya who was too polite to say that she had grown up on Gandhi and listened as though India's history was unknown to her. One afternoon when Nora read aloud from her book, Maya could not contain herself.

"Ah yes," she said, "these are excellent ideas, but my father was being a good landlord and he died poor because of this new India. Perhaps that had to be, but nothing is so simple. For instance, you must think that Gandhiji was also a husband. Husband is lord to Indian wife. Now I am asking you, did Gandhiji's wife wish to do untouchable work, clean latrines, give away her jewellery? She did not, most certainly not, but he was her husband. And when they went to England, who decided? And who decided that she will be brahmacharya? That means celibate. What woman can be celibate if her husband demands otherwise? He could not think that a woman has sexual needs."

"So, you don't think that much of Mahatma Gandhi?" Nora asked, surprised.

"Oh yes, yes, I think very much," Maya said, "it was the Mahatma who brought womans into the freedom struggle, not just trailing after men. And he saw our qualities as a boon in the struggle because he is seeing that we can resist without violence. This is how I do. Mr Basai calls it my silent treatment. Gandhiji called that truth-force or love force. None-violence means to live a life of love. And he believed that womans can do much better than men. I think so he's right.

"Gandhiji was bringing great advantages to women. The idea of liberation is not new to us Indian womans and men."

171

"But it seems as though so little has changed," Nora ventured, "matchmaking, dowries..."

"Ah," Maya said, "everything must happen in good time. How to replace tradition? Even Gandhiji was knowing this.Who will experiment with life of their own child?"

While Maya was selecting Indian sweets one day, Nora wandered into another shop and discovered out of date newspapers and magazines. There was one with Indira Gandhi lying in state on its cover. All that had happened in Delhi seemed past now, especially since the television news had moved on to the elections but she bought the back issues and ploughed through graphic images of the violence all over India. It was only then that she realised how cocooned they were in Agra. Television coverage of the aftermath of the assassination had been discreet to say the least, and because the Basai's daily newspaper was in Hindi, she had not realised the full extent of the riots in different parts of the country or even in New Delhi. And the men had been careful not to speak about it. Agra had been an island of peace. At the refugee camp in Delhi there was a family of twenty-one widows. Fourteen of the men in another family had been killed. A picture from one paper burned into Nora's brain: a woman stood as a dog carried off a piece of her son. And in Kanpur where Mr Basai had gone on an errand, there had been mayhem, but he had not mentioned it. The stories revived Nora's memory of the train, and she felt that she had colluded in the silence over that terrible time even though when they were alone, she and Maya often mentioned it. "I am Missis Dennis Ryan ... we are all ladies in here," Maya mimicked. Reading the papers, Nora realised how fortunate she and Maya had been and wondered where had she got the nerve. It irritated her to realise how their experience of the riots had been passed over so condescendingly by the men, and the way in which, occasionally, the oldest of

172

the men referred teasingly to herself and Maya as "heroines".

Nora was surprised that Maya did not wish to look at these magazines, and neither did any of the other women. What had happened was past. What was the sense in reading about it? "I wish to let this terror go. It has passed," Maya said softly. But somehow, its revival brought the two closer, even though the magazines disappeared.

Nora found she was writing more letters home:

... the election is a foregone conclusion. There hardly seems need for one. Not even the Tweedle Dum and Tweedle Dee situation of home, she wrote to Derry. The deputy Prime Minister is still referred to as Rajive and Indira is fast slipping into mythology, taking her place among the gods. Her son vows to walk in her footsteps, seeking friendship with both East and West to continue the crusade against the global arms race. And to root out poverty and corruption. Some of the English language papers, which arrive when they are out-of-date, are anti-Indira now. I suppose because it is getting less dangerous. And most people accept that Rajive will be assassinated too. And he seems so nice and tries his best even though he never wanted to be a politician in the first place, much less Prime Minister.

Maya teaches me a little Hindi every day, but she'd rather speak to me in English and I usually end up practising on Virgoe.

Whenever I think I understand a bit about India, something contradicts it. For instance, Indira Gandhi married the man she loved, not even her religion. And she ruled as a widow. Widows are supposed to be invisible in India. Maya's mother-in-law had to be dragged away from her husband's funeral pyre because she wanted to throw herself on it, commit sati. Always these contradictions, it's what scrambles the mind in India. Don't I sound like a proper memsahib? But I love it here. Been reading Mahatma Gandhi.

When I mention him, it's like bringing up Jesus at a Dublin 4 dinner party. Love, Nora.

Nora ordered English language newspapers and reading them gave her confidence to join in the conversations with the men, but when she did, it felt as though she had broken out of purdah.

"Why all this blaming of Sikhs in London and New York?" she asked, "even I understand the consequences of bringing the army into the Golden Temple. There must have been another way. It was like attacking St Peter's in Rome."

There was silence.

"And I saw the police standing around in Delhi, twirling their lathis in the middle of the looting and burning!"

"She was also being their Prime Minister," Ravi Basai said too gently, "because they are police does not mean they do not feel. Also he continued evenly, "foreign Sikhs are supplying money for arms, but they live safely away."

"But police must be impartial," Nora said, "although on the other hand Mrs Gandhi could not put up with the Golden Temple being turned into a fort."

Maya's eyes tried to warn Nora, but she was in full sail: "There has been stupidity all round. Mrs Gandhi might have lost the election, now Congress will have a landslide." Even as she spoke, Nora knew that she had gone too far.

"She is attempting to understand politics," beamed the old man, "this is because she is a heroine." Nora had come to learn that in India a heroine meant a film star and she fumed. The men waved their heads about in understanding.

"Your daughter is still happy in her hostel ?" Maya quickly asked of her neighbour as she poured tea into his cup.

CHAPTER 19

On the third of December Mr Basai hurried in and switched on the television: "There is disaster in Bhopal," he said, "a gas leak from the Union Carbide Factory. The trains are full of people for the hospital here ..." and he waved his hand for them to listen.

In Bhopal people were fleeing from the poisonous cloud of the worst industrial disaster in the world's history. Thousands were dying and there was not enough hospital space, too few doctors, too little of anything. Ravi Basai shook his head. "They ran into the wind carrying the gas, into their own death trap, inhaling," he said.

No one had an appetite for dinner. On top of the assassination and the riots, Nora thought aloud, as if that wasn't enough.

Mr Basai sighed heavily as he mixed dahl into his rice: "Ah, if you run, naturally you must breathe deeply and with each breath ..."

Nora stared at her plate.

His words have fallen on her food, Maya thought. "Eat a little," she ordered, "Nora, Kumari. Mr Basai? Starving will not help this thing. We are fortunate."

"Correct," said Mr Basai, but like Nora, he left his food.

The news from Bhopal grew more gruesome as the days went on and Nora felt uneasy as Western business interests were revealed by the disaster.

"We will see," said Mr Basai with a cynical shrug, "what Union Carbide do to make amends. So, they

175

send a plane load of money, doctors even? No, but a plane load of American lawyers are in Delhi. Yes, yes."

Meanwhile, Maya cleared off the table in the grain room so that instead of her work on the Taj Mahal there were account books and wedding lists, and the bicycles, tools and other household things were moved elsewhere. As mother of the bride, Maya had space of her own and she locked the room when she was not in it. A steady stream of tradesmen came to see her as the business of the household focused on Kumari's wedding.

Nora poured over reports of Bhopal and Maya dragged her out in search of more and more sarees. Nora imagined them stretching along the track from the railway station to the next town. They would certainly run up the Taj Road. Sarees were purchased three at a time, although so far, mostly for the "boy's side". Dissatisfied with what Agra had to offer, Maya took Nora and Kumari on shopping trips elsewhere, but nothing took Nora's mind off Bhopal. People's detachment from the tragedy shocked her. Even Mr Basai seemed to have lost interest and she was the only one who mentioned it in conversation. She thought that there was probably more talk about Bhopal in Dublin.

"But, it is Bhopal, not here," said Maya, "so we are fortunate."

It was only when Nora heard that Mother Teresa was in Bhopal that she realised that detachment was not indifference. It was not that Hindus were uncharitable, they simply did not believe that it was their business to try to change the course of people's lives. Karma. This time around it was the people in Bhopal. Next time, who knew? And Nora was disgusted that Western businessmen still haggled over culpability. "Five hundred pounds each would be a fortune to them," she wrote Ciara, "and the Americans could settle the case later. Even five hundred rupees would be a help to any of these families."

Maya was heartened by so few wedding cancellations

in the papers. For weeks there had been notices: "owing to the death of ..." some explained but most were a simple notice of a change in plans. "Everything passes," said Maya, "that is the mercy of life."

Ravi Basai was in a good mood when he announced that he had seen a group of foreigners on their way to the ashram for Western seekers. "That is where the big money is to be made," he said, "I will retire from my law firm and set up an ashram. You can be my manager," he told Nora.

Nora was touched by his teasing. It made her feel accepted, but reminded her that she could not stay forever. Basai's joke became a fantasy as she saw herself in saffron robes, coolly serene and surrounded by eager seekers.

Kumari was too quiet and moped around the gramophone. "That is the way of engaged girls," Maya replied, "they are off on a cloud. She is going and coming, but is not with us, thinking of her beloved only."

"But is he her beloved?" Nora asked, "how can he be?"

One must tolerate, Maya reminded herself, Nora is a foreigner. My dearling is a foreigner, and so she is not understanding. She waited until Nora was in a better mood and asked: "You are upset about Kumari's marriage, isn't it ? There is no reason. This is how we do. Try to tolerate, my dearling." Nora smiled at the endearment and Maya's studied preoccupation with her wedding list.

"Marriage must be," Maya said, "we might be wishing otherwise, but it must be. Marriages are made in heaven," she continued recalling another phrase from her long ago English teacher, "even if I search all over for a boy for my daughter, still the match is made in heaven, who is to know what will turn out? No matter if it is love match or our way. I said to you before that you people marry the people you love, we love the people we marry. Who can say what is better?

177

We have chosen well for our only daughter. Who is knowing our child better than we do?"

"I'm sure you have done your best," Nora murmured.

"I am not heartless mother," Maya said, "I have even chosen so that she does not have to live with mother-in-law until she is older at least. The boy is posted out of station, so they will live alone while they are young."

Nora was impressed: "That was deliberate?"

Maya nodded, "Ah yes, I am knowing my daughter, she has not enough tolerance. Things are changing in India, in places like Bombay and Delhi. But, we hear these love matches are falling down. How many parents will wish to take such risks? To experiment with daughter's life?"

Maya looked into Nora's eyes.

"For instance, if I do not give dowry like law says maybe it is alright. At first the in-laws will say we do not wish dowry, we do not make demand. But people who mention demand at all want something. I know. And later they say to my daughter or someone in their house is saying: 'you brought nothing with you,' maybe it's a sister-in-law, not even the mother-in-law. And then my daughter is shamed. It is too late. A beggar is treated like a beggar. At your place, a bride does not need anything of her own? Tell me how this works?"

"A couple become engaged and they share ..."

"Ah yes, but what do they share?"

"The couple earn money before they are married and ..."

"They earn so much?"

Nora was about to say that Irish couples started with less when she thought of Ciara's wedding presents from herself and Dennis.

"The important thing is that they are free to choose a partner for themselves. In Ireland there used to be dowries and matches," Nora said, "in my grandparents' time."

One day, Maya produced a magazine: "Is it true that at your place you have strangers to look after the children when you go out? Called baby-sitters, isn't it?

And this says that you make a small baby sleep in a room alone. The writer has just returned from England. This is terrible, Nora. Of course, this is why you are having molesting of children in England."

"I am Irish," Nora emphasised, for it seemed that Maya could not grasp that Ireland was not England. "England is across the Irish Sea."

"Ah," Maya said, "so you are not having these baby-sitters at your place?"

The theme returned again the day Maya came back from visiting a sick neighbour: "I have just heard the saddest, most awful thing about your place. Tell me true, I can bear. Do you put people in a fridge and tie a tag to their toe when they die? This neighbour's daughter is in Australia and she wrote this thing."

Nora was tired.

"My place is not Australia. Ireland is as far away from Australia as India, I think. If a person does not die at home, where else could they be kept but in a morgue? It's not like a fridge you put food in."

"And the tag on the toe?"

"I suppose so relatives will get the right body ..."

"They would not recognise?" Maya was horrified.

"Maya, please ... I saw a dead body thrown on the back of a rickshaw in town the other day. It was wrapped in cloth. To me it was an upsetting sight, I . ...

"Going to the cremation ground, no tag on toe ..."

Nora was silent. She had questioned Indian ways, now the shoe was on the other foot.

"It is not your responsibility, dearling," Maya said as she put her arms around her, "and neither mine. I too must tolerate."

As the wedding drew nearer, Kumari lost weight and became more listless. Maya was with Dadiji when Kumari approached Nora.

"Archana said that I must speak to you about something," she began, "it is about my marriage."

She was silent for so long that Nora said: "What about your marriage?"

179

The girl dug one thumb nail into the other on her lap and stared at her hands. "I am nervous, you see," she said, "I am always shivering when I think of the first time we will be alone. Do you know what I am saying?"

"Yes," Nora replied, "I think that I do. What does your mother say?"

"We did not speak about it. Always before she says that girls do not like that part of marriage. And none of the girls who have married will tell me anything. They say I will find out as they did. They are laughing at me."

"But your mother?" Nora prompted.

"She says I must tolerate. I know the husband is lord, but I fear I cannot tolerate this thing. I will be the cause of much unhappiness only, if he tries to do this to me I will not be able to tolerate. What then?"

"Perhaps you are thinking too far ahead," Nora said helpless. "The first time you are alone, are you expected to ...?"

"Oh yes," said Kumari, "Nina was not afraid and she said she would tell me, but now I will be married first. Perhaps she will never marry now, even though it was not her fault. She may not get a second chance."

"Perhaps you are thinking too far ahead," Nora repeated, "maybe you will want to make love with him when the time comes ..."

"Oh no. Did you enjoy?" Kumari asked.

"Many people do" Nora said, "many women enjoy sex, you know ..."

"How can I enjoy?" Kumari said, "I only wish to tolerate, but I do not know how," she had covered her face with her hands and Nora took them down. "Would you rather remain single?" she asked.

"Oh no, I must settle," Kumari was alarmed. "I wish to be a married lady and my parents are wanting me settled. What will I do if I am single? I cannot always remain here. No, I will marry, but I think only of this. They say I will find out. That I will tolerate this thing, all women do. What I will do?"

"First, you must stop calling it 'this thing'," Nora said. "You are giving me goose pimples, the way you say that. Have you met your fiancé?"

"Yes, when he came to our place with his parents. He said I was nicer than my photograph."

"And you like him?"

"He wrote me a letter. It was a nice letter."

"How do you know he is not just as nervous?"

"Nervous?" Kumari looked puzzled.

"Probably he has never made love before, and he is expected to know everything because he is a fellow, and maybe he doesn't. Maybe he hopes you won't be so frightened."

"Boys are not virgins," Kumari said, suddenly calm, "even so, his brother will instruct. He will know."

"Suppose you can ask me questions," Nora said, "I will try to tell you what is likely to happen. The first thing to remember is that you have all your lives ahead, it doesn't have to happen on the first night ..."

Maya could not spend money fast enough. Merchants beamed as she approached, but Nora made her uneasy. "What I can do about Bhopal?" she repeated, "I have duties here as you can see."

Nora thought about joining Mother Teresa, but like most people with that fantasy she confused wanting to join Mother Teresa with wanting to want to do it. Instead, she declined invitations and told everyone she was feeling unwell and needed to rest alone. As the family set off without her, she felt virtuous.

Maya thought she understood. R.D. had told her that foreigners could not bear poverty or suffering. It frightened them. Sometimes foreigners did not see anything except hardship in India. That only, none of her glory. Such foreigners criticised everything, even the dust. They knew all. In one visit. As if everything was perfect at their own place. "I just can't stand it," Nora said, failing to explain why she wanted to stay home.

Maya was soothing. She could not fathom how Nora's staying at home would make the slightest difference to Bhopal, but rest was always good. Nora had a soft heart. The softness of a woman's heart was not a matter to be taken lightly. She saw to it that Nora was left alone in her room.

Women brought Nora flowers from their gardens, sweets from the shop near the Sardar bazaar, food from their kitchens and remedies for fatigue. They sent her get-well cards and gifts of sandalwood and fragrant oils. And Nora found herself admitting how much she had in common with them. Mothers of brides. Ciara's wedding and all the shopping, parties and presents had cost a tiny fortune. The price of my dress, much less Ciara's, would have gone a long way in some poor Irish family. One doesn't see poverty like this at home, but there is so much more poverty than we see. How am I any better? Because I brood about it, tut tut about Bhopal, and the poor? What use is that, when I haven't done any better at home. Mrs Byrne works for me because she is poor, just like Thangamani and Uma.

Nora recalled the times she had laughed at the idea of Derry going out on a wet night on some cause or other and failing to persuade her to go along or join anything. Now, she saw that it was because she hadn't cared enough to get involved. People were entitled not to care. How much did the troubles in Northern Ireland impinge on their lives?

Daily, Nora had stooped to the beggars in the Indian dust. In Dublin she had clicked past blanket-wrapped mothers and their babies sitting on the pavement in cold and rain, resenting that their presence spoiled her moment. What made her so bloody bountiful here? Was it that even India's distress was exotic? Maybe it was all the silk-wrapped women. That reminded her of all the new silks she had bought. And there were wardrobes of clothes at home. It wasn't the shopping or the silks, it was the whole business of weddings which engulfed her and separated all of the women from a larger world. What could she do about it? She came out of her room, and sent money to the Bhopal Fund. It took so long at the bank and she came into the sunlight with such a sense of achievement that she had to remind herself that all she had done was send a money order.

Maya was relieved.

"This human race is pathetic," she said, "but I am glad to welcome you back."

Matchmaking resumed in earnest. Nora knew it was going on when Maya and her friends fell into deep discussion in Hindi. Archana, the widow's daughter was often mentioned and she gathered that the girl had not been offered the match in New York. When snap-shots were produced, Nora slipped from the room. She hardly knew Archana, but she feared for her being of such low value in the eyes of those who would decide her fate. Nora thought matchmaking was not unlike the electioneering which gathered momentum in the background, merits proclaimed, one party measured against another. Elect this girl for that boy.

On Sunday she had read about the continuing tragedy of Bhopal and was reading the matrimonial columns when before she could stop herself she burst out: "Maya, this one is looking for a girl with no bra. Green cards are one thing, even colour and caste, and there's another wanting a girl with a submissive nature, but no bra? No bra ..."

Maya bent over the paper: "Where? Impossible. Point this to me?" Nora pointed.

"Colour, caste no bar," Maya read, "a mistake. They do not care about colour and caste and you are knowing very well it is bar, not bra, teasing only."

How am I supposed to know, Nora thought, nothing would surprise me now.

During the week before Christmas, Nora and Maya were sitting in the garden when in the distance they heard the unmistakable din of wedding music. "Ah, a

183

baraat," Maya said, "this mourning time is past, come, we will see." And they hurried down the narrow laneways leading to the main thoroughfare to watch the bridegroom's procession to his bride.

As they watched, Nora was suddenly swamped by a sinking sensation. The feeling settled into sadness until it dawned on her that she was the odd one out. Standing beside the delighted Maya, the feeling puzzled her before it dawned upon her that this carnival excitement was all about mating. The celebration of coupling permeated the air and left her lonely. She watched, but she could not join in.

How could young blood resist this season of weddings, she thought, all the seasons that had prepared them for their own season? Now, she thought how marriages were "arranged" beyond the matching and the business, the blood fired in preparation, nature turned on by ritual. Ritual became romance, and forced the couple together as surely as romance led Western couples to ritual. Why should these young people fight against tradition? The alternative to arranged marriages was as frightening to them as arranged marriage would be to Ciara.

Nora and Maya strolled slowly back through the narrow lanes, past the family with the hairy black pigs, the furniture maker, past the grain merchant with his plum calf who came to nuzzle Maya and past the child carpet-weaver and the children who called: "Hello Auntie," and kept calling until both women answered. They strolled with their arms across each other's backs, linking or holding hands, but touching until they approached the courtyard, both aware that the time for parting would never be right.

Nora's dream came back, but the snake just lay there, sluggish, keeping her from her rest. And jittery, she spent a lot of time thinking. After Kumari's wedding, what? Sometimes the repetitive activity of the household so clogged her senses that she longed for familiar things, but going home meant leaving

Maya whose voice grew hoarse when she said: "Yes, I am realising you must go dearling. I ask only that you stay for the last possible moment."

Even on Tuesdays, there were callers, although not so many. On other days, women arrived as early as ten a.m. and Nirmal good-humouredly ferried tea and snacks from the kitchen. Their trips to the Taj Mahal, of which neither tired, were fewer as Maya became busier.

Each morning the priest's bell was heard when he came to make puja with Dadiji and left the holy mark on her forehead. Then came the milkman who ladled from huge cans on a wheel car, and added the tilly sup that Nora remembered from her childhood. After that, the vessel woman came and made kitchen utensils gleam as new with ash and water and her bare hands, followed by the vegetable man whom Maya defeated over price most days and referred to as "that thief". There was the spice grinder, the video man on his bicycle, the tailor – too chaste to measure Nora – the little massage woman who worked on aches and aggravation, and the jeweller whose work continued to cause Maya to shake her head in frustration.

By the end of December, Congress (I) were back in power and Rajive Gandhi was the darling of the electorate. It was a Christmas without turkey because even if they had been able to find a bird, Maya did not have an oven in which to roast it, but there was a pudding from Derry, and the surprise of an artificial tree with presents for Nora who had posted hers from India in November. And on New Year's Eve there were calls from R.D. and Mother Bridgid and one from London which never came through.

The house was filling up with Kumari's dowry of furniture, household effects, sacks of grain, sarees, jewels, provisions, as well as all the things needed for dozens of relatives staying and daily visitors. The pace quickened and extra servants appeared.

Women came, simple villagers with the confidence of

185

relatives in the fine city house. Their work-hardened hands played drums, and they sang about brides, mother-in-laws and bridegrooms. City cousins were due later.

Wandering about the house, Nora stopped asking what the words of these ancient verses meant. Even when they were explained to her she could not grasp their significance or hilarity.

The women were romantic and skittish about weddings, delighted with their release from routine as they performed old village dances for each other. Endless refreshment flowed from Nirmal and his assistants.

Gradually, Nora lost the privacy of a room of her own. At first women just popped in without knocking, but then Sunita Auntie's suitcase and carrier bags appeared. Finally, Sunita Auntie arrived. She was Mr Basai's sister, and pushed the door open with her bedroll: "Ah," she said, "here is plenty of room." Nora was lying down with the blinds drawn, but Sunita Auntie's voice tore the air, shouting to women and children playing on the roof. Her personality took up as much space as her girth. Sunita Auntie was awake before the Muslim call, last asleep, and always talking.

Nora spent little time in her room. She wandered about fascinated by the social and religious ritual. The courtyard was busier than the bazaar. It was the arrivals place, where guests relaxed with tea after their journeys, and where the servant tended the luggage which invariably contained homemade pickles. Groups of women partied, children played, and Maya's mother-in-law sat in front of her door, the focus of respect in her white sari. A backdrop to all was the hiss of pressure cookers on kerosene stoves.

The sweet-maker sat upon a large table between two vats of sizzling ghee and produced an endless flow of buttery, golden ladoos, and honeyed whorls. A baker brought trays of gold and silver confectionery and a man sat in a corner of the dining room rolling beetle nut and lime into parcels of dark green leaves. Each day, the caterer produced dozens of piping hot samosas for breakfast before the real cooking of the day began, and his bearers brought trays and pots of food to the kitchen in addition to what was prepared there. Stacks of banana leaves replaced dishes, but even so the vessel woman had to bring her two children to help Uma. They sat in the trough under the kitchen taps, their feet in the water and scrubbed the pots.

The dobhi's bed was under his work table on the back verandah. Nora watched him fill his huge iron with hot coals to heat the water in its base and hour after hour he steamed lovingly along miles of silk and swayed his head as guests laid down sarees for pressing.

The women and girls were crowded into the rooms at one side of the house, the men and boys on the other. A marquee provided extra dormitory space.

Ashoke stayed in his room with friends to watch video films. From six o'clock in the evening they sat on beds in the dark and ordered cokes and pizzas. Nirmal bought them from a tourist place. It was quite a distance away, but he went by auto-rick, delighted to do it for Ashoke.

Nora and Maya were rarely alone now. And Maya seemed sad and somehow older. Nora mentioned this to Sunita Auntie who nodded understandingly: "It is expected. The mother of the bride is losing her daughter. How she can look happy or young?"

All the activity and intricate ritual dizzied Nora who tried to steal snatches of sleep when Sunita Auntie was downstairs, and it was then her snake came to weary her. It seemed to Nora to be losing girth as she found her own waistbands tightening from food rich with ghee.

CHAPTER 20

About ten days before the wedding Maya's brother, Mamaji, arrived from his village. Nora wondered how he had got such a name. Maya looked surprised: "Ah yes, you are not knowing all Indian family members have a special name. Mamaji is mother's brother, and he has special duties. He has come soon to attend to wedding affairs."

She did not say what these affairs were, but Nora saw that Mamaji took a trip to Kumari's in-laws armed with an important envelope and drove a brand-new car which he did not bring back. And when one afternoon, Kumari's jewels were displayed Nora was reminded of the young woman in New Delhi with her "Boycott Dowry Weddings" notice.

The priest arrived. His door stood open to the courtyard. His room was small and freshly white-washed, with a shrine, a garlanded picture of a guru on the wall and a narrow bed which was changed every day, so that he always sat on linen befitting his purity.

"Panditji" sang prayers in a soaring, whirling voice that stilled people. Otherwise, he poured over documents, meditated and held court. People waited in line to speak to him about their part in the ceremony. And he ate. Nora had never seen anyone relish food so much.

As Maya got busier Nora became dependent upon Mamaji's pregnant daughter-in-law, Sita, to explain ritual. Again and again Nora learned that this or that ritual symbolised the family, a branch or a root of the family tree. Each family member had an official part to play. The pandit and Mamaji were central to a lot of ritual such as the planting of the supporting pole of the pandol and the preparation of a place for the sacred fire around which the couple would make their vows.

Day after day, Nora sat in the bride's room while women worked on beautifying Kumari. For an hour each day, a village woman massaged Kumari's limbs and slipped out when the girl drifted off to sleep. And then at last, she lay on cushions while the mehndi on her hands and feet dried.

Now, on the morning of the wedding, the pandit had still not announced the precise auspicious time for the ceremony. He stretched over the astrological charts which he had spread out in the middle-room the day before and his presence made a huge hole in the centre of the house.

The holy man poured over the paper as he crawled across it. Now and then he would fold back another section, and exclaim: "Acchaa," with a great air of significance and sit back on his pink soled feet to ponder further. Maya brought a chair and with a great sigh of patience sat down on the edge of the horoscope to wait.

At last, shortly after four in the afternoon, the women of the bridal party went to the hotel driven by Ashoke and Mamaji while another car followed with their finery. Dadiji watched them leave.

"It's a pity to leave her behind," Nora murmured to Maya as they drove.

"Ah yes," Maya said, "but at least she is not insisting to hide entirely while her granddaughter is being married. Mr Basai told her that this custom of widows staying away from weddings is superstition only, nonsense, but still she is not moving. She lives in past only. Forty-five years she is a widow, she was wife for five years only. Truly, to be widow is a sad fate for a lady. Even now, she will not take salt even though doctor said."

Kumari turned and looked pointedly at her mother who said: "We are already late for this beauty business."

It was dark when the hairdressers had finished, and the bride sat in her suite, her hair entwined with flowers. Eventually, everyone helped Kumari into her heavy lehnga of gold and red silk, encrusted with Rajasthani embroidery. Her veil was like a golden cobweb. Jewels adorned the bride in sixteen places and Archana stood back to admire her handiwork.

The beautician painted white and gold flowers of rice paste over Kumari's brows and cheek bones. She was dotting the centre of each flower with red when a boy burst into the room.

"He's coming, he's nearly here," he told Kumari, "he is in a special tonga with four horses, not a car, not on a horse and neither on an elephant," he said and Nora guessed that both their bets were proven wrong.

"Go, Nora Auntie, go and see," Kumari urged, her neck stiff with the weight of jewellery parting her hair. "You are watching baraats, now see ours. See our bridegroom coming. Please do not miss ..."

As Nora hurried along the windowed corridor which overlooked the gardens Westerners appeared from the bedrooms at that side of the hotel. The lawn was covered with rose petals, and a red throne awaited the couple under a canopy of flowers. The canopy was similar to the one in the Bombay synagogue, but the scene reminded Nora of department store windows at Christmas and her head had started to fill with clock-work toy-makers and reindeer when it was jolted clear by an explosion of perfume.

"They go to a lot of trouble to impress tourists, don't they?" said an American woman beside her. Nora felt the sting, even as she realised that tourists would get that impression. If this woman only knew how much more there was to it. She smiled at the woman and hurried on.

Teasingly slow, the noise came closer, until they could see fire-works spraying the stars. Virgoe arrived with tourists to the hotel door and stood restlessly sniffing the excitement until Nora stepped forward to speak to her. Children straggled backwards into the driveway before break-dancers, acrobats and a crowd of musicians in red jackets and gold turbans, each doing his own thing.

Nora felt the triumphant presence of the bridegroom long before he came into sight. Flares were held precariously on high. Uproar drowned all, even though it was fifteen minutes before the bridegroom's horses pulled his blossom covered tonga through the gates of the hotel.

He's nice, Nora thought, he has a lovely smile, the snap Kumari has makes him look older, too serious. Probably because he was having the picture taken. "He's just a boy," and her eyes filled with tears.

Prakesh was dressed in a Western suit with a plumed turban. A small boy in gold satin sat on the bridegroom's knee and Nora smiled at the symbol. The child tried to scratch his head through his turban. Showers of blossoms and roars fell on the bridegroom as the performers halted his horses from moving towards Mr Basai and the reception party on the steps of the hotel who surrounded the pandit waiting at the hotel door with his puja tray to perform the welcoming ceremony.

Nora spied R.D. in the reception party and smilingly waited for him to look her way, when something made her turn her head. Sarla was glaring at her. Nora stopped smiling when she realised that the women with Sarla were unfriendly too. She recognised them from Delhi, but they all busied their eyes elsewhere. Supporting Sarla, against her, Nora flushed as the women greeted other women, smiling extravagantly, inclining heads. Ladies at a wedding. Sarla still glared as she moved on.

Nora looked back at R.D. and saw that he had seen

her and Sarla. His eyes moved from one to the other before he greeted Nora with brief formality. Nora's sense of belonging evaporated as she realised that he was being careful not to be seen. She had never been in such a situation. They had talked about her and condemned her. They were punishing her. Home wrecker, she told herself dryly. Dangerous woman. Ridiculous. How dare they? Who did they think they were? As if ...

Maya had warned her: "Sarla is a simple village girl, she is not understanding foreign ways. She saw you and Rajendra in the study and that is enough for her. You are in her bad books always."

"You know it was nothing," Nora had answered, "a mere trick of memory."

"Ah yes, I am knowing," Maya said affectionately, "but to her it is not nothing, she is going to stand guard against you. A fierce guard. He is not an angel, but as wife she will naturally not be admitting that, she will blame you only."

Her mood spoiled, Nora made her way back to Kumari, choosing a way that avoided Sarla. Maya was leaving the bride's suite. "He is a very handsome young man," she told the bride, "much nicer than his photograph."

"I wrote and told him what you advised," Kumari said smiling. How on earth had Kumari managed to put such things in a letter? Kumari waited for the bathroom door to close after Archana before she said: "He wrote back not to worry, we will discuss, co-operate. We have exchanged more than one letter. At least we are pen pals, I think that thanks to you it is not going to be difficult, Auntie."

The warmth of the girl's gratitude was soothing. As she looked down at the fond Kumari, and recalled the sting of Sarla's glare, Nora thought, how could R.D. be friendly when he had to contend with Sarla?

It was another hour before Kumari, eyes downcast, came slowly along the bridal path in her heavy gown and jewellery. Prakesh came through the trees at the other side of the throne, accompanied by his men folk. Nirmal, spruce and wide-eyed, stood where he could be close to Ashoke, regal as a prince.

The pandit led the couple in prayer and Sanskrit recitation, as with lowered eyelids, each put garlands of flowers and sandalwood about the other's neck. They did not glance at each other as they sat on their throne for more prayers, showers of rose petals, photographers, the video maker. The garlanding done, the crowd swarmed towards the feast and the tourists, assuming that was that, moved off.

Nora found Maya sitting outside the banquet room. "She is fasting," Mr Basai explained, "for daughter's marriage." His mother fasted at home. Kumari had fasted all day and said: "How can I eat now with this face and hand jewellery?" Nora went in search of a teaspoon, and the young women surrounding the bride laughed as Nora fed scraps of rice and curried vegetables through Kumari's barely open lips.

R.D.'s father flitted from woman to woman. Lighting on Nora, he said: "You are aware this hair of yours is like fire in the moonlight?"

"How is Nina?" Nora replied.

He slumped into his years.

"She is here," he said, "she is somewhere, no doubt. It is too difficult for her to come to a wedding, no one expects you understand, but she is bold. I believe that she wrote from her hostel in Bombay that she will not come. Also, she is promising her mother she will not attend. A wise decision, but she changed her mind. Now she must face all this."

"It would be a pity for her to miss Kumari's wedding," Nora offered.

"A pity yes," he said, less nervous, "however, she need not be so bold. Modern girl you see. Of course, no doubt she must not be ashamed, after all who is blaming her?" He gave a hugely liberal sway of the head at the same time as he sighted something behind

Nora: "And I see that my daughter-in-law is bearing up nicely. So," said Mr Das, "things pass, everything is passing, yes? India survives. We are not destroyed by this disaster …"

Did he mean the assassination or the cancelled wedding? In form again, his eyes went back to Nora's hair and rested on her lips: "I hope that you will be visiting my house again before you leave India?" She did not have to answer. He had lit on another woman.

"We are still having hours to go," said Sunita Auntie, laughing when Nora stifled a yawn on the way back to the house in one of the wedding cars. The holy fire burned in the garden under the pandol with its decoration of bugle blooms shining white in the sky's glow, the scent of night blossoms coming in waves on a soft breeze. People were settling down.

"Sit, come Nora Auntie, sit here, it's going to be a long night," a voice invited and Nora looked down at the young woman who patted the cushion beside her. It took her a moment to recognise Nina. She had seen the girl at the hotel and not realised it was her. More than once, the silver embroidery had caught her eye, the elaborate hair-style. Nora had got the impression of someone older, more sophisticated. She sat down beside her.

"You arrived late?" Nora asked, as she tried to identify the change in Nina's face.

"Yes, the train was late. I just got to the hotel in time for the garlanding." Uneasily, Nora felt that this was not the Nina she had met in Delhi, the quiet bride. Her face had lost its softness, or was it her hair done up like that? The make-up too pale? But it was something else. And she saw again the look on Nina's face when the cancellation of her marriage was announced. Nora could not have said why it frightened her. She wanted to ask Nina how she was, but instinctively held back. As she tried not to stare, Nora saw that Nina's lipstick was a sharp, drawn on shape, filled in with vivid colour and wondered if the girl's mother had seen it.

194

"A mysterious girl," R.D. had said and Nora realised that Nina was cause for worry. Thank heavens Ciara had never been "mysterious". How easy it was to get the wrong impression. She recalled Nina in R.D's car on the way from the Imperial Hotel to the house. So young and shy.

People had been awkward with Nina because of her cancelled wedding. A couple of the girls had said she was courageous to come. She hated that. She need not have come, but she wanted to show them. She could not stand anyone to think that she was afraid to face this wedding. Now she was fascinated by the foreigner who had come all this way for a wedding and seemed so calm and interested in everything. Free as a bird. What it must be like to go and come as one pleased, not have to answer to anyone. That's what she wanted more than anything. Just to be free. In London or Paris or even New York.

Nora watched the bride. Kumari sat with eyes downcast, never looking at Prakesh. The fire blazed between the priest and the couple and Mr Basai and Mamaji stood near, somehow involved. Nora realised that this part of the wedding was mainly a family affair. She could hear the voices on the roof and see threads of smoke. They must have lit fires.

At the garden wall, young blades flaunted their freedom as far away from the pandol as possible while the girls squeezed in close. Nora was attempting to follow the ritual and said: "It seems so complicated."

Nina stretched her legs as much as space would permit. "It is not about these two. They must sacrifice for the family. They do not matter, only that they are a new shoot. That is why each family member has a part to play. These two are duty bound. They must adapt, and they must multiply." She laughed, a bitter little laugh. There was silence until Nora spoke: "How are you, Nina? Have you recovered? What happened was so hard ..."

"Hard for Indira Gandhi," Nina said and before Nora had thought of a reply, Nina repeated that laugh. She

195

was looking in the direction of the ceremony: "Kumari was very worried about married life," she said, "she made me swear to tell her all about it after my marriage. Now I am not married. Naturally, I cannot tell." Again she laughed. "We are seven hundred million people in India," she said, "so there is a lot of this thing going on," she mimicked Kumari. "People are coping with this mystery. What is your opinion?"

"I think she'll be alright," Nora said, "she's settled enough now, not so nervous. We had a talk and it seems to have helped."

"Oh, a talk, you had a talk?" Nina said "that I would like to hear. You are knowing about this thing in your country?"

Nora stared coolly, but Nina continued: "After all, what is so mysterious? No doubt you have counted on the fingers of two hands what a man and woman do in bed? Kumari will find out. She will find out without delay, have no fear. I would like to be fly on the wall." And she squirmed into herself chuckling.

The fingers of two hands, Nora thought, glad to slip away while Nina spoke to the woman who sat down on the other side of her.

Most people paid scant attention to the ceremony at this stage, knowing that it would go on for hours and so they chatted or rested. Nora strolled about and was at the edge of the garden again when she found herself standing beside Sarla.

"I am asking you something Mrs Ryan" Sarla began.

Here it comes Nora thought in dread. The woman's face was congested with emotion: "Do not encourage our daughter to go to your place, against our wishes." Sarla struggled for control, her face flushed: "Kindly respect parents' wishes ..." Nora was about to tell her she did not know anything about Nina going to Ireland, but Sarla continued: "I am telling you as mother. We are against this. Do your duty only. Do not encourage." And she walked away.

CHAPTER 21

Relieved that R.D. was not mentioned, Nora wondered what all that was about? I've no designs on her daughter, she thought. She's welcome to her and her ugly little laugh. She reminded herself to make allowances for the girl, but there was something about Nina which unnerved her, something that went deeper than a reaction to her cancelled wedding. Nora could not put her finger on it, but whatever it was, it was frightening.

Wearily, Nora looked at her watch. It was three a.m., and she decided to follow Sita's advice about lying down for a while during the long ceremony. She was about to enter her room when she heard the faint snoring from within. She closed the door and went in search of a quiet corner. Everywhere she looked people were resting. On the lower landing, she turned hopefully into the narrow hallway which led to Ravi Basai's study. The door opened when she turned the handle. The room was empty, but she hesitated. The inner sanctum. The retreat to which Ravi Basai disappeared. And where the men came to drink whiskey, leaving the women to take tea with Maya. Not even Ashoke came here. He'd hardly object to my using it in the circumstances, Nora thought, and in any case he need never know. He's under the pandol. And I'll be back in the garden before the ceremony is over.

The room was comfortable, with leather chairs, book cases, a cabinet, but nowhere to lie down. A chair would have to do. And then she saw the bed rolled out on the desk. Of course, Basai's bed was occupied by three women now. She switched on the ceiling fan, slipped off her shoes and sank down on the desk sighing with comfort. She lay thinking about Nina. Was the girl intending to leave India? Ought she speak to R.D. about what Sarla had said? Was he aware of Nina's state of mind? It was natural for the girl to be upset, but ... I'll talk to Maya first, Nora decided before she fell asleep.

R.D. saw the glow of Nora's hair in the moonlight as he realised that she lay on the desk. The silk of her dress hung down, giving the appearance of an altar. He had been looking for her earlier to smooth over whatever damage Sarla might have done when he had seen the women together and the startled expression on Nora's face before she disappeared. He had come to Basai's study in search of a whiskey.

For several moments R.D. stood looking at Nora in her sleep, forgetting his need of a drink. She was so fragile, her face incredibly pale with those freckles on her nose. In the heat of sleep there was a mist on her upper lip. He recalled that same dew of perspiration caused by the mildest spice when they ate dinner together. It had always caught his heart. He blotted it gently with a finger print. She sighed and moved, baring the inside of one knee so that it shone white. He barely touched it with his lips. She did not move and he kissed it again. She sighed again as he gently brushed his lips along her thigh.

In her sleep, Nora caught the smell of sandalwood, faint and tantalising. She breathed in to capture its headiness and rubbed her thigh. The scent of sandalwood grew stronger. Something touched her nose and she brushed it off with the back of her hand. She moved luxuriously, sighing, and in that moment R.D's life narrowed down to this room, and this woman he had once thought he had won so long ago. And then lost. The pain of that rejection, all the years, the surprise of seeing her in Delhi were in the passion that rose as he burrowed in her neck and she started awake. He kissed her mouth and she felt the silk of her dress fall away as he untied it and covered her breast with his hand. She did not immediately realise that this was twenty-two years later.

Nora walked towards the garden, ghee spluttering in the fire, as the ceremony drew to an end. Mr Basai looked about to cry when he handed his daughter over to Prakesh's father who took Kumari's hand. The couple poured more offerings into the holy vessel.

At last, the pandit tied the knot between the bride's sari and the tail of the groom's khurta. Taking tiny steps in the small space, the pair walked around the fire four times this way and three times the other way. One of the aunts sprinkled vermilion powder, the symbol of a married woman, beneath the jewels which lay in the parting of Kumari's hair. Nora saw that Maya's face was grief-stricken, and Ravi Basai walked quickly away from the pandol into the house. Soon everyone went to lie down, but only for an hour.

Nora had become accustomed to waking with different people, but she was amazed to find the bride lying beside her with her friend Archana who was still asleep. "I am exhausted," Kumari said.

"Where is the bridegroom?" Nora asked.

Kumari looked surprised "He is with the men," she said.

Exhaustion was shaken off in the rush to get ready for the morning ceremony of kavole, the husband's first meal in the home of his bride's parents. Nora was impatient with this ritual since Maya had explained that the bridegroom would not accept food if some demand of his family's had not been met. And as Maya pleated her sari, Nora asked: "This is just a formality, isn't it? I mean the bit about Prakesh making a demand at the last minute?"

Maya swayed her head : "It is not up to him only, don't forget. This is last chance for in-laws to see that all is correct. Also, to establish boy's status in this house. Don't worry, we are prepared to meet if he makes demand."

The women were boisterous with excitement. This ceremony was their's alone. They prepared to honour "the boy", to celebrate a son-in-law in the house and banish any little dissatisfaction that might be lurking among Kumari's in-laws. And, ever after, Prakesh would be received as a lord in this house. Hurrying breathlessly, the women giggled over jokes to tell, as they attended to the preparation of his food. "No, no," Maya advised, "he is liking coffee only, no tea. Let Nirmal fetch it."

"That cushion is too awkward," another woman said, "he cannot be comfortable."

Sunita Auntie, spruce in claret silk, sat importantly behind a small card table as Prakesh and his men were settled: "Do not eat until demand is met," one woman reminded him mischievously. Otherwise, Nora could not understand what the women were saying to him, the jokes they told. Seductively, they coaxed and teased Prakesh, giggled at their own boldness. They playfully slapped each other and some drew their sarees to hide embarrassment. Such a joke. What a thing to say. Prakesh obviously enjoyed it all, the naughtiness of the bolder ones, or being treated like a baby by another. Nora could have sworn that he gurgled for Sarla. The older women were closer to Prakesh and caused him to squirm and grin. His men roared with laughter, thumped his arm.

"Look at Kumari's sister-in-law," Sita whispered to Nora, "that is a good sign." The woman beamed approval, and Nora recalled Maya saying that sometimes the sister-in-law had more power than the groom's mother. It's going well, Nora thought, amused to see that Dadiji glared as always.

All the while, women lined up to hand envelopes and

bank notes to Sunita Auntie. Managerial, she entered each gift in the ledger in front of her. "It's so we know what to give back," Sita explained.

An "A-a-a-h" went up and Nora was just in time to see Prakesh close his lips on a mouthful of food. The women fed him with their fingers. A woman stuffed in the next mouthful of food as Sarla bent over him. She said something and everyone laughed. Sita, still beside Nora, was convulsed with laughter, her hand on her belly. "She told him to lick," she gasped.

Eventually, Prakesh held his hands up, unable to eat any more, but the teasing continued until the groom's brother rose. It was time to leave. People hurried to get ready to accompany the bridal party to the station.

As Nora came downstairs, she felt something in the air even before she saw Ravi Basai's face. It was drained of colour, each muscle forced to behave. Maya's face was bent over a puja tray. Another ritual, Nora thought, nobody mentioned this. People in the hall stood back from the little group. Kumari was closest to the open door, with tears on her face.

"It's the leave taking," Ashoke said to Nora.

Mr Basai spoke to his daughter and straightening up, she blew her nose and adjusted the sari on her shoulder. She stepped forward and lit the incense on Maya's tray, waving the smoke in a little circle. Then she took some rose petals and sprinkled them along a couple of yards towards the open door, saying something in a steady voice.

She returned to the tray for rice which she sprinkled with the petals and spoke again.

Ashoke translated for Nora: "Kumari is saying 'all that I have had here, all that you have given me, I leave behind forever.'"

Rice and roses, thought Nora and could not control her tears. Not until Ashoke's translation had Nora fully understood what the Basais were about. They were handing over their daughter, not simply in marriage, but giving her to another family. So much depended upon their choice of in-laws for Kumari.

Ashoke helped his grandmother to the gates to see Kumari and Prakesh off. They touched the old woman's feet, and she placed a great hand on each of their heads saying something that sounded to Nora like the whispering of a crow. Huge tears rolled down her face and she swiped at them with her sari, the way she did at flies.

The couple were driven twice to the top of the lane before the third time when they left for the train with the wedding crowd who saw them off. Nora saw Ravi Basai bend low to say something to his daughter before she boarded the train. A look of sheer worship crossed her face as he stood tall again, impassive.

Mr Basai drove back in silence. Maya sobbed. Nora's throat was sore with emotion. A bird pecked at the remains of the rice around the door, the rose petals were bruised into the marble of the hall. "She will be different when she comes back," Maya said, "bride's always are. She will realise that childhood is gone and time of being daughter of this home is past."

People were leaving. R.D. came to say goodbye to Nora, formally, because Sarla stood beside him. Nina swung in the hammock waiting to go with the party from Bombay. Maya, with dark circles under her eyes, packed boxes of ladoos for the girls at Nina's hostel and other departing guests. Mr Basai announced his intention to "drink some whiskey" and three or four men trouped after him.

Nora sat on the charpoi where on the day after she arrived, she had lain to sunbathe and amazed the servants. They had spluttered past her, crept up the steps and peered through the railings, stifling giggles. "They have never seen anyone in the sun," Maya explained, "they are thinking that you are crazy and you are becoming entirely pink, is that your wish?"

Now, Nora watched a woman salvage the food from

the banana leaves which all week long had been dumped under the neem tree beyond the back wall. She filled her sack with the scraps as birds scavenged around her. Behind her, she could hear people getting ready to leave. They all belong somewhere, Nora thought, and have to get back. Even that woman. Nora was uneasy over what had happened with R.D., although it had clarified so much for her. And it was time to think about leaving. I won't leave too soon, she thought, I will give Maya a chance to recover from this, but she knew that whenever she parted from Maya would be too soon.

At 6.30a.m. Nirmal followed Maya into Nora's room with breakfast trays. Nora's tray had a plate of golden French fries arranged around a bowl of tomato sauce.

"Oh Maya," Nora said, as Maya put the tray in front of her, "I didn't have to have chips. I only meant ... I mean I don't really miss anything at all about home, but the women coaxed out of me what I missed. It wasn't serious ..." Nora realised that the women must have informed Maya that her guest craved chips.

Maya was smiling. "It is a tiny thing. A small craving is so simple to put right. Who would not try? Archana told me how to make these potatoes. First some tea?" They sat on Nora's bed, the tray between them. The chips were crisp and dry and freshly sprinkled with salt. Nora dipped one into the ketchup and feeling herself flush because of the chilli in it, managed not to wince: "Delicious," she said.

Maya sipped her tea. "Thangamani and Uma are gone," she announced, her eyes pained. "My widow and her daughter have left. I am being fond of Thangamani, always. Mother-in-Law says I must go to my village and bring new servants and this time to be sensible. She is like a general this morning."

Nora was surprised. So, touching mother-in-law's feet was no mere formality. "She says I had not business to bring a widow to cook and a widow with a girl was bound to be trouble. I should not have sent

Uma to school ... She had no need of school. Thangamani's brother took them last night. A match is arranged for the little one. She is being settled."

"But Uma is only twelve," Nora said, "isn't that against the law?"

"Ah yes," said Maya, "and who will enforce the law, tell me that? The poor are not knowing such laws. This year her uncle has offer and dowry, who knows about next year? They are peasants working hard. Laws? They try to survive only. My mother-in-law has given strict instructions, no widows and no girls. I will go there today. You will come?"

As she prepared for the journey Nora thought that she had not even begun to understand Maya. She had been so blind. It was not simply that Maya had a mother-in-law living with her. Maya was a daughter-in-law in this traditional house. She had come here as a bride and been the one who had to adapt and obey. Maya's freedom was only as much as her mother-in-law permitted. Nora could see the old woman watering her tulsi plant in the courtyard and wondered if Maya had to ask permission to bring her there in the first place? And was it alright to stay so long? She realised that she had not recognised how Maya must have battled for freedoms which she had taken for granted. Little freedoms that must have been wrested inch by inch from entrenched tradition.

Nora picked up the sari blouse Maya had dropped. It had a pattern of tiny flower buds and wrinkled under-arms. She buried her nose in it. Again and again she breathed in its beloved scent. Her face flamed and she sat down on the bed. She recalled their first meeting, how she had recognised Maya's eyes and how her heart had jumped. Now, she knew that Maya shared these feelings. And she seemed so at ease in their relationship. Nora thought that Maya was like India, complicated and beautiful. Both took on new ways, but neither lost her ancient depth. Like India, Maya was open and hidden, forever a surprise. They would probably never quite understand each other. And it did not matter. She had thought that she knew Dennis.

Nora could hear the clink of bangles and went into the middle-room to find Maya in a yellow sari: "It will take four hours to be going there," Maya said.

"Four hours is not very far, why don't you go back to your village more often?" Nora asked.

"It is far away in reality, maybe not hours. It is not acceptable for a woman to return too often to her parents' home. We will stay overnight, there is much to do. A letter is there for you since yesterday afternoon. On that little table."

Nora picked up the envelope, surprised by its bulk. There was a chatty few pages from Derry, who enclosed another letter. Inside that was a third letter. The first was from "Anna Bell", a name Nora did not recognise, but the address on the unheaded note-paper jumped from the page, The London Adoption Society. Nora sat down on the edge of the divan. A social worker, Ms Anna Bell, was asking her if she would like to meet her daughter!

... we did our best to guide this matter through the orthodox channels. Now I feel that the best we can do is to attempt to soften what will undoubtedly be a shock for you.

As I'm sure you are aware, there is now a law which gives adopted children the right to their original birth certificates, with the possibility of contacting their natural mothers. Your daughter, Sara, has been determined to do this for several years. She has been intent upon finding you. When I examined your file I realised that you left us a forwarding address at the time of her adoption and that, furthermore, you wrote to provide your new address when you got married.

Adding it all together, I had a letter ready to post to you, advising you of Sara's wishes, when she rang to tell me that she had actually gone to Ireland. She told me she had "hunted down those Boylans and discovered my Ma married a Dennis Ryan". I'm afraid that Sara called at your home outside Dublin. She was told that letters would be forwarded to you in India. I believe that she did not divulge her identity, but since I have no doubt that Sara is capable of finding some way of tracing you, perhaps even following you to India, I have agreed to write and enclose her letter. I'm afraid Sara can be most headstrong.

I suggest that you take your time in deciding what to do about the enclosed letter from Sara. It is natural that this news will come as a shock, and you will need time to decide what to do. So do take your time. Sara assures me that if you do not wish to meet her she will be satisfied with your photograph.

Sara, Nora thought, suddenly furious. But I called her Patricia. Her name was Patricia and then Wren-bird. My little Wrennie. They've changed her name. Nora's hands shook as she opened the last letter. Wrennie, Wrennie.

Dear Nora, or can I call you Mum? It's hard to know what to call you though I've thought about it a lot. Since I was told I was adopted I've wanted to know all about you. At last I got in touch with the agency, but they didn't make it easy. I'd love to meet you, I think I'm like you, even if it's just once. I've left home and work in a boutique. Mummy and I don't quite hit it off. Anyway, that's another story.

Mrs Bell says I'm not to write too much, to give you a chance. I thought she was going to keep putting me off forever and my friend, Sadie, said "why don't you go to Ireland and find her? You could be lucky. It's a small place." So that's what I did. It was easy. The neighbour in Cork, Mrs Lynch, remembered you well and knew all about you and got your address from the telephone book. She even rang and checked. I told her I was the daughter of a friend you had in London. Mrs Lynch was

*at your wedding, she said it was on an island? I
thought she'd sussed it when she said I reminded her
of you, but she says you have red hair and fair skin. I
went back to Dublin and knocked at your hall door. The
woman said she was your sister Derry and well, you
know the rest. That would make her my aunt, wouldn't
it? She's lovely. Reminds me of a smashing teacher I
had once. Mrs Bell says you'll have all kinds of feelings
when you get this letter, and not all good. Does it feel
like being haunted? If you'd like a photo of me I'll send
it. I'd send it now, but Mrs Bell says better not. You
needn't meet me unless you want to, but would you
please send a photo of you no matter what you decide?
If we could meet just once? Just to see how it goes? I
don't want to make trouble for you. I just want to meet
you. If it freaks you out or if you feel you can't, then
maybe even next year, when you get used to the idea?*

Nora was about to offer this letter to Maya when she
realised that she had lost contact with what was going
on around her. Nirmal was holding the tiffin carrier by
its handle with the luggage on his head, and Maya
was carefully wrapping her paan for the journey. Nora
followed Maya outside feeling herself dragged along by
her own body. She wanted to speak, but her tongue
ached at the back of her throat and she did not know
what it was she wanted to say. She put the letters in
her handbag, and climbed clumsily into the auto-rick.

It was eight o'clock, yet the sun seemed too hot at
the same time as Nora felt icy spiders crawl over her
back, under her sleeves and down her arms. She
closed her eyes against the sun. Wrennie. Poor little
wren bird. You know. Wrennie, her contented baby,
was a woman now. And she knows, Nora thought, she
knows I left her. I gave her away. Never mind why. I
did. I left her. And she's back, it's all caught up with
me. Everything that I hid and tried to forget. Her heart
pounded with excitement until she felt tired.

In her mind, she found herself back at the

beginning, herself and Wrennie lying in the hospital bed.

"Is bad news in there?" Maya asked, glancing at Nora clutching her handbag. "Someone is ill? Family problems, always for womans there are family problems."

"It's a bit of a shock," Nora said. "I'm not sure if it's good news or bad news ..." She shivered, and instinctively Maya massaged her back, so that Nora felt the spiders' icy feet driven outside the circle of Maya's hand.

"Ah yes, you can tell," said Maya, "in the heart one can always tell."

"I can't talk about it yet," Nora said, "perhaps on the train. I have to think. Though how ... one second I feel terrified and the next so happy and this shivering."

"We can go tomorrow to the village," Maya said, "if you are not well it is better you rest and ..."

"No," Nora said, amazed at the firmness of her own voice. "No, let's go. I'll be alright."

As they bumped along, Nora was back in the hospital in London, back handing her baby over to Eleanor Conway and Sister Clare. Wrennie's face was round and content in the pink and white blanket, her weight warm along the inside of Nora's forearm.

I might not have given her up, but for Sister Clare, Nora thought. Or if Sister Clare had been the usual run of nuns. Sister Clare was young and a stunner. "A few mothers who have kept their babies are coming to tea on Sunday," she told Nora. "Come and talk to them. That will help you decide. Bringing up a baby is hard to imagine, you know. It's not all cuddles. I couldn't manage a baby on my own and work and all. Some girls think they can. And a few can. Come on Sunday."

The mothers were all Nora's own age, scruffy but not trendily so, as though they had not been told this was the "sixties". Each seemed so alone around the tea table. And, like deprived children, they clung to their recently acquired treasures.

What would happen to those babies? Probably they would grow and be alright, but what about the mothers? Their vulnerability terrified Nora. Perhaps she might cope slightly better, but how? What would it be like for the child? And how could she bring the baby home to Ireland. Her father had died earlier that year, her mother still in grief. More than two decades later, Nora blinked at the thought of a girl bringing a baby home to Ireland in the sixties. Irish girls who had got pregnant had gone to England for abortions or adoption. One could do it now in the eighties. Barely. It would depend, she thought. Nora stumbled out of the scooter and felt herself leaving Sister Clare. Sister Clare was rocking Wrennie in her arms and Nora was walking away, feeling a scrap of agony dislodging from the mass which was not yet completely numb, like a barely audible whisper. The pain had slept where she had laid it to rest, never daring to waken it. Nora still held her handbag by the clasp, aware that her arms ached with loss as Maya led her through the crowdedness on the platform, through the battery of noise and smells.

"Nora?" Maya gently pressed her arm, "Please say you are sitting here!"

"I'm OK, just a bit funny, Maya," Nora said. "Get the tickets. I'll be fine." Nora watched Maya and Nirmal go and closed her eyes. She opened them to get away from Sister Clare.

A tiny girl in a red sari was being dragged along the platform by two women in a group of people. The girl was veiled and bejewelled. Her eyes were enormous and frightened, widened as though she saw what she most feared. The women dragged her, jingling. She clung to the station platform with her heels, her toes curled stiffly above their rings. Her eyes caught Nora's who saw that she made a decision before she spoke to a young man who wore a watch on top of his shirt sleeve. He glanced in Nora's direction, and told the women to let the girl go. She scurried across the

platform and sat up beside Nora, her feet clearing the
ground, smiling. Nora could feel the girl's relief. About
fourteen, she thought. From beneath the veil, the girl
said: "Good-morning!"

"Good-morning," Nora replied softly.

"Good-morning," the girl repeated even more politely,
and Nora saw a nun standing in front of a class. A
Loretto nun? The girl giggled nervously, and slid along
the bench on her bottom until she was touching Nora.
Why me? she wondered. The girl sat too close and had
to twist her neck to look up into Nora's eyes. Nora
sighed, the girl had brought her back to the present
and it felt weird being on an Indian railway station
waiting for a friend to buy their tickets. A special
friend, Nora thought as she recalled Derry's book. And
yet Maya knows nothing at all about me. Not of my
life, Dennis, my children. Children. It had always been
"daughter". Now she was thinking "children". Nor did
Maya know about R.D. Nora wondered if she was as
like Ireland as Maya was like India.

"Good-morning" sat contentedly while the group who
had brought her sat on their luggage or their hunkers
chatting. There was a pyjama clad fellow and two
young men in Western dress. Nora looked down at the
girl whose hand went to her mouth, her wrist heavy
with glass bangles. Beneath her veil, ear-rings danced
and flashed, and above her sari-blouse was an ornate
neck-piece. A daub of red powder marked her
forehead. A bride, Nora thought, as her thoughts were
drowned by a shrill whistle.

Like a street of blackened houses somehow shoved
along, the train slowed into the station. Impatiently,
young men threw their belongings out and jumped
onto the platform. The whistle shrieked again, while
people poured from the train and others pushed
forward to board. The girl squeezed closer to Nora.
One of the women from the group came and caught
the girl by the wrist, jerking her off the bench. "No!"
Nora protested and realised that there was nothing to

be done. The girl pleaded until her captor stopped and waited. "Good-morning," she said. Nora's throat was dry so that she could not reply before the girl was dragged off.

Maya, exuding triumph, was back.

"I have achieved this task," she said. She returned Nora's passport, watched to see it put away, and held her arm along the platform, followed by Nirmal . They could not get to the train because of the "Good-morning" girl's party. The girl sobbed brokenly and tried to sit down on the spot so that people had to make their way around the group.

One of the women who was not wrestling with the girl gave Maya that conspiratorial look that women exchange over the heads of girls, the look that sneers: "She can't win", or "She'll learn, we all suffered it".

Maya did not acknowledge the look, and she spoke to the girl who relaxed and stood upright for a few seconds, attempted courage. Then, she broke again, whimpering. The older man spoke to Maya in Hindi and Maya swayed her head slowy, avoiding the woman's eyes. "Come," she said taking Nora's arm, "come". They shared the coach with a man who read *The Hindustani Times* and three women in burka.

"What was wrong with the girl?" Nora asked.

For a moment it seemed as if Maya would not reply, her face clouded before she said: "A bride going to her in-laws' house." It was obvious that she did not wish to discuss it further but Nora had to know.

"Which was the husband?"

Maya hesitated."The one who spoke to me," she said."He said he understood. She was going to a good home."

Nora did not say anything. The bridegroom was probably older than the girl's father.

Maya was gazing out of the window. Nora took out her letters.

...and I almost forgot to tell you, the daughter of a

*friend of yours called to the door. She put me in mind of
someone, but I couldn't think who. Dark eyed, olive
skinned, could be Italian. A girl called Sara. She
wouldn't come in for coffee. She has a cockney accent.
All love, Derry.*

Nora read Anna Bell's letter again and felt angry:
Why couldn't they handle things properly? Suppose
Wrennie had arrived in the middle of Ciara's wedding?
She read her daughter's letter again. Sara. It was a
nice name, but no better than Patricia. You'd think
they'd have the decency to leave the child with the
name her mother gave her, Nora thought. Funny the
way things worked out, she had never thought of her
as anything but Wrennie. In London there was a girl
called Sara with a cockney accent who was waiting to
hear from her.

"I've found my mother," Nora knew she would tell
that friend of hers, Sadie. "I've found her and she's in
India and I've written to her." She imagined the stir
that would cause. She told herself that not many
people got a second chance. She could turn back the
clock, make it up to Wrennie, but then how could she
ever really do that?

Nora's mood kept changing, peaking with excitement
and then suddenly plummeting. What would Wrennie
think of her, would she be what she expected, or
imagined or hoped? Maybe it was better to let things
be. But how could she? Another rejection? She winced
for the girl. Even as she thought that she could not let
Wrennie go a second time, Nora felt angry, trapped.
How was she going to face this child?

"You have been far away," Maya was saying, "I think
you must be knowing every word of this letter by
now."

Nora passed her the social worker's letter. Maya
arranged her sari and settled down to read. Nora
watched her frown as her eyes travelled back to the
top of the page to begin again. Maya read slowly until

without raising her eyes, she held out her hand for the other letter. After a moment, she squeezed Nora's hand. "Ah-h-h," Maya said at last as she handed the letters back and pressed her other hand on her chest. "But this is a thing. What you must feel. How you will do? We must discuss ..." and then incredulous, she ran out of words.

Never had the women been more conscious of their difference and yet the closeness between them. Through Maya, Nora felt that she had discovered that women have a universal culture. Now, this flowed as a warm undercurrent beneath their separate thoughts, but even so, Nora felt exposed. What Maya must think. She can't possibly understand, thought Nora, it just confirms what she thinks about the West, full of loose women, people not caring, wild girls, babies put out for adoption. Tags on toes. How can I convince her that I didn't sleep all over the place? If only she knew the truth. Oh God, a few months ago, life was so normal, a husband, daughter getting married. Normal or what passed as normal.

In fact, Maya's amazement was tinged with admiration for Nora. To think that she had imagined her correct for a Western woman. She did not smoke and had not accepted a drink even when Mr Basai offered her whiskey, Maya recalled. She tried to imagine these things happening in her own life. Having a baby in secret. Giving it away. Surviving. And Nora had got a husband after that, even. Presumably without help from anyone. In India even if marriage could be arranged after such a thing, the child coming back like this would be a disaster. A whole family destroyed. West was different, Maya decided. Even so, Nora had suffered too much. Ah, but for mother to find the child again. That must be a miracle.

"Sometimes a nightmare can begin with a miracle," Nora said.

Maya was startled at Nora reading her thoughts. "Ah

213

yes," she said. She glanced up at the man with *The Hindustani Times* and seeing that he slept, continued: "but reverse is also true. You will meet Kesruji in my village. She is old, so holy. She lives in a house with one room only and there is always light there. It is special place. All the women go to her and she is knowing all things. She will ease your heart. And she is speaking English. All womans love Kesruji, and it is not necessary to tell your trouble. She is knowing. It is fortunate we must go there." Maya lowered her voice to a whisper.

"Since she was small child the goal of her life is liberation from rebirth, you understand. Her family respect this. She did not bleed and this sign was plain. No marriage was made for her. Kesruji is special soul."

Briefly, the train stopped and Nora spied the wedding party making their way across the fields. The women dragged the bride along. Nora wondered what the girl would do if they let go of her. As the train moved on, there were masculine cheers from the window of the next carriage. Nora watched until the heads of the group were hidden by a crop of yellow. The bride was the first to disappear.

Nora sensed Maya's shame.

"It's not only in India that a girl can be so helpless," she said. "What puzzles me is that motherhood is so powerful, but equally, just as powerless."

"Ah yes," said Maya, "but who would like to be a man? It is hard the life of womans, but comes a day every bride is mother-in-law. If she has a son..." Her shoulders expressed confidence in the reward awaiting her. "And not every woman can be a Phoolan Devi," Maya added aware of Nora's fascination with Phoolan Devi, the recently captured gang leader of a mob of outlaws.

Nora had read that there was a Bombay film being made about Phoolan, whose English name was Flower Goddess. But no sooner had Nora read one story about Phoolan than she came upon another that contradicted it. There were so many Phoolans, the terroist, the towering Amazon on a horse, Phoolan the runaway bride, the rape victim, the man in disguise. Nora had bought a magazine with Phoolan's story. She was married at eleven to an old man, ran away, took a lover, was dragged back to her husband and brutally beaten, ran away again, was jailed for something she did not do, raped in the jail by the prisoners and guards, escaped, became a gang leader and avenged herself by killing 22 people, shooting them down one after another in a row.

"This lady dacoit had the police of two states helpless," Maya had boasted. "Police on high chairs lost their positions because this girl could not be captured. She had so much furiosity."

The photograph of the dacoit had revealed only a sullen girl, tiny and plain.

CHAPTER 22

When they stepped outside the station at the end of their journey, Nora recognised Chitra, Mamaji's wife, whom she had tried to talk to at Kumari's wedding, but had found her so shy that the conversation had dried up after a few sentences. Now Chitra prepared to touch Maya's feet, but Maya manoeuvered an embrace instead.

Nora noticed how sophisticated Maya appeared beside her country relative. Both sarees were lovely, but Chitra's tika mark was the same powder as she wore in her hair-line, and smudged. Maya wore the crisp red dot which she peeled from rows on a piece of sticky paper each time she dressed. Nora came across these dots stuck on mirrors, or on the wall in the bathroom, wherever Maya discarded them.

"It is traditional mark of married lady," Maya explained, "but these days it is more like a beauty spot. In old days it was meant to distract men's eyes from other things."

In the crush outside the station Nora leaned on a stall for support but snatched her hand back when she felt something wet in her palm. The stall was heaped with animal skins, oozing pink slime in the sun. Sickened, she rubbed her hand on her skirt as Maya closed her eyes in revulsion and led her to the car which shone beneath layers of polish and had white curtains at the windows held back by red sashes, and a shrine on the dashboard. The driver wore a shirt with palm trees and "Florida" written on it. He honked his way through the crowds and Nora's head throbbed so that she longed to reach where they were going. When at last they were free of the market, they came to the level crossing which cut the town off from the fields. The railway gates were closed, but people climbed over them on to the tracks to cross the fields on either side or cycle along the hot road.

Children crowded round the open windows of the car. One of them smiled directly at Nora and stretched his fist over her skirt. "What have you there?" she asked and the boy opened his hand and dropped a little snake which wriggled wildly in her lap. Maya spoke angrily to the boy who laughed and retrieved his snake by the tail.

"They are harmless, these snakes," said Maya, "but boys are happy with mischief." On the other side of the car a woman was pressing in on Chitra, holding up a sack in each hand. "She wants us to pay her for mongoose and cobra fight," Maya explained.

"Say no," Nora pleaded and Chitra closed the window.

The train passed and they drove over the tracks with the bullock carts, cyclists and burdened pedestrians until they were alone on the road, bumping giddily past fields of crops on either side.

Suddenly the driver scooped coins off the dashboard and threw them towards a man with a wild beard and saffron robes, who sat under a tree. The driver's coins landed on the confetti of money at the man's feet.

"Throw a coin," Maya told Nora, "he is the road guru. He is praying always for the safety of all who use this road. The driver says that this guru has prevented many accidents on this road."

Nora threw a coin, and found that her arm ached from the effort. She thought that she had never felt so tired and confused. Her back was crawling with icy sensations again.

"I will take you to Kesruji," Maya consoled, "she will give you much advice about everything. Kesruji is very wise, you will see."

"Here is my village," Maya announced as the car turned into a narrow roadway between a field of ripe wheat and a row of ochre and golden trees, a stretch of poplars, jack and neem trees. Beyond the trees and their dark, tangled undergrowth flashed the surprise of gold; a field of marigolds for garlands. The field women in vivid sarees rose to look at the car, soothed their backs, and slowly waved.

Maya had told Nora so much about her childhood in this village, but Nora was not prepared for the dismal dwellings of the village sweeper cast on its outskirts. Small children shone like jewels in the dust where the smell of poverty hung heavy in the air.

Quite suddenly the village became alive with colour as they passed the sari printing works with vats of dye and endless cloth. Maya had told Nora sarees came from factories, their plainness providing employment for so many and were sent back to cities as high fashion, though never as colourful as the spattered dyers.

An old woman shelled peas in her doorway, another picked over rice. The barber clipped away in the sunshine, an old fellow rose upon his elbow on a string bed to spurt red spittle in front of the car. Here a boy massaged old shoulders, a little bottle of oil propped against the man's hip, and another boy made newspaper cones ready to fill with something yellow from a plastic basin.

Surrounded by children, too young for school, a dhobi worked with a black flat iron upon a table. The fire which heated the iron was on the ground behind him and with his bare feet the man rubbed at the heat burning into his legs. Nora longed for an end to the journey as sarees covered a field, and the sing-song of lessons came from a school-house. A camel and a man shared a tall hut. The man puffed on a hookah, the camel chewed. The car passed a temple, a spice vendor, women threading marigolds, and a potter. Everywhere, animals ambled hot and underfed, flicking their tails, looking to quench their thirst. People stared at the car and children ran alongside the windows.

Council Development read the brass sign to one side of the hall-door. "Now, you are at my home," said Maya. "Here we are. Inside, there is the government office for village development work." As she spoke, Mamaji came through the door, smiling.

"Ah," he said, "our Irish sister, you are entirely welcome here. And you must call me Simitra. Mamaji means mother's sister, so I am not your mother's sister? Your presence is a good surprise."

Chitra made a modest movement of her head in an acceptance of credit for her husband's pleasure. Women crowded the doorway, sarees modestly down over their foreheads and Mamaji suggested rest and cool drinks to the air before he disappeared. He could be seen through the window of his office. He nodded at them, happily.

In the courtyard, one woman pumped water from the well and two others brought it to Maya and Nora. Two women motioned Nora into a basket-chair in the courtyard, the hub of the household here. She sat down, relieved. Everyone else sat on their haunches. A girl brought cooling lassies with cardamon before Maya disappeared with Chitra to discuss the purpose of the visit.

Left alone, Nora was at a loss with the shyness and giggles of some of the women. And soon, the few faces she recognised from the wedding were lost midst all the strangers who came and stared at her. Some brought tiny babies and toddlers, beautiful wide-eyed children.

Sita, who had grown huge in the ten days since the wedding, translated for the group. Nora focussed on the little ones. It delighted the mothers, but after Maya had been gone for an hour, her nerves were frayed. She longed to be alone, to think about Wrennie, and was exasperated by the way the women pulled the sarees down over their foreheads and peered out at her. Their scents fused, heavy in the heat and she could not escape the steady gaze of their eyes.

"How many children you have?" a woman asked.

"One," said Nora, "I mean two," she said flustered, and felt the ice at her back again. She sighed with weariness and immediately two pairs of hands were upon her, pressing and massaging. Someone brought pungent oil and caressed her temples. Eventually, their voices faded.

Nora was amazed to wake in a room, dark except for a candle. She was covered in a Lucknow quilt. A Moghul batik hung on the wall, and rose-oil burned somewhere near. "Can you open the window?" she asked Maya who was sitting on a cushion on the floor beside her.

"Better not. The moon is full. It is wiser to protect you from it. Perhaps it was foolish to bring you travelling with this letter of yours, and the moon full."

So, I was right, Nora thought. All her life she had been wary of the full moon believing it drained her energy and affected her concentration. She tried never to leave her head exposed to the moon's rays while she slept. And her avoidance of full moon-light had become a family joke.

Maya's cool hand touched Nora's face. "How do you feel? When I came back you were fine, but after dinner, no more. We laid you here and you kept talking about a little bird, a wren. You have not had this disability before?"

Nora shook her head, knowing now that she had been ill since morning, shivery on and off, with the sensation of slipping away. She did not immediately remember the women massaging her before she'd had a rest and gone out with Maya. She recalled touring the village; pink sand-stone houses, huts, shacks, a jumble, she decided, until she realised its sprawling shapelessness had a pattern, the centre of which was Maya's house. A landlord's house.

The young man, Krishna, and his wife Shanti had come to see Maya and remained silent while the sweet-maker negotiated. Krishna would be paid to cook and run the house, his wife would help him. The question of her payment was not mentioned. Maya gave them money, they would follow in two days time. The sweet-maker escorted the women home.

Nora remembered the smells as they got ready for dinner. Everyone seemed to have been involved in the preparation of the meal, including Maya's brother. And then the food had been brought to a table in this room. Nora looked around and found the table in the opposite corner to her bed. She and Maya and Simitra had sat on the floor at the stump legged table while Chitra brought them dish after dish of amazing food. Those who were not cooking, watched them eat. It had seemed to Nora that the entire village looked on, crowding into every scrap of space on beds and cushions and the bare floor, so that the darkest corner glowed with eyes. Sita had taken her to wash her hands on the bench under the tree, given her scented soap, and poured water from a jug over her hands. Later, she had presented her with a spoon. Remembering all the attention, Nora felt embarrassed, especially for Maya who had brought her here. She had passed out over dinner. She must apologise, but now there were voices at the door.

Kesruji, Maya's holy woman had arrived to bless the visitor. "You will see her?" Maya asked and did not wait for a reply. Kesruji was tall and thin and wore a cotton sari. Her hair was white and her face wrinkled. Kesruji placed her hand on Nora's shoulder, and murmured a blessing.

"You have fever," she said, her voice as deep and soft as her eyes. Nora had expected the holy woman to be like a nun, but decided that she was more like a priest, and although she thought no better of priests than of nuns, she was immediately convinced of Kesruji's holiness. The old woman studied Nora: "You are attached to solution that has no problem. You must detach yourself from this thing. It spoils your life. If there is no solution, there is no problem."

"I don't understand," Nora murmured.

"Yes, you will understand," said the old woman, "your heart is drying around this attachment. Your desire is always for something you do not desire. If you wish liberation from this thing I will work?"

Nora nodded.

"In India you have found what you journey towards," she said, looking into Nora's eyes. "You do not know yet what this is, but you will know. You will be surprised. Isn't it? It is unfinished business from the past life. Also, something from the past has returned. This is plus, not minus. As for your health, I will tell you that you are better today then you are tomorrow. This is not serious illness, but nuisance. You will be well again to see your daughters. Pray, you must pray."

The word "daughters" reverberated in Nora's head even as she thought that she had not come to India to find a guru; there was enough religion in Ireland.

Kesruji answered her thoughts. "I am not seeking to bring you along my path. This is not for you. Pray the prayers your mother taught you, remember her god. Also, you are having a dream, it is necessary dream, do not be afraid." Kesruji left soon after that, and Maya stretched to touch the hem of her sari.

"I have never fainted before," Nora whispered to Maya, "I must have picked up something."

"Perhaps. Or perhaps dearling, those letters were too much," said Maya softly. "Kesruji says dream will help to make you well."

"Did you tell her about the letters?" Nora asked.

"She says there is older problem than letters, but it will unravel. But problems are coming with these letters. We must discuss."

"I'm not sure," Nora said, "I don't think I can ever explain how I feel, what has been going through my head. Such confusion. So unreal one minute and too real the next. I suppose you've thought it odd that I would come to India alone? My husband and I have parted suddenly. This is why I came to India. The wedding invitation gave me the idea to get away. At first I wasn't going to accept, but my aunt said it was a heaven sent opportunity. Just what I needed and she was right. Aunt Flo is in her seventies and she's getting married. She's a great character, buckets of courage and common sense ..."

Maya was puzzled by the marriage of Nora's aunt at such an age. How could such a thing be? She put it out of her head and thought about Nora. At their first meeting she had sensed a numbness in Nora and put it down to a Western way of being. Later she had wondered if it was an attachment to an old grief. Not an unusual thing, she thought of several people she knew who had a dead bit in their hearts.

"Is your husband knowing about the baby?" she asked Nora.

" No," Nora said, "he never knew."

"What means suddenly, this parting from your husband?" Maya asked.

"I mean it came as a shock. We were going along fine I thought. Although things were never quite right between us. We were not compatible. That was the word the doctor used. He said the chemistry wasn't right. It obviously wasn't."

Nora was embarrassed. She sensed that Maya heard her words as self-indulgently Western, and it seemed impossible to explain her relationship with Dennis. She was aware that there was something about it that she herself did not understand. How could she have been so oblivious? Since her thirtieth birthday.

"So your husband is wanting to take another wife?" Maya was asking.

"No," Nora said, "not like that. He's not very interested in women. Anyway, you can't get divorced in Ireland. You see the way we were wasn't a married life. I was

223

miserable when we were younger and I, well, we decided that when Ciara left home or got married, we'd go our own ways. That was over thirteen years ago."

Maya was trying to understand. "But you say thirteen years. This is not sudden?"

"In a way sudden," Nora tried to explain, "it came as a shock to me, but Dennis meant to go all along. I mean he behaved normally, but it was in his mind. And as time went on, I forgot about the arrangement. For a while things were strained between us. I mean after we decided, but it just sort of faded and I forgot the whole incident. It was gone until he brought it back. We had agreed we'd stay for Ciara. She had a happy childhood. And gradually, I suppose, I settled for what I had, but Dennis never forgot. I realise now that's the way he is. I shouldn't have been surprised. I don't know," Nora's voice shook, "he just waited and then announced that it was time. He told me a couple of weeks before the wedding. Imagine. Knocked the stuffing out of me. And then he left the day after."

Ashamed, Nora's voice trailed off. She did not want to face all that now, thinking about her own part in it threatened such humiliation that she could not bear it. But Maya pressed on.

"So," she said with realisation dawning in her voice, "Mr Ryan is being like sadhu, holy man? Ah yes, but that can be boon for wife." When Nora did not answer, Maya puzzled: "But if the marriage was not arranged, why did you do it? Why did you marry?"

That's a good question, Nora thought and said: "I think I wanted something normal, somewhere safe after what I'd been through. Perhaps I wanted to do something right for a change. And Dennis was right in that sense. He was, I mean, he is a lovely man; kind, intelligent, civilized. I'm still not sure why he married me. We got on well together, liked the same things. It just wasn't enough."

"And now you will take divorce?" Maya asked again.

"I can't," Nora repeated, "Ireland is a Catholic

country and divorce is not allowed. Not even for non-Catholics. Anyway, why bother. I'd never marry again."

"You two must be reconciled?"

"No," Nora said, a little impatiently. "People just break up in Ireland." As she said it she realised it seemed incredible and that now she was like all those other people with a broken marriage in Ireland. An outsider. A race apart. I don't care, she thought, but if I did?

"I don't want to think about my marriage now," Nora said, "it's an old problem."

"And your daughter Ciara," asked Maya, "how will she feel about finding out she has a sister?"

Nora had thought she knew what Ciara's reaction would be in any circumstances. Now, she faltered. "I'm not sure," she said. "Ciara is my sole heir. That's occurred to me. Have I the right to change that?"

"And also you must consider her in-laws?" Maya asked. She got up and brought a basin of water and a towel to wash Nora's face. "I think all these things roaming in the head are making you ill. It was not wise to travel today, tomorrow might be better. Now, we must attend to that handbag of yours. We will pretend you have just read these letters. So, they are read. What to do about this bolt from the sky?"

Maya leaned forward to dry Nora's face and sat back in her night sari, waiting.

"It's not one feeling," Nora explained, "it's like an attack of feelings. Sometimes, I feel I'm still twenty. It's like living through the whole thing again. No, not again. Living it now as if now was real and then was just a dream. I feel I'm in London and pregnant and don't know what to do. Yesterday, I even felt such relief when I thought my period was coming. And then I get so excited at the thought of Wrennie. I named her Patricia you know. They changed her name to Sara. Wrennie."

"Ah yes," Maya said softly, "like a little bird."

"When I think of her looking for me ... and then the idea of it makes me cringe, all the trouble she had finding me. If I meet her what will I say? How do you face a child you gave away?"

Nora sighed deeply. "I was twenty years old," she began again. "In the sixties I had to go to London. I thought if I didn't get to London I'd die. Away from home. Freedom. Art College, the Beatles, excitement, a real love affair. But it wasn't a real love affair. It was the pressure of the time. I was in London and a love affair was part of the scene. Is it very difficult for you to understand what I'm talking about?"

"It is hard when you talk fast, but I think I am understanding this. I was also hearing of the Beatles, even in this village. Now, I am glad not to be Western woman. I have not the courage. So much freedom, but who will protect? Who was the baby's father?"

Nora longed to tell Maya about R.D.but she held back and lost the moment.

"He was Indian," she said. "We were just young people in London in the sixties. Marriage had never entered my head and it never occurred to me that he'd ask and when he did I just couldn't. How could I go off to India? Yes, I know, if I'd cared enough, but in a way it was lucky I didn't. It would have been a disaster. Imagine me as an Indian wife, calling him Mr,and living with in-laws. Of course I know there are such marriages, but ..."

Now I know it wouldn't have worked, Nora thought.

"And he stayed there ...?" Maya asked.

"No, he went back to India that summer and was married by Christmas. His father sent for him. I couldn't understand how he could agree to an arranged marriage if he wanted to marry me, but he went home and got married. And never knew I was pregnant."

We had parted before I knew myself, Nora thought, and even if we had still been together I wouldn't have told him.

"It was R.D.? "Maya asked and seeing the frightened roundness of her eyes, Nora shook her head: "No, no. Of course not. It doesn't matter who it was now.

"Anyway, I got help from an Irish priest and landed in a home for girls in trouble and you know the rest. It was an impossible situation Maya, I wasn't callous. My father had died the year before, my mother wasn't well. It was a hard time for the family. How could I tell them and I couldn't face it on my own. How could I keep her? I mean, imagine if it happened to Kumari? Well, Ireland was like India in those days. Now, she's found me. I wonder if this would have happened if I hadn't come to India. I have this weird feeling that by coming here I've somehow turned the clock back."

Maya was crying.

"I am feeling how it was for you this suffering. Like cruel teeth of a trap." She got into bed beside Nora. "Your face is so pink. It is your heart bubbling over, I think. Tell me," she placed her hand over Nora's heart, "what would you do following this only?"

"I want to meet Wrennie. I know it is probably too late to be her mother, but I am her mother. Here, so far away, it seems like a dream that's possible; maybe it will be different, home in Dublin."

Nina came into her mind. "I mustn't expect her to be perfect just because she's my child, and she may be disappointed in me. Probably will ..."

They talked until Maya fell asleep with her arm across Nora, her foot curved over Nora's ankle. Nora lay thinking about her infant daughter and now and then Nina's face floated through her mind. Uneasy feelings about Nina had haunted her since the wedding and were now part of her fears about Wrennie. Wrennie must have been unhappy to have decided to track her down. How could she cope with that? She had no experience of an unhappy child. Ciara had always been so sunny. But Maya was right, thought Nora, this reunion was a miracle. How did one cope with a miracle?

A few years ago Wrennie's return would have been disastrous. Or would it? She realised she would have responded to it as a disaster so the rest of the family would have done the same. But I'm a different person now, Nora thought, I think it's great and I'm not going to let anyone make a B movie of this. They'll take their cue from me. Dennis, Ciara, Derry, Aunt Flo, Mrs Byrne, all my friends. In her mind she wrote letters to Ciara. She rehearsed telling each of the others and realised that, after the shock and the questions, they would all be with her and say that she should have told them, but they would realise why she could not. Wrennie. She could not decide whether to write "Dear Sara" or "Dear Wrennie".

Again, Nora's back crawled with ice and her face burned. The heat seemed to come from the weight in the back of her head. Maya murmured Hindi in her sleep and caressed Nora's arm. And Nora lifted Maya's hair off her face and surrendered to the weight of her own limbs.

Nora woke shivering. They were in a railway sleeper, alone. She was stretched across a seat and Maya sat on a cushion on the floor beside her. "We are almost home," Maya explained, "back in Agra. You have fever, perhaps a virus. Please take some of this." She poured the liquid between Nora's lips. Not since childhood had Nora had medicine from a bottle and her faith in it seemed to spread as the red syrup slid down her throat. Maya looked strained.

"What happened, how did we get here?" Nora asked. She was getting hotter and hotter and her eyeballs felt dry.

"It is another day since we talked," said Maya, "the doctor came and said you must go into our village clinic. I thought this is not wise for a foreigner. My brother helped me to get you here. We will be in Agra while it is not yet hot and I will take you to the nursing home. It is like Western hospital. You will see. Our doctor has given a note for Agra doctor."

Nora dozed off again. When she woke the train was in the station, and Maya went through the door and locked it on the other side. Air conditioned, Nora thought. She tried to get up, but any movement made her nauseous and she seemed to float in her bunk until Maya's apple green sari appeared and two spruce looking bearers placed Nora on a bier.

From a great distance, Nora heard Maya's instructions, as she was lifted onto the platform and carried along. So now I've become one of those sights on an Indian railway platform, she thought, and craned her neck to look around. As she whispered encouragement, Maya's hand pressed Nora's forehead back. At last they stopped and Nora felt her limbs being arranged into a car. Maya got in after her, propped Nora's head with a cushion and held her steady as the driver jerked through traffic. She pushed off her shawl, but Maya warned it was "too cold" and tucked a blanket tightly around her. Unbearably hot, Nora felt trapped, but too weak to protest.

They left the noise behind them for a while, the road free of traffic until they drove through grand gateposts topped with white eagles. "The European Nursing Home" Maya read from the plaque before they drove up a tree-lined avenue.

"Maya," Nora thought, overcome by gratitude. "Darling Maya."

Hands of unseen people lifted Nora onto a stretcher, and carried her over gravel, up steps, and across slippery floors as Maya kept pace alongside, talked excitedly in Hindi.

With relief, Nora's head touched the flatness of an Indian pillow, but she was too weak to talk. Maya lifted her head to give her water. Nora's feelings for Maya took all her energy as she smiled a smile that brought tears down her cheeks.

"It is because you are so good to me," she managed to say.

"And I must leave you in hospital," Maya said, "but I

229

will return soon with some things you need. Also, I will bring a camera. The second you are well we will need a camera. I am going Nora, but I am not leaving."

"I love you," Nora whispered.

"Ah yes," Maya whispered, "I know this. I also."

CHAPTER 23

"Why are you all alone in London, Dad?" Why indeed? He felt that he was going to cry. That took him by surprise. There was no point in feeling sorry for himself. It was natural to feel a bit flaky after all the years. Although away from Nora, he did not feel guilty or inadequate. Or not quite so inadequate.

He had intended going to a play on Saturday night, but the only person he knew was a woman he had met through the gallery, and when he rang her number he got an answering machine. Relieved, he decided to go alone, but did not get around to booking a ticket. There was really no need, he decided, he'd pick one up at the box office. He had a sense of there being odd spaces left in theatres. Single seats only, he seemed to remember being told so often in the past. There was always an empty seat waiting for the odd person. As things turned out, it was a rain drenched night and Dennis stayed at home.

He had taken to engaging himself in conversation, chatting back and forth in his head. He did not mind sitting through a play alone, he told himself, but would rather enjoy it in fact. It was the interval that was awkward. Still, in time he would get used to that too. Being alone felt uneasy. Even in a crowded theatre it felt like being in a vast space by oneself, a bit like being at sea without that exhilaration. It was a bad idea to hang about the flat at the weekend. A mistake to leave oneself at a loose end with time to get bored.

He ate rashers and eggs and watched television, but could not stop thinking of his life in Dublin. It had not been perfect, but a lot easier than this. It was not as though it had been a bad marriage. He and Nora got along together in so many ways. Not bad friends. Shared interests. They had reared a child together after all, that took a lifetime. Nora was getting on. It was not likely she would find the missing link now. Him neither. Not that he'd attempt that again. He could have been so content with Nora. If only. If she could just have settled for what they had. He had been more surprised than he realised when Nora had let him go without a fight, taken aback by how easy it had been, even though he had not planned what to do if she had wanted him to stay. And recently, it had begun to dawn on him that he had not thought things through well enough. He felt let down. If she had made the least attempt, perhaps. Now, everything seemed so unreal, an anticlimax.

Had he meant to leave for good? Yes, he told himself, it was the only thing to do, but he had never imagined it being like this. Never imagined it at all really. He knew that he was not too good at imagining and he felt cast adrift. Alone in his flat, it was as though everyone else had left the world. He'd had to do it, he told himself, especially when she hadn't shown a hint of wanting him to stay. Dennis could not have said why he had to leave. He had simply stayed with the plan after they had agreed on it. Nora had never given any indication that she might have changed her mind. And nothing else had changed.

Nowadays, his thoughts often dwelt on that weekend of Nora's thirtieth birthday. By the time they had finished dinner that Saturday night, his mellow mood ill-equipped him for what had happened. How could one be prepared for such an ordeal? He remembered he had been especially nice to Nora and had her birthday present organised.

Nora was in her sunken bath of bubbles in the

centre of the Cleopatra effort she had converted from
the Georgian bedroom. He had never felt comfortable
in that room with the silk screen and the tricky coral
lighting, mirrored wall, plants, plush carpet and all
the antique glass bottles everywhere. It made him
clumsy, afraid of knocking over things.

No one else they knew had a bathroom like that and
he thought it a bit much.

He recalled how Nora looked that night as her auburn
hair caught the light from the chandelier of glass soap
bubbles, her neck rising above the cloudy water.

"It looks like ass's milk," Dennis had said, smiling
down at her with admiration and tensed at the
expression on her face. She had taken his good-
humoured affection as an advance he had not
intended. He had been drying himself with a towel
and was suddenly aware of his nakedness. He tried
to appear nonchalant as he got out of the bathroom.

As he settled in bed he assumed the mood was past
when Nora arrived scented and expectant. She'd worn
the twenties night-gown and stroked his stomach.

Even when he continued to read she had kissed him
on the mouth. Remembering the rest, he squeezed his
eyes tight. In the morning, Nora announced pleasantly
that it was time they had a talk. Because she was
thirty now. They had to sit down and talk.

He'd been in good form after the week's sailing on
Flanagan's boat. Flanagan was a riot in Kinsale, the
lunatic. He had been on watch when he woke them
with a roar from the wheel: "All hands on deck ye
buggers. Look at this. Come up here. All hands, all
hands."

And out of sleep, they had all scrambled on deck,
bewildered at being roused on a calm night.

"Look there lads," he said holding onto the wheel
with a grin splitting his face. "Look there. Look at that:
water and stars and sky as far as the eye can see. Not
a cunt in sight. How about that?" The men had
groaned. Flanagan was a gynaecologist. Poor Flanagan,

233

Dennis thought. Tinkering under women's bonnets. Not something he'd fancy himself, and Flanagan was not that far off the mark. A life on the ocean wave.

Life had been free of that during the years since then. Ever since that night. It had cleared the decks for him. Not that he'd ever been allowed to forget. There were always the barbs and reminders. Sex was probably like everything else, he'd told himself long ago. Either it was your thing or it wasn't and yet you could say you didn't care about anything else, but not that. People took that as a personal insult. Flanagan understood. Men understood better than women. It was supposed to be the other way round. Still, he missed Nora. Surely they could still be friends. Things need not be much different than they were. They could start again with a new understanding and leave the past behind. They must at least discuss the future. Perhaps, if he wrote and laid all the cards on the table. He jotted down a few headings and then put it in his wallet for when something else came to mind.

The day only began for Nora when Maya came and placed her hand on her forehead. She waited for it as one might the chiming of a clock, felt its healing, and smiled when Maya sighed with the relief of being back with her. She was convinced that it was Maya's care rather than the medicine which brought down her temperature.

After three days Nora's condition was diagnosed as P.U.O. – pyroxia of unknown origin. The diagnosis impressed Maya who said firmly: "Now, you will feel better," as though the sound of its name would shrivel the disease in Nora's body. Nora sat up between her long periods of sleep and Maya took the photograph for Sara. And when Nora asked for a magazine, she did not bring it because she could not find one which did not mention the on-going horrors of Bhopal. Instead, she brought the Gandhi book.

When at last Nora was hungry Maya brought a flask of chicken soup.

"Chicken broth?" said Nora inhaling the absence of spices, "did you get it from the hotel?"

"No," replied Maya, "I asked my non-veg neighbour and she was glad to make it for you. She agreed that it would build your strength. I read in an English magazine that broth of the chicken is good for invalids. It will make you pink again, help you fight this illness and the chicken was so fresh, not from the butcher's shop."

Maya tried not to think of the bird's last moments. The poultry man had told Nirmal to take a bird from the wire cages in his yard. The chosen chicken fought hard and escaped twice. Bravely, Maya had trotted down the lane after Nirmal who handed over his prisoner to the executioner, the servant of the neighbour. There was alarming commotion when the chicken got free for the third time. Maya joined in its final capture by standing to block the gate. Her neighbour's servant cornered the bird on the roof of a shed and before Maya could turn away, the fellow had chopped the bird's head off and was plucking out its feathers.

How was it possible that these things would not be in the soup about to be eaten? Ah yes, the magazine article about food for invalids had advised chicken broth, but Maya worried. True, it was an English recipe and Nora was a Britisher, but she could not forget the sight of the victim in the steaming soup with its yellow eggs floating about. A mother hen, not a chicken. Mother hen soup.

"Just the soup," she murmured to her neighbour, "not the body." On her way to the nursing home she had gone to the temple to make an offering on Nora's behalf while Nirmal stayed outside with the flask of soup.

The doctor refused to discharge Nora.

"I am perfectly fine," she said assertively, "I would be

more comfortable at home." He was not used to being spoken to like that and looked ruffled, but Maya understood. The soup in Nora's veins was making her fierce. She was affected by the creature's desperate struggle to escape.

"Maya, there's no need to fuss so much," Nora said," I can eat the hospital food."

"You will not eat hospital food," Maya replied firmly. "Here, I believe, they are cooking good meals, not typical of hospital, but there is not necessity for you to eat. You are not being without a soul in this world."

Nora argued that she was not a fussy eater. If she could eat at all she did not care what she ate so long as the spice was not too hot. In Ireland, she would eat hospital food if she were in hospital.

"Ah yes," Maya said, "I am hearing that. And in such food there is nothing. No love. Here, relatives are always cooking, even in the wards. And you have me, not just surrounded by strangers, only." Her voice softened. "So that is settled."

That afternoon they composed a letter to Sara. It began: "Dear Sara" and took over an hour to get right. Nora was tired and unsure. "Is it a bit gushy?" she asked Maya, "after all, I haven't seen her since she was an infant. It's not as if she remembers me."

Maya was also tired.

"What is this word 'gushy'?" she asked.

"It means saying too much with too much emotion, I think … mostly it means over-doing it and sounding insincere."

That decided Maya. Her face cleared and she picked up the letter, folded it carefully with the photograph of Nora within its sheets, her bangles jingling as she spread glue on the flap of the envelope and pressed it down.

"How can a mother be gushy?" she asked, "too much about a thing as this? A stiff upper lip is perhaps good for a soldier. Are you in the army? You do not feel this gushy?" she pronounced, waving the envelope slightly in her hand, "this is for your dearling daughter."

Once the letter was posted, Nora thought less about Sara, but more and more about her marriage, an attachment, Kesruji had said, that had dried her heart. An apt description of her problem with Dennis, Nora thought. An attachment not unlike what had happened long ago with R.D. Why had she taken so long to admit that her response to his love-making had always stopped short of passion? There was nothing new about that. But my heart is no longer dry, she thought.

CHAPTER 24

Nora realised that she was on the mend when the snake came back, as though the thing knew that she had been too sick to cope with it. And she felt caught again, trapped by this dream that was not like a dream. She was relieved to see that it had lost so much girth, but its movements still drained her.

"Of course it has returned," Maya said, "Kesruji said it is necessary. Bulk is a symbol of grossness, that I know, and the snake can be bad energy and growth. Both, I think. But if it is getting less, we will see what becomes of this visitor."

Wearily, Nora found herself praying as the holy woman had suggested. And even though the dream became more frequent, she kept on praying, encouraged by the example of the old man who meditated under the tree opposite her window.

After the first ten days in the European Nursing Home, Maya asked daily to take Nora home, but the doctor simply repeated: "When temperature is gone for twenty-four hours." The weather was pleasantly cool, like a good Irish summer, but towards one o'clock the air outside her window grew dense with spices and Nora's temperature increased so that she felt the need to lie down.

And Maya sat in a chair not so close to the window on this "winter's day" chatting and ready with the answers to Nora's undying curiosity about the Indian way of life.

At home, Maya was often sad. Ravi Basai struggled

238

with his own thoughts. It was hard to bear, being without a daughter in the house, and he assumed that it was this alone that pained Maya. He had not imagined what it would be like without Kumari. She had always made him feel good. "Daddy!" she'd exclaim when she opened the gates for him each night. He must get used to it. She would be fine, he consoled himself. Since she was born, he had worked for her wedding, her dowry, and now it had been all perfectly managed. Kumari's in-laws were well pleased. A nice boy, good family, what more could a father expect than to see a daughter settled? Naturally, the house was quiet, all her little friends gone too. But so quiet, and such emptiness.

Maya missed Kumari and realised how alone she was going to be when Nora left too. Naturally, Nora must leave. She had always known Nora would go home, but the letter decided it. Her dearling must go and meet her daughter, the daughter of an Indian father. That brought Nora closer, made her less of a foreigner.

Maya worried about Nora going home to be alone with no husband, no son, no mother-in-law, not even servants. Terrible. Perhaps it was different in Ireland, but how could it be? Nora would be all alone in a house. Why had fate brought them together if they must live on different sides of the world? Why? Only time would tell the answer to this mystery.

Maya was leaving to see Nora when her brother rang. "Sita has given birth to triplets. She has given Pavan three daughters," Simitra said and Maya winced at the accusation in his voice. It was her fault. When the doctor suspected twins, Chitra had wanted Sita to have "the test that tells the sex".

"Let it be," Maya advised, "even if one is another girl, the other will probably be boy. Maybe two sons," and Chitra had obeyed her elder sister-in-law.

In the night Sita had delivered twin girls, fallen

239

asleep exhausted and later surprised even the midwife with the third child. Daughters. I should not have interfered, Maya fretted. Now, all those girls. All might not live, but one must not hope. The existence of the three tiny brides tormented her all the way to the hospital.

"Triplets?" Nora asked, amazed, "not even twins, three of them? Oh Lord. What a handful. Well, at least there are plenty of people to mind them. It could be worse. Oh, that's three weddings, isn't it? Well, please God. Poor Mamaji. I must remember to call him Simitra, since he asked."

Her remarks calmed Maya. Nora was right. One must accept. What else? One must not think ill on these lives. If the babies live, we must accept and the worry will become an everyday thing. We will help. Mr Basai will be generous. Four to educate, dowries, weddings, poor Pavan, poor Simitra. Surely all three cannot survive?

Nora was talking about presents for the babies "... and something extra special for Sita, poor Sita, what a night's work. She should have three presents."

She does not understand at all, thought Maya. And yet she is right, she corrected herself. One must accept. I am thinking like a mother-in-law because she is gone, but I am not mother-in-law. Worse things than this must be accepted. Each day a little more. All may not live, Maya thought again. No, I am not wishing that, she told herself, it is a simple fact only that not all souls come to the world to stay.

There were two letters for Nora. Aunt Flo wrote to say that she was going to have her wedding at number forty-five.

Your house would be ideal. That way more people can be at it and I want Peter to meet all the people we know. Just close people. We can spend our honeymoon going back to New Zealand. Also, I intend to invite Dennis to the wedding, but Derry has some sort of bee in her bonnet, and says I should ask, so I'm mentioning it. He has always been one of my favourite people. She also says to tell you about Mrs Byrne, she's expecting and having trouble with that husband of hers again.

Dennis's white envelope was registered. What was he sending her? Just a letter. The length of it surprised Nora. They had not exchanged many letters through the years, but even on the telephone Dennis had a format. He'd say he had arrived safely, mention what artist he was going to see immediately, and finish by reminding her of something he'd asked her to do.

Dear Nora, he wrote now, everything is fine, except for the weather. I envy you in the sunshine. Business is slow, though I have a couple of young Irish artists and three pieces were sold before they went up. Is there anything exciting in the way of modern art out there?
Ringing India is a day's work. I got through to Agra the other day and a boy answered, at least it sounded like a boy, and he just kept shouting. I could hear him perfectly, but it must have been Hindi. Obviously he could not hear me. Infuriating, and impossible to discuss anything on a line like that. However, on second thoughts I realise that the phone would not have done for what I want to say although it would have been nice to hear your voice. We have so much to talk about and I want to say certain things. Twenty-one years is a long time, we can't just leave things. By now, I'm sure you've realised that we've been a bit hasty.

"We," Nora murmured. She read: *We need to think about the future and talk things out. You can't stay in India forever. I know you think that I went rushing off, but that decision we made was always there, between us. And if I'd assumed otherwise, that would have been as bad. I can see now that since that night I was never*

241

free of guilt and it was that which drove me to leave. Not that I don't still feel guilty, as well as missing you, but more adequate in myself even though I don't blame you for being so fed up with me. Also, it's not beyond the bounds of possibility that as the bride's father I was affected by wedding nerves the same as anyone else. I've thought a lot about us during the past months and you're the only person in the world for me. It may not be the sort of love you want, but if we could just talk. I can't help hoping that you might like to live in London for a while. You always did enjoy London. After all, we get on so well together for most of the time, except in that way. But surely now we are both getting on - sorry - I'm going to be fifty-three, it should not matter that much. If there was anyone else for you, anyone who could make you happy, I could let you go without a fuss, but there isn't, is there?

We could talk when I go to Aunt Flo's wedding. I expect she'll ask me. I'd hate to miss her wedding. You wouldn't want me to, would you? After all these years Nora, I feel that we've been hasty. I can just hear you repeat that sarcastically because I know you think our parting was all my fault. Perhaps you didn't intend to go through with it after all? It honestly did not occur to me, until it was too late, that possibly you might not have meant what you said about taking your life back when Ciara went. As a matter of fact that phrase of yours: "I'll take my life back," always hit home. In a way I did take your life and make you unhappy. Or rather, I failed to make you happy. I know you think that it didn't bother me and it's true that most of the time I was content, but when you cried or said something sarcastic it certainly did bother me. And always feeling in the wrong isn't easy to live with.

Now I'm going on too much. I've promised myself not to read this back because I might not send it. The one thing I want to say is that I think we should try again. At this stage in our lives, maybe we could get together on a different basis.

That idea you have about me marrying you for an alibi simply isn't true. I'm not homosexual. You were wrong there. There must be a lot of people like me. We just don't hear about them and it's not surprising that they don't declare themselves, because it is alright to be anything but disinterested in sex it seems. Especially men. I can't believe that marriage is so dependent upon sex. And we did manage to have Ciara. I'd better stop. Even from this distance I can feel you getting annoyed. All I want to say is that it seems such a waste, and could you think about it?

All my love always, Dennis.

He must have made notes, and the idea of him adding to his list in that methodical way he did before a business appointment, brought her to tears. "Could you think about it?" she heard him say. All alone in London. And she was annoyed with herself for thinking that. He was the one who had left. He left, announced it like that, two weeks before the wedding. He ruined the wedding for me, she thought as the feelings she had tried to leave in Dublin overtook her, and now here he is with his bloody "there, there" noises, making me feel guilty. Why the hell should I? He chose his moment and went. Got his pound of flesh. What other reason for such timing? Through all the years, he couldn't forget what happened but suddenly he thinks he can. Con-bloody-vient!

Nora wept until she was worn out and fell asleep.

Later, she reread bits of Dennis's letter and then all of it again. Glimpses of herself and Dennis blinked on and off but gradually, as she gathered her courage, the images stayed. And at last she was able to face it all.

Her thirtieth birthday. Time to do something about things. Politely, she had told Dennis that she wanted to talk. Seriously.

"No time like the present," he had said and she began: "Do you have any idea what it's like for me living a celibate life?"

243

She had not meant to say that, had rehearsed something quite different, but it had come out and in that voice. Her polite request for a talk had put him off his guard and the look on his face said "not that again".

"Is this the most important thing in the world?" he asked.

"It's important to me," Nora said, and when Dennis remained silent burst out: "It's important to the vast majority of people, it's why men and women get married. It's the reason for two sexes for God's sake."

"Perhaps that's the cart before the horse," Dennis said quietly ..."However, if we are going to have a talk let us observe the rules of discussion ..."

"It's not an academic debate," Nora raged, "sex is not a foreign food fetish. It is not unusual for husbands to make love to their wives. I haven't some kind of abnormal slant on things."

"We have a good life," Dennis continued, "a child, friends, we're very lucky, but naturally if you focus ..."

Nora had thought a lot in advance about this conversation. It was going to resolve everything. They would lay the problem bare and decide on a solution. She had rehearsed speeches and here was Dennis with no sense of all that.

"What's wrong with you?" Nora asked, "or is it me? Tell me then, what's wrong with me?"

His calm enraged her more.

"No, it's you," she had said. "You're like a fillet of fish. Your attitude about sex colours everything, no I mean it drains the colour out of everything. I'm married and I might as well be an old maid. I feel so cheated. Give me back my life, then. You bastard, why did you bloody marry me?"

"Because I love you," Dennis said, "please don't upset yourself. We can talk ..." He stopped at the sight of Nora's face.

"That can't be why. That's rubbish. That's not why you married me. I know. Don't think I'm a fool. I was your alibi. Wife and child, everything looking normal, you're a ..."

"And suppose that's true?" Dennis interrupted.

"And suppose that's true," Nora mimicked, taunting, "just so long as it looks right in public. The doctor says lots of women are in the same boat as me, lots of his patients have husbands who just got married to have an alibi, or hope they'd change. Well, you haven't. Were you afraid of being found out? Is that why you scurried into marriage? Because that's what you are, isn't it? Admit it. You're queer, a bloody ..." and she choked on the word.

She felt his disgust as he walked out of the room.

"I'll get you a cup of tea," Dennis said.

"Come near me with tea," Nora screamed, "and I'll hit you with it, you puff."

In her Indian hospital bed Nora flushed and was relieved to remember that in those days the word "gay" described someone like Aunt Flo and "closet" was an American cupboard. And she found satisfaction in admitting that even had she known the term she would not have shouted "closet gay". It had been all she could do not to shout worse. Later, she had wondered where she'd heard the ugly things that had been on her tongue. Did she really feel like that about homosexuality? And yet she'd called him those things. The intensity of her feelings had made her joints ache and her viciousness had hung about the house for days. Dennis had taken to the Other Room. When his birthday roses arrived for her she had simply left them in their cellophane on the hall table.

Eventually, they both had recovered enough to talk. It wasn't as though they did not care for each other, share so much in common, or have an otherwise pleasant life, they had agreed. They could be responsible, remain together until Ciara was married or left home, whichever happened first. Here Nora's rage threatened again. What about her life, her needs? But she could not have said, even to herself, that anything was more

245

important than the child. Now, she realised that there were no words for saying something like that in Ireland in the sixties, no words that questioned sacrifice for the sake of the children. "For the sake of the children," Nora thought, had become a code for the impotence people felt in a country where they could not end an unhappy marriage. Naturally, she had sacrificed her sexuality for Ciara's sake. Anything else was unthinkable, and Nora wondered that such a thing had even crossed her mind. Ciara came first. It was not as if he drank or went with other women, as her mother would have said. They would finish the job they had started and then be free to go their separate ways. If only it had been that simple, Nora thought, and did not let herself dwell on what had happened with R.D. and Leo.

"Not the most important thing in the world." She hated the way Dennis said that. It brought to mind the no-smell of nuns, loose false teeth, watery cabbage, floor polish.

What Dennis wants now, Nora thought, is things the way they were. She felt that "talking" would be a trap. What was the point? And if she rejected his request would it be the "tag on toe" behaviour that so horrified Maya? More and more she tried to look at herself through Maya's eyes, wanting to be blameless. As Nora felt the aching loneliness of lying beside the sleeping Dennis, she hoped that Maya would understand. She decided not to answer Dennis's letter until she felt a bit better. More detached. She had intended writing about Wrennie, but that would have to wait too.

In Victorian times, Nora reflected, Dennis would have been appreciated as a good husband. He was the perfect gentleman, she thought. Mr Ryan, a man who rarely bothered his wife and even then was quick about it. Nora had been amazed that such a non-event had caused Ciara's conception. Less intimate than an injection. And during the pregnancy she and Dennis had got along so well, become like brother and sister, a relationship that was comforting until Nora's hormones returned to normal.

Dennis's honeymoon virginity had embarrassed Nora and gradually revealed itself as a chronic state of mind. That first awkward time was the blue print for their sex lives. He didn't even notice that I wasn't a virgin, Nora recalled sourly, forgetting that this had been a relief at the time, and she had decided that such thoughts were beneath Dennis. She'd thought that perhaps he had not been inside her long enough to know that she was not a virgin, a few thrusts was all, a restrained grunt and he settled down to sleep on his own side of the bed. Virginity was expected of an Irish bride in those days, and Nora remembered thinking, as Dennis slept, that in preparation for being a bride she had succeeded in becoming a virgin once again, one of the thousands of Irish girls who had come back from England after a baby or an abortion.

In the seventies, it had been easy for Nora to diagnose Dennis's sexual performance, a description of which jumped at her from women's magazines. Where once she had lapped information about house and garden and tips such as having something white at one's throat to hide the tiredness when hubby came home, now there were endless articles on sex, and problems like premature ejaculation that a woman could solve.

"It's curable," Nora assured him. Curious how all those articles imparted nothing about sex but the mechanics. Even then, she had sensed that something more subtle lay beneath their problem, something less obvious.

It took a while to get round to finding a therapist in Dublin, and when they did, Dennis hedged over going, and by the time he was ready to go, she'd gone off the idea. Eventually, Nora prepared the way and they went to "see about it" together. In the doctor's office there was a lot of chat about Sunday's game before any mention of "this little problem". The doctor seemed as reluctant as Dennis and having listened, asked a few questions without looking at either of them, said that he thought that they had left it a bit long. It would be difficult to put right now. Still if they felt they wanted to try, he gave them exercises he'd had copied from a book.

"Can we buy the book?" Nora asked.

"No, one chapter at a time. Anyway it's a text book."

Nora found the exercises boring. And felt guilty about that. Dennis snored half way through their third session.

"Sorry," he said, when irritated, she gave him a shake, "it's the heat." They were, as the chapter suggested, on the rug in front of the fireplace.

They were permitted to go only so far each night, and build up to what, in her mind, Nora called the "grand slam". Except that things never got that far. Dennis enjoyed the massage, but when it was her turn he did it all wrong. "Tell me how?" he asked, but she was too irritated. Then one night she said: "Oh let's forget it."

"You decided to give up," the doctor said.

Nora did not answer.

"We knew it would take commitment, co-operation from you both. You've both become so negatively conditioned. Trained yourselves away from it so to speak. The idea is to do the same thing in reverse. With positive conditioning. Perhaps you might like to think about psychotherapy ...?"

"Look," Nora had said, trying to keep her voice even, "Dennis is simply not interested. He's just doing the exercises for peace, he doesn't think it's important."

"Does it matter why he's doing it?"

"Of course it matters."

The doctor sighed heavily.

"Do you think he might be homosexual?" she asked.

"What do you think?"

She had been thinking so much about that, but felt disloyal, regretted having asked this fool of a man.

248

Dennis mentioned Nora's crankiness to the doctor. "Is it cranky to want a normal married life?" she asked and never went back to him again. But she couldn't leave it at that. Even if she and Dennis did get along well on one level, she was aware that she was getting along less and less well with herself. A love scene on television made her uncomfortable. She felt so lonely. And eventually, it was only when she had succeeded for a while with yet another diet that she felt any sense of self worth. It was the next doctor who provided her with the alibi theory. Now, the more she went back over it all, the more Nora became angry and confused and she took two of the Valium she had brought to India against emergencies.

At last Nora returned to Maya's house where the family doctor ordered further bed rest. Maya was with her when they heard Ashoke's motor cycle and the sounds of Nirmal opening the gates for him. Maya was still tidying her sari when Ashoke strode across the roof from the stairs. He slid back the doors of Nora's room: "Mother, how could you do such a cruel thing? Why did you not speak to me? Divya's parents are coming. They will take her out of college, back to the village and she is a first rate student. You have put all the blame on this girl. Am I not a man? It is all my fault, my doing, but she is punished ..."

He was moving backwards as though by the power of Maya's fragile hands as she held them up on her way towards the door.

"You are not seeing our guest is resting? No *namaste*? This is not the place to discuss. Come!"

They bumped into each other at the door before they disappeared, but Nora could hear them.

"You must explain to her parents that it is my doing," Ashoke insisted, "do not let them take her away from medical college."

Maya answered in Hindi even though her son continued in English as they moved out of ear shot.

Maya brought milk laced with ground almonds.

"What happened with Ashoke?" Nora asked. He had not come to say goodbye.

"I have done my duty," Maya replied, "and he is thinking I am enemy. One day he will realise the truth and be grateful. Even my mother-in-law heard about this matter, a lady who does not go out of the courtyard. She is concerned. I spoke to a friend who spoke to the girl's parents. The matter is settled."

"But Ashoke is so worried that she will be removed from college."

"Agra has not the only medical college in the country. If this girl is so smart she can enter elsewhere. Also, she was not appreciating education when she was telephoning my son."

"Telephoning? Is that all she did?"

"That is sufficient. Also, they were seen together." And Maya emphasised: "They were seen at the Taj Mahal itself. It has gone far. She will snatch this boy away."

Nora looked at Maya in silence. So much for Mr Basai's claim that "this caste thing" was not a consideration in his family, that it was going from India.

"Don't look like this, you cannot understand," Maya's voice shook, "all is wrong, this girl is wrong for Ashoke. He is also much too young. Her family is not for us."

"Wrong caste," Nora said.

"Not caste only," Maya replied.

"And it's always the woman's fault isn't it?" Nora said softly, "even poor Sita is in the dog-house for producing girls. I cannot believe that you will ruin this girl's career to protect Ashoke. I cannot believe ..."

"Then do not believe, if that is your wish," said Maya and turned away. Nora was left open mouthed, unaware that Maya trembled outside the door of her room. She has no idea how an Indian mother must work for all the family, Maya thought. So many things

to consider for the good of the family and now so many
worries at once. Pavan with all the daughters, this girl
trying to spoil Ashoke's future. And Nina. Nora did not
realise that Nina was such a problem, always talking
about going to London, insisting that she would find a
way to be free. At least she could protect Ashoke. She
could make such a match for him, but she must be
careful. And in the end he would not hurt his mother.
Not Ashoke. Let the girl's parents have the worry of
her, no doubt they would not object if she snared
Ashoke. How could a foreigner understand such
complicated matters of India?

These differences were bound to arise, but they
always shocked both women, left each feeling
misunderstood, disillusioned, and insecure in their
relationship. East is east, Nora thought unhappily in
her room, it is no use pretending otherwise. Mean-
while, Maya vowed that if she ever went to Ireland she
would be tolerant, or at least pretend to tolerate how
matters were there. She would not say anything
against girls and boys searching each other out in
public places. One must tolerate.

It was not anger that lay between Nora and Maya on
such occasions, or even disagreement, but a shared
bruise that was healed out of their desire to bridge the
gap and end their individual loneliness.

Nora woke with a fright to shrieking, wailing, and
voices pleading. In her bare feet she went downstairs,
stopping to listen now and then. What was
happening? Were they having a row? Perhaps she
should go back up, but the distress in Maya's voice
compelled her to continue.

The noise came from Dadiji's room where Nora found
that Mr Basai and Maya were bent over the old
woman, pleading with her between talking to each
other in Hindi. The old woman thrashed about on her
bed trying to get free of them while Shanti, the wife of
Krishna who had replaced Thangamani, stood with

startled eyes and her sari pulled forward on her forhead like a hood.

"She is having a nightmare," Mr Basai told Nora, "it is necessary to hold to prevent her from hurting herself."

His mother's fever heated the room. Her wide eyes focused on something unbearable as she tried to break free.

"You hold," Maya panted in exhaustion. "Hold her here. I must give medicine."

Nora moved awkwardly out of the fear that paralysed her, and pressed the old woman's hips to the bed while Maya poured medicine onto a spoon and carefully tried to find her mother-in-law's mouth, but the old woman jerked her head about, splashing the liquid off the spoon and kept repeating something. Mr Basai's face was calm with understanding as he held his mother's shoulders, but tears ran down Maya's face.

"Again that dream," she said, "it has been years. I thought it was gone."

"What is it?" asked Nora.

"The custom is to break widow's bangles. Glass bangles are symbol of marriage." Maya said as she made another attempt with the spoon.

"When Father-in-law died, women had to force her, break the bangles off her wrist. After that she was ill for one year, a terrible year when Mr Basai was a small child. It is the high fever that has brought on this nightmare, look how she is protecting her wrists. Ah, the medicine is in." Maya had clamped up the old chin. "At times she wished to die, no doubt, but her father-in-law saved her from harm."

Nora watched the old woman's struggle. "Tell her to break the bangles herself," she said, and the family looked at each other.

"Do as she says," Ashoke said to his parents. Mr Basai hesitated before speaking to his mother. Again and again he pleaded with the old woman until

252

Ashoke nudged him out of the way and put his arm around his grandmother, tenderly coaxing. "Dadiji," he kept repeating, encouraging and promising, until at last the old woman quietened. Either her grandson's voice had penetrated or the medicine had worked. Tentatively, everyone took their hands away, ready to grab her again. She lay back and stared at her huge hands. Tears ran down her face as she turned her naked wrists back and forth looking at the bangles of her youth. Then she squeezed the fingers of one hand together to slip them through. She handed the invisible bangles to Maya. Now, Dadiji made her other hand small enough to squeeze off the rest of her bangles. She stared again at her wrists and suddenly grabbed the bangles she had given Maya and threw them hard at the floor. Nora jumped as she imagined they smashed.

Mr Basai turned away.

His eyes wet, Ashoke rested his cheek on his grandmother's head while she sobbed, until she began to retch. And she continued to retch as if trying to cough something up. Everyone was petrified as her body worked with jerking movements. At last, something seemed to dislodge. Invisibly, it came up and out and the old woman stared at it beside her on the bed. The rest of them stared at the empty space on the sheet. The old woman breathed deeply several times as if to prove to herself that she could, before she lay down, sobbing as one prepared to cry for a long time. Ashoke wrapped a blanket around his grandmother, and with his eyes told everyone else to leave.

Tea was brought and Ravi Basai took his cup to the middle room. Maya and Nora sat in the garden. "That was a wise way of yours," Maya said, "how are you knowing this solution?" But before Nora could answer she said: "Drink your tea, I wish to show you something."

What she wished to show was on the wall of Ravi Basai's study. Nora thought it was a portrait of Ashoke wearing a turban which had been moved from the middle room.

"No," Maya said smiling at the youth, "it is not Ashoke. This is a portrait of my father-in-law only two years before he died. For so many years she is mourning the death of this young husband. She was married for five years only, widow for forty-five. So I can tolerate even when she is fierce. Something else I will show you."

Maya opened a cupboard and took out a portrait of a matching size. It was her mother-in-law in all her aged fury.

"R.D. painted it," Maya said, "he brought it to the wedding. One day it will hang beside this boy. Who will guess that they were husband and wife?"

The paintings, the room were too much for Nora. She shivered and realised that she wore only her nightshirt.

"Come," Maya said, " we both must take rest."

Nora slept through Virgoe's early morning grumbling and the Muslims, and even the sound of Ashoke's cycle taking off. The women were drying their hair in the sun when Dadiji came out of her room. The whiteness of her sari dazzled towards them: "Your health is improved?" she asked Nora abruptly.

"Yes thank you," Nora said, surprised that the elder spoke English. She studied Nora. "See that she does not catch cold," she ordered Maya, "and give her cow's milk to drink." She turned and struggled back to her quarters.

In the freshness of early morning, Nora watched the young married couple play where the pandol had been, the lawn still patchy after the wedding ceremony. She could hear the mali working around the corner of the house as he prodded the dry earth with his hoe, muttering: "Ram, Ram, Ram," and thought that Kumari's laughter mocked the old man's preparation for the next life. The appearance of the bridal couple must have driven him away from where he usually worked at this hour.

Kumari and Prakesh were back at the bride's home after a month of marriage, before travelling to Prakesh's post in Orissa. The visit was traditional. In the orthodox way, Kumari was back to reassure her parents before she settled. The visit demonstrated, Maya had said, that the bride's in-laws were treating her well and recognised the respect due her origins. Prakesh was singing and dancing around the bushes, like the hero of a Hindi movie working up to a love scene. From a safe distance, Kumari, still in her night sari, was imitating him in a squeeky, ridiculing voice.

Nora went to have her bath from the two buckets of water standing ready. Yesterday, she had written to Ciara:

... arranged marriage seems to work as often as ours, and strange as it may seem, I don't look upon it askance now. Admittedly, the relentless way it's brought about can be frightening, with so many considerations.

Kumari didn't want to get married, I'm sure, but she didn't want to be single either. It's hard to be single in India, although around Gandhi's time there were many women who didn't marry because he so believed in celibacy as a positive thing. In any case it controlled the population and it left them free to work for India. One hears of them, women in their sixties who have sacrificed themselves in the cause of others. There isn't much of that idealism left, I think, but maybe more than I know. Certainly, not much population control. Young people seem to fall in love after they are married. They might as well. Isn't it surprising how we do what's expected of us without even realising that we are, or for that matter, what is expected?

When Nora had dressed, Prakesh and Kumari were still in the garden. Maya was sitting behind a tea tray under her rose arbour and Nora joined her to sip tea as the newly-weds horse-played around the jasmine

255

tree. Maya seemed edgy. At last she sighed: "Oh dear".

Nora followed the direction of her eyes. Kumari had the garden hose turned on Prakesh. He was yelling, his white khurta drenched, an arm across his head as he ducked under the water to take the hose.

"This is too much," Maya said. "All this playing. They are not children. All the time is the same this playing. What I will do? We did not settle our daughter for child's play. What I will do?"

"So," Nora said to Kumari who had come to her room, "marriage is not so bad after all?"

Kumari blushed: "I will say this is your doing. On the wedding train itself we talked about what you said, about getting to know each other first. Prakesh says you are a wise lady. He agreed that we have our whole lives as you said, but we were both so worried about this first night, so we have postponed. You were right, he also was worried about this thing. We have decided to wait."

Nora heard Dennis's words, *not the most important thing in the world.* Perhaps if both people felt like that, but then what had she done? And she could not bring herself to inquire how long the couple had decided to wait.

CHAPTER 25

Mr Basai made his voice cheerful. "Come, I will drive you to the Taj," he said after the three turned, sad from waving Kumari and Prakesh off, and Nora realised that this was the beginning of the end, the last time they would visit the monument before she left India.

Reminded that he had not always been in the mood to take Maya to the Taj, Ravi Basai would have shrugged at the foolishness of youth. Now, he understood women better. His wife had explained to him that those awkward silences of hers were "for thinking" and sometimes to avoid saying what was better left unsaid. He could never guess which it was but he knew that a visit to the Taj improved matters.

Ravi Basai had been alarmed when he first saw Nora at Agra airport, hair glinting red in the sun and white trousers, but after all, the Irish woman had given no cause for worry and had adapted to the household very well. It was a pity she must go, but naturally, she must. Odd that she came without Ryan, but men had work. And he thought that he might permit Maya to visit Ireland. The women had become like sisters, it was too bad that Maya must lose such company in the home. She would have more time to think about Kumari now, but that was no more than the nature of things. And there were the triplets and Ashoke. Mrs Nora would be gone when he came back from his mango groves, Mr Basai thought as he parked the car outside the Taj Mahal. He would instruct Ashoke to come home and attend to her departure. As he handed the Taj entrance tickets to Maya, he said to Nora. "I regret that you must leave before I return. I hope that you have a pleasant journey. And do not forget this ashram for Western seekers which we are planning to establish."

"Oh," Nora said, "thank you, thank you so much for everything," and standing on tip-toe she kissed Ravi Basai's cheek. "Thank you for having me, for such warm hospitality."

He had prepared himself to shake hands with a woman, which was awkward enough, and now he glanced around to see if anyone had seen. "Have a safe journey," he said aware that he still held Nora's hand. He shook it until she took it back.

"You too," she said, and found herself at a loss of what else to say.

"Yes, yes," he replied swaying his head before he hurried off.

"He is not accustomed to kissing," Maya said, "but he is realising affection."

Nora watched Mr Basai get into his car and felt a tinge of guilt. She wondered what he thought about herself and Maya. "He was so kind to me," she said.

"Ah yes," replied Maya, "naturally."

As they passed beneath the portals of the Taj, Maya began: "look, in this light how clear are the flowers all over Taj. Shah Jahan was thinking of fresh flowers here forever I think, but even he must compromise. So instead they are flowers of the semi-precious stones of India looking like real flowers."

She's branding my memory, Nora thought, as though I could ever forget this place, and the time we've spent here. Her sadness sharpened.

They stayed until closing time, clutching at the minutes even though each told herself they would be back there together. And driving away from the Taj Mahal in a taxi, they looked out of opposite windows to hold back their tears.

They roamed around the shops in the bazaar where they had spent so much time, and in the cool of the evening took snacks from the vendors - hot cashew nuts, grated potatoes spiced and sizzled crisp on a griddle. Maya fed bite-sized puffs to Nora who winced when the spice exploded in her mouth but distracted her from the ache in her throat. And in the rug shop Maya bought Nora yet another "reminder of Agra," a beautiful prayer mat. "It will easily fit in your case and you can hang it on your wall," and while she was paying for it Nora bought one for her knowing that Maya would use it for meditation. Reluctant to end the day, they did not leave the bazaar until the mats grew too heavy and awkward to carry.

Maya changed into the sari with the elephant border and helped Nora pleat the coral silk they had chosen together in Rajasthan.

Their supper was laid out as a picnic on the roof, with lights floating in tiny clay boats midst the dishes, and because the moon was almost full Maya put up a large black parasol to protect their heads.

"I had a letter from my husband," Nora said, "he wants me to come back."

"Ah yes," Maya said, "I am sure that he does. A husband will be lost without a wife, isn't it? Probably the poor man is suffering." She tore a paratha and waited for Nora to speak.

"I don't see how I can take him back," Nora said, "I feel so angry, and what is the point? I used to get so ... so lonely with Dennis. We never had what you could call a normal marriage." Nora was suddenly embarrassed. "We have one child, but ..."

"Poor Rajendra is also not having a son, but he has these two nephews, so ..."

"No, it wasn't that, although I dare say we might have had one, but Dennis prefers to be celibate." There, it was said. Nora's throat relaxed.

"I also would prefer that," said Maya easily. "A

259

woman must have children. But otherwise? He has philosophical reason?" She knew of only two types of men, those like her father and the opposite, like Mr Basai. There were few like her father these days. Mr Basai was even more demanding since the vasectomy, but how could a woman complain when there was no fear of pregnancy? Everything passed, she thought. Now he was getting older.

Nora had considered showing Maya Dennis's letter, but could not. Instead, she said: "Dennis's letter made me feel guilty. It must have been awful for him too. I always blamed him, didn't let him forget. Even when I did not care anymore, something would remind me and I'd blame him. It could be just something on television that reminded me, started me off."

Nora found it impossible to express what she felt about her marriage, how cut off she had come to feel. Even from herself. She remembered the feeling of dishonesty she had sometimes, as though she and Dennis were pretending to be something they were not.

"We lived like brother and sister," she said. "I don't like the thought of him being lonely, but I can't go back to square one."

"Square one?"

"The way I was before, before I came to India, before we met, half alive, and so alone. Numb."

"Indian womans do not think sex is so important ... For most of my life I have not."

"But you were worried about Kumari?"

"Ah yes, she must produce first, but after ..." Maya swayed her head.

"They seem so happy," Nora said.

"Always this happy, happy," Maya said, "there are other considerations. If happy even, one cannot stay like that all through the life. A different happiness, more lasting, comes from duty." She did not look at Nora. "In my country," she continued, "duty is first, always first thing."

"And our duty to ourselves?" Nora asked, "what about us? You and me."

"First are many duties. Why you and me, we came together I cannot know. There is reason, no doubt. For now we can dream, but we cannot live fairy-tale happiness. Reality is there." She was sure that the slippery goal of happiness was the cause of much misery in the West and in spite of an effort to be tolerant, she said: "and in West, how many happy people you are having? More than we? Who is knowing? Not so simple."

"The thing is," Nora said, "I thought I'd be happy if only I had a normal marriage. Now, I'm beginning to realise that wasn't what I wanted. I mean I only thought I wanted a marriage. I did not see when I was young that I might not be the same as other girls, not want what was expected of me. What I expected of myself. And I wanted to be like everyone else. I couldn't admit to myself that I might be different. I thought Dennis made me feel rejected, but after all, I chose Dennis. Maybe I'm bi-sexual?"

Maya was not sure what that meant, but said: "A person is the way she is. Sometimes we cannot be that way. We have to do one way and smother other. Wimmen," she pronounced the word carefully, "have not the choices. And always, we must try to include, not destroy."

She watched the ant wriggle into the fold of Nora's elbow and reaching out to take the pale arm, she brushed the insect away. "It has not become brown," she said. Nora turned her arm over and placed it beside Maya's. "Barely beige was all I hoped for," she said, "and yours has not become white."

Maya stroked the golden down on Nora's forearm and leaned forward to caress her throat with the back of her forefinger. "Everything is the way it is supposed to be,"she said. A balm of healing spread through Nora. Everything is the way it is supposed to be, she repeated to herself, and thought that she must keep telling herself that, hang on to it as she felt Maya's hair cool and smooth against her cheek, while Maya sighed at the feel of Nora's curls against her ear.

In the mirror Nora could see the silken pool of sari where it had slipped out of its folds onto the floor. Maya woke and moved back into the hollow of Nora's shoulder.

"I was sleeping?" she said, "I left you alone?"

"I slept too," she said, "it is gone four in the morning, my favourite time in India when things stop ..." She was interrupted by a blast from a transistor radio across the roof tops and they laughed. "For a moment or two," Nora said.

"The earth wakes first, doesn't it?" she asked Maya.

"No," Maya said, muffled against Nora's breast, "the workers in the sugar cane are first. If you sit out there and listen, soon there will be sounds in the sugar field before the Muslims call, then maybe the earth and the insects."

"I still can't hear that, it's too far away."

"That is because you do not know for what you are listening." They were silent for a moment before Maya spoke. "I wish to tell you secret."

"What secret?"

"Secret I have never said. No one is knowing this secret, but now I can tell. I had love like this in college. After my fiancé married other one, there was someone. A girl from my own village. We were so happy. Like now, while everyone is sleeping, no others in the world, just we two. She said we must go away together, maybe Calcutta, but this dream of hers is impossible, entirely not practical. How we can do such a thing? She came to my wedding. It was torture for her, but all her family members were invited so she must come. A match was found for her at my wedding. Often at weddings it happens like this. She was married one year and one half year later. I did not go to her wedding because mother-in-law was ill that time, so I always remember her at my wedding only. I see her now," Maya rubbed her forehead with four fingers. "She looks at me with such a look in her eyes. I was in the back of the bullock cart leaving my village, all my dowry things around me. I felt bad for so long knowing that she comes before husband in my heart. No, please, let me say all. I could not love husband like that. Like this. I used to wish he was woman. Foolishness. He is always husband. Not cruel husband, just husband. Good husband, it is only fair to say. For years I felt like, like ..." Maya searched for a word. "It must be like exile," she concluded pleased with having found the word. "Exile," she repeated and Nora held her closer.

"This love of mine was married. She was a brave spirit, but how could she tolerate being a wife? To her it was violence. I could tolerate, but she ... She died giving birth to her first born. A son, she had. In that way, at least, she was triumphant. No one could say against her. Even so, I think that upon the cremation ground itself, marriage was arranged for her husband." Shivering, Maya suddenly sobbed.

Nora held her, overwhelmed by realisation. She had taken Maya's obedience to tradition for granted. Traditional, obedient Maya, as brave as India, but Maya had not deluded herself. She had not passed her time in longing for the right man, or wasted time in longing for the man to be right. As I have, Nora thought, and quite suddenly Nora felt that she was no longer angry with Dennis. And that was enough for now, she had more thinking to do but not now. Contentedly, she followed Maya into sleep.

Had the snake whispered her name? Maya was still asleep. Nora waited, aware that something different was about to happen. She stared ahead able to see the snake on the carpet beside her bed, as though through the side of her head. She saw that the creature br-e-a-t-h-e-d slowly, carefully, seeming within its swollenness to have just discovered how to breathe.

Nora felt herself compelled to breath in rhythm with the creature and with each breath found herself able to breathe deeper still.

She closed her eyes upon a feast of air and when she opened them the room was bright.

The snake grew slimmer. With each breath it had stretched longer and as it did Nora felt her own body lightening. The snake began to squirm, imperceptibly at first in pace with the depth of its breathing until it gradually gathered speed upon more shallow breaths and became all movement, travelling fast within its coils without displacing itself or going anywhere. Again, Nora rested her eyes. When she opened them the snake was even thinner and squirmed still faster. As she watched it become as thin as an eel, she recognised the familiar feeling of acceptance and distaste she felt when she looked into a mirror.

Now, instead of its scaly murky brown, it had become softly green, but recalling its former bulk and grossness, Nora sickened with revulsion. The snake moved smooth and fast within coils without beginning or end. There was a moistness at its centre, a greener greenness that somehow became liquid, a pool into which the snake began to slip away, sinking, slithering ever thinner beneath the surface of the water.

A cloud dimmed the light. Nora felt an umbilical cord slither from her vagina as she had twice before and knew that the snake was still now, only its breath above the water. She closed her eyes for a few seconds and then for the first time since its appearance in Bombay, Nora turned her head to look and forgot to breathe. Floating on a little pond was a lotus blossom whose petals had been pushed open by a glow of light. The flower closed slowly upon dewy drops until it became something else in a pool of light and although she could not see what that was, Nora knew that the heart-shaped light was her own.

She felt as though she had shed a heavy coat in the

264

heat. She was free, light with relief. And scoured clean. She sighed, thought about more sleep when the call to prayer rose above Agra, and Maya stretched her arms high above her head and opened her eyes.

CHAPTER 26

On the way to Bombay, R.D. had the feeling that
everything was going to work out after all, and realised
how jittery he had been lately. The daily whiskey had
become too many. No harm done. It had been whiskey
that led him to Nora in Basai's study. She'd promised
to see him in Delhi and added, she wanted to talk to
him about something. Why couldn't she say what it
was about? Probably Nina had invited herself to visit
Ireland as a chance to run about, get to London. She
would understand that this was more out of the
question than ever now. She would drop all that
nonsense when she heard the news.

Things had gone so wrong for Nora's visit. He had
hoped that with Maya's co-operation they could
arrange a trip together. Kerala. There was something
about Nora that had not changed at all, some essence
that at times made the past more real for him than
today. He'd like to have shown her Southern India. It
had occurred to him in the study and he had planned
to get Maya to organise it. But the assassination had
changed all that.

He should not have taken such a risk in Agra.
Naturally, he did not regret ... but everyone had
suffered enough, he must keep his nose clean. There
was no question now of inviting her home.

Sarla was no fool, she had been wary of Nora at
their first meeting, and she would have been like a
dervish if Nora had stayed around after she came
upon them in the study.

"Good," she had said when the women left to visit Vimla, "now there is peace to do what one must."

No, R.D. thought, not the house. Anyway, he and Nora needed privacy. Maya would understand and together they could take Nora to the airport.

Sarla had made a remarkable recovery during the past week. The renewed offer from Singh: "Let us put all this behind us and get on with the wedding," had stunned her at first, and she could not believe that things had taken such a happy turn. Even in her most desperate prayers such a solution to the disaster had never occurred to her.

Deepak Singh had recovered to take his family's reins, and Sarla felt herself rescued. She was suddenly starving, but did not wish to appear immediately recovered, for she was well aware of the effect of her devastation upon her husband and the rest of her household, but gradually, little by little she would improve. "I will take milk and almonds," she told the servant in R.D.'s hearing, and was rewarded by the look of relief which crossed her husband's face.

From the beginning, Sarla had feared what might happen if the charts were not consulted. An astrologer would have seen and avoided disaster. That simple thing done, they would not have acted in the dark, like fools arranging everything as if there was no greater power than their own wishes. Even the Britishers had a saying: "Man supposes, God disposes." Sarla knew that her father-in-law was of the same mind, but had remained silent. She decided that the old man was afraid of being thought old-fashioned in front of his foreign educated son.

This time, things would be done properly. She would make a pilgrimage, and the path would be prepared, the auspicious day chosen. And it was agreed to have the horoscopes matched. She had taken the girl's chart from the box in her almirah, the chart her husband had said they would not be needing when the match was being arranged, and chose a moment

267

when her father-in-law was in conversation with his son. The old man shrugged. Naturally, these things meant nothing, he cajoled R.D. They were superstitions only, so what harm? The charts had been matched at the Basai household so why not here? And if it made the woman happy? There was no arguing with that. It had been like a tomb in the house since the wedding was cancelled.

R.D. was pleased with himself. He had chosen well for his daughter, Singh's attitude proved that. He was a sound and honourable man. After all that had happened it would be understandable if he had changed his mind about Nina for his son, and about getting mixed up with a Hindu family. He admired the way Singh was not swayed by it all, would not place blame where it did not belong and refused to be dragged down to that level. He had made the point that his Sikh family had as little to do with Mrs Gandhi's death as the Das family were responsible for retaliation.

As the train raced towards Bombay, R.D. decided to make it up to his friend with a brotherly gesture. Singh's house had been cleaned out by the mob. Jewellery, sarees, money, a gift would be appropriate, and no doubt appreciated after the losses suffered. There had been no dowry demand. Yes, thought R.D., a gift between friends. For the sake of their children. And why not? It was only fair.

Although he would not allow it to intrude on his thoughts a sense of Nina niggled at him. And he convinced himself that this news would change his daughter's attitude which was probably temporary in any case. Almost a wife, she had turned against the whole idea.

"Daddy, I prefer not to marry after this. Please," she had repeated, "let us forget about this wedding business now. I was going back to college later anyway, so let me return to Bombay and finish there. It is fate I tell you. I did not say before, but I must not marry. I do not wish to be housewife. If you give me the money it will cost I can start a different life. We can discuss this together. I will not have need of in-laws and a husband. I have no desire for this, please believe. I was doing my duty only. No marriage, I beg you?"

He had ordered her not to speak to her mother of this. Where had such an idea come from? Shock, it must be.

"And what will you do without a husband, no children, yourself only," he had asked, and more gently: "Parents do not live forever. I thought you liked this boy?"

Nina did not answer the question.

"Don't you see, Daddy, you are spending so much money for my marriage, but if I have money I can make a good life. When I qualify I can work. Marriage is not essential for survival. I am not eager ...."

"Suddenly, you have this notion. I cannot take this seriously. We will fix a future for you, never fear."

"Please Daddy, I thought of this before, but I could not say. The assassination changed everything. Fate has taken a hand." Her father was looking at her in silence as he often did when he wanted to pacify her without giving in.

She grabbed at the opportunity. "Even let me wait a couple of years to see then. Only, not so soon only, I beg you, do not think of another match for me until two years at least."

"We'll see," he said.

He had not enjoyed going against Sarla in the matter of Nina returning to study in Bombay. She had so wanted to keep the girl at home, safe from gossips who knew that she had gone home to Delhi to be a bride. Sarla had pleaded with him, puffy eyed and plunged into another collapse. And being fed up himself, R.D. had decided to let the girl go. She would be better out of the house for a while, a change of scene could work wonders. And so he had taken Nina back to her hostel in Bombay.

After a decent interval, R.D. had intended to try for another match, perhaps in London. He did not want to believe his eyes but at Kumari's wedding he saw that his daughter did not look well. Sometimes it happened as quickly as that. The girl had lost her bloom. Time was a consideration. The idea of a London match had occurred to him after they heard through the brother of one of Nina's friends at the hostel that Nina was saving her money to go out from India. He had calmed Sarla with the question: "So, if she has enough for the fare, how will she get a visa?" Yet, he worried that Nina could find a way.

When R.D. visited Singh the convalescing man sensed his worry. "My son has the notion that the marriage was not to be, you understand. It is not that he is not liking your girl, naturally not that. He is uneasy about marrying a Hindu after what happened." He shrugged."This will pass. We will not heed. The children will do their duty and all will be fine. Let her do this set of exams, live at her hostel. I am glad to have your Nina for my daughter-in-law. All will come well. In time, you understand."

R.D. sighed. Tonight he would take Nina for a meal at a five star, and let her choose which one. She would like that, probably the Taj. He would tell her the news then. And tomorrow they could go shopping on the Queen's Road, more wedding sarees for the women, especially the Singh women, so much had been destroyed when the Singh's home was attacked. Then on to the gold market. These notions of hers would pass. Naturally, she had suffered a shock.

R.D. was always wary of a woman's change of heart even in lesser matters than this, a wariness that had its origin in the blow dealt by the young Nora when she had turned him down in London. Utterly unpredictable. It had never crossed his mind that she might not accept his proposal after she had let him make love to her.

It was only since Nora's arrival in India that R.D.'s

memory had begun to present the past like a cat laying its dead prey at one's feet. Even inviting the Ryans to the wedding had been done in response to the invitation to their daughter's wedding. He was, after all, a civilised man. A man of the world he told himself. He was bound to return the courtesy of their invitation. He had not expected them to accept, and he was taken aback when Nora came alone.

For years R.D. had refused to think about his departure from London. There was no point. His dream had died, and a month later he had obeyed his father's call. Things were destined. He had agonised, struggled to overcome his beliefs and sense of duty before deciding that he had to have Nora as his wife. And after all, his proposal had meant nothing to her. How that had seared him. It had all been for nothing, about nothing. He had forgotten who he was and become just another Indian fool sucked in by foreign ways. But he had got himself back on course.

Now he could not dismiss Nora from his mind. After all this time she was back. In India. Alone. That first sight of her on Basai's desk and he was a young man again. When she came to Delhi ... but he must be careful.

As R.D. came out of Victoria Terminus, he hailed a taxi to take him to his hotel and rang the hostel. There was no answer. He showered and rang again. This time he was left holding the phone when the girl who said she would fetch Nina had not returned after ten minutes. He rang again. Engaged. If he did not reach Nina soon, she would have gone into the dining hall and eaten the "filthy food". He took a taxi to the hostel.

The grounds were full of girls, and the chowkidah recognised R.D. and unlocked the gates. As R.D. strolled about he realised that his daughter's friends had become women. Quite a crop. When he did not find Nina he asked the Fernandez girl who had come for the wedding: "Is Nina somewhere about do you know?"

"I think she is in her room Uncle," Patricia Fernandez said, "I'll go quickly and fetch her." She hurried off, dhopalta blowing, and he sat on the stone bench to wait. He was enjoying the polite attention of a few of the girls, aware that he charmed them, when Patricia came back, calling: "Usha? Did you see Nina? She is not in her room. The door is locked. Her father is waiting."

"I saw her laughing with Leela, maybe they are in Leela's room. I am going there now, I will send her," the other girl said and Patricia saw that R.D. heard and nodded as girls crowded past him, smiling acknowledgement. Within minutes the dining hall was full, the yard was empty and the building seemed deserted.

He wrote a note.

Dear Nina, I came to take you out for a treat. Where are you? I'll ring first thing in the morning so take the day off and we will go shopping. Daddy.

He beckoned through the glass at Usha and as she took the note from him, he noticed her warm scent. "Please," she said, "come and eat with us. There is room at our table?" It crossed his mind to invite the girl to dinner. Instead, he declined her invitation.

Usha shrugged and aware that she had not called him "uncle", R.D. smiled.

The girls hung about in R.D's senses as he made his way to his favourite restaurant at Colaba. He was surprised by their effect on him, a bit uneasy with his reaction to Usha, although since the episode with Nora in Agra he found himself more aware of women. He welcomed this as a new lease of life, he had become far too settled in the past couple of years. After all, he shrugged, he was a man in his forties, and living a monk-like existence during the past months. He had permitted responsibility and worry to make an old man of him. Not any more, he decided as he pushed open the door of the restaurant.

Unlike most Indians, R.D. preferred eating out. He found restaurant service relaxing, a rest from the relentless attention of his wife who scurried back and forth from the kitchen and hovered, never sitting until his father left the table. R.D often felt dissatisfied with the food at home, but never said so. He knew how hard Sarla tried to please him. The trouble was that she had no idea how non-vegetarian dishes should taste because she could not bring herself to taste them. And it was from her village that, through the years, she had brought one dull cook after another.

Over dinner, R.D. thought about Nora and the pinkness of her face when they ate at London's Bombay Duck. The faint mist of perspiration on her upper lip, even though her food had no chilli, was the same when she lay asleep on Basai's desk. In London he'd never been able to take his eyes off her tender skin, the light of her hair.

"You're staring again," she'd say, and more than once: "Red heads are fierce you know, watch out." He had been surprised by her lack of fierceness. Remembering, R.D. thought that girls in London had never behaved like virgins even when they were. They seemed so free up to a point, impossible to anticipate. In bed, they were no more co-operative than an Indian bride. Nora had been so shy, so unsure. Sometimes, he and some of the other foreign men at the college had agreed, English girls did it because it was expected of them, but R.D. was convinced that he had not taken anything for granted.

Shaking himself out of the past, R.D. took out the letters he had been given as he left the house for Bombay. The writing on one envelope looked like a woman's. The post mark was January fifteenth, a week ago. A New Delhi post mark? From Nora. Clever of her to get it posted in Delhi, a letter from Agra might have been noticed. He was glad that she appreciated his position, and must have understood the formality of his farewell in Agra.

The letter began chattily and continued:

In spite of all the trouble, I've enjoyed India. She

273

recalled some of their East, West differences of years ago. *I feel I understand you better now,* she wrote, *now that I know India.*

He smiled. In three months, she knew India. She confirmed that she would meet him in New Delhi as promised and wanted to talk to him about something that she could not write. He thought that Sarla was probably right about Nora encouraging Nina to "visit her over there".

The rest of the letter soured R.D.'s mood. Nora regretted what had happened between them. It must not happen again. She loved someone else. She did not mean to be brutal, but that was the simple way of putting it.

Maya had booked a room for them at the All India Women's Conference Hostel where she was a member, and they could not have visitors there, so she would like to meet him over a meal. She deeply regretted any pain she might have caused him. She was sorry and hoped that they could meet in Delhi. With increasing rage R.D. reread her letter. She deeply regretted. So. Again, she regretted. But at the time it was only when she realised the risk of someone coming in on them that she had resisted. He was sure of that. Hadn't she said that there would be more time in Delhi?

Why hadn't she told him about this someone else then? Instead, she had said: "Someone will come. We can't." He could feel those fragile little hands on his chest, pushing him away.

"So, I will lock the door," he replied and had gone to the door, but there was no key.

She was on her feet, fixing her dress.

"No one will come," he said, his arms around her again, "nobody comes here."

"But you did," she said, "and Sarla or Nina or anyone ..." and she stopped to listen, placing a finger on his lips. "I'll see you in New Delhi," she said agitated, "I am leaving from there for Ireland. Anyway, there is something I wanted to talk to you about."

"What?" he murmured against her hair.

"Please R.D., we'll meet in Delhi. I'll come a couple of days early."

That sounded better: "Very well," he said, "I will find Basai's whiskey while you go back."

Furious, he put his glass down so that it banged on the table. Again. What a damn fool he was to fall for her pull and push game all over again. At this stage of life. How could you ever understand women, especially this one. All that play-acting, like a wife's modesty.

In love with someone else? Why hadn't she said? Someone else. In Ireland? Then what was she doing in India? Was that the reason for the break-up of her marriage? More likely that Ryan got fed up with her last minute changes of mind. Her unattainable offerings. There was another difference with these people, an Indian would solve his problem without disturbing the family.

When R.D. left the restaurant, he walked bad temperedly towards his hotel, with his good meal forgotten, and in no mood for sleep. Without making a conscious decision, he suddenly decided upon another destination, and smartening his step, soon turned into a busy gully dense with smells. There were vendors to one side, rubbish underfoot, shops on the left, hawkers and pimps who lit on him. Those who would not be ignored he swotted off with a movement of his head as anger hastened his way through the congestion.

Bangles jingled invitation from the verandahs, but he did not bother to look up. He was going to Clara's. He had gone there for the first time a decade ago, but had not been for a couple of years.

"Ah," Clara greeted him, "a long time, no see, eh? Last time you were thinking of settling your daughter?"

Sipping his Scotch, R.D. said: "Her wedding had to be cancelled," and brought her up to date.

"I am hearing many such stories from Delhi, but if all is ending well for you, that is fortunate. Now, I am settling my granddaughter ..." She swirled her drink in her glass, "and it is my turn to pay. I have expanded business, you'll see even my own private room is in use now. She is reaching sixteen and I give first rate dowry ... The younger the better, isn't it? Marriage is like this business. Everyone wants new, fresh." She was interrupted by a knock on the door. "Ah, that is you," she said, "the room is ready now."

R.D. had never been in Clara's own room. At one end was a living area with a kerosene stove upon which a kettle sat ready, with teacups on a cloth embroidered with flowers, and milk jug and sugar bowl covered with muslin. The television was draped with velvet. There was a trolley with bottles, a bowl of spicy snacks, a tin of dutch biscuits, an armchair with a footstool and an English landscape on the wall.

In the opposite end of the room from where R.D. had entered, was a large bed protected by a mosquito net. On the wall beside the bed, facing the door, hung an oil painting of an Indian village scene at sunset, all browns and oranges aglow in flame.

R.D. studied the picture for some minutes, tried to see the signature before he sat down, took off his shoes and lay on the bed. He turned down the oil lamp on the table under the picture.

This was more like it, he thought, aware of the whiskey's balm. Life was now. He had been acting the fool.

He was squinting at the picture again when he realised that the girl was there, her scent strong as she lay down beside him. She was slim and long, partly undressed. He stretched away from her to turn up the lamp. The light came on more brightly than he expected, but he left it and turned back. He looked into the horrified face of his daughter.

Her mouth shaped his name silently for seconds while she saw recognition turn to bewilderment and bewilderment become rage on his face.

"Daddy," Nina whimpered, "A-a-h-h. No-o-o-o-o-o."

Chapter 27

Leaving Agra reminded Nora of emigration scenes from her childhood. Even people she had barely met came and bid her a lingering farewell and though she promised to return it was obvious that most people did not believe they would see her again in this life. The servants and several of the "lady callers" cried, and the spice grinder's eyes looked about to spill red tears as she swayed her head in sadness and turned away.

Virgoe knew that she was leaving. Nora heard her grumbling and padding the spot where she was tethered, and slipped next door for yet another last rub of her cheek on the elephant's hide. When Kalu tried to lead the animal to the river she pulled away and would not be persuaded out of the compound. "It is a week since she smells you are going," Kalu said, "she is remembering those wedding sweets too well."

Nora had ordered a wedding treat for the elephant, sweetmeats made of chappati flour, molasses and cane in balls weighing more than a pound each. Halfway through eating the first one, Virgoe had trumpeted her pleasure and a crowd had come from the wedding house to see what was going on. "A most auspicious sound," Sunita Auntie had pronounced, and small infants had been passed under Virgoe's belly that they might grow up as fearless as an elephant.

People had brought so many farewell sweets for Nora, and now she brought them to share with the elephant who waved her trunk over the basket but would not take anything.

"I'll be back, I promise," Nora pleaded with her as she put a sweet to her trunk, and as though she understood, Virgoe took it and put it in her mouth, but then she sucked some of Nora's dress into her trunk so that she was almost lifted off the ground, and could not move. Kalu produced his whip, but Nora would not let him use it.

The pair stood there for more than ten minutes, while Nora stroked and coaxed the elephant and was not at all sure that Virgoe would ever let her go. The last minute callers slipped through the fence into the neighbour's compound to see what was happening and picking up Virgoe's grief, stood around dabbing at their eyes with the corners of their sarees. Maya had guessed this would happen and busied herself with re-packing Nora's cases to fit in farewell gifts.

Kalu was impatient with the giant female as everyone gave advice as to how she should be managed. Nora was feeling the strain of being held by the elephant with her feet barely holding the ground when Maya's mother-in-law appeared and shouted something in Hindi. Virgoe let go of Nora's dress. "She is evil cow today," Dadiji said but Nora had felt the tear roll from Virgoe's eye and held back her own while she nuzzled the wrinkled grey hide.

"You will be late on account of this elephant," Dadiji said gently, her face as fierce as ever. "You go. She must take water."

As she left, Nora felt the ache of Virgoe's grief on her back.

Ashoke drove them to the station, very much the man in charge. Having made every provision for their comfort and for their dignified boarding of the Taj Express, he offered his cheek for Nora's goodbye kiss. Nirmal, dreading what the foreigner might do, jumped to join his hands in salutation.

The women settled on the train as happily as

children on a school-trip, with thirty-six hours before they must part. Time to say anything that has not been said, thought Nora, time to make plans.

As they sipped their first cup of tea of the journey, Nora asked: "What will happen to that girl of Ashoke's?"

"Since you have pleaded her case, I must be merciful," Maya said in that way Nora always thought was joking, but which never was."

"His grandmother will speak to Ashoke about this matter. He will not displease her for anything, that I know. And my mother-in-law is wise in such things. He is young. True, the girl is also young, but she is knowing to snatch him. We will see."

Earlier, when Nora had found Maya packing bedding to take with them she decided against staying at the hostel in Delhi. There was no point in sacrificing comfort just to keep R.D. at bay, and she was relieved by how easy it was to get Maya to change to the Maurya Sheraton, "as my guest as I have been here." The idea amused Maya: "Why not? Certainly, I can be tourist in my own country. I can enjoy five star treatment."

And she accepted nothing short of that. Nora sensed that word of Maya spread among the staff so that they jumped to her every whim. Room service brought several people with the order and Maya had no difficulty in finding something for each one of them to do.

Nora spent most of a morning telephoning her goodbyes to Bombay. Sophie made her promise to return to India and Mother Bridgid told her that Leo was gone with tourists to Aurangabad, "but I will tell him you said goodbye".

"Ask him to give my love to Parvati?" Nora asked and there was silence before the nun said: "Yes, yes, God bless your journey."

They strolled around the hotel shops, visited the much scarred Connaught Place, and the Mahatma Gandhi Museum, but for the most part they enjoyed the gardens or cocooned themselves in their room. Maya had phoned R.D.'s house from Agra and learned that he had gone to Bombay and guessed that he would be back in time to see Nora off.

Nora was aware that R.D. had not been in touch. She wanted to tell him about Wrennie, but did not want to sacrifice any of her time with Maya.

On the morning of her last day in India Nora woke to find that Maya was not there although breakfast waited on the table. She knocked on their bathroom door, then put her head around it. Maya was sitting on the floor of the shower stall with two jugs and a bucket, giving herself a bath. And Nora realised that she must have ordered the utensils from room service.

"Why don't you use the shower?" she laughed.

"Avalanche," Maya replied, "it is too much. I prefer Indian way."

"Nonsense," Nora replied, "wait, I'll show you," but Maya was up off the floor in a flash.

Over breakfast she said: "You will fix with your child, your husband? You will return next year for our season of weddings?"

"Next year?" Nora panicked "But you said. . . I mean that's so far away. You promised to come to Ireland, to miss the heat and the monsoon, that we would travel together."

"I think I will not be able to spend so much money," Maya said quietly, "the government is not permitting to take out of the country and anyway there is not bottomless money."

"Please do not allow money to be a problem," Nora said and realised that Basai might object to her sending Maya tickets. She would send them anyway, after all she had lived in his house for months. He had even insisted on paying her hospital fees as well as never letting her put her hand to her purse for anything else.

"There are three more girls in my family now," Maya continued. "All may survive. How can I take pleasure trips? I said that Sita should not take amniocentesis. Now, I must share responsibility. No, do not shake your head. It is my doing that these three girls are born. It is my fault. We cannot ignore. Mr Basai agrees we must share responsibility. You are not understanding that in India these babies are sister-cousins to Kumari and Ashoke."

They avoided the subject for the rest of the day, but that night in bed Maya asked: "And still, what do you know about Indian ladies, or I about Western?"

"We know each other well enough," Nora replied. "Do our entire cultures have to come into it? I feel as if I have always known you."

"Ah yes, in here," Maya said, her hand over Nora's heart. "But even when new ways are possible for womans, wimmen I mean, the old ways are there. Life is jumble. We must include, not destroy."

"Why not keep the good things from the jumble," Nora said, "and let the other things fade away, the old ways that hurt us."

"Same ways do not hurt everyone," Maya replied, "and fear is also there." They lay for a long while, each aware of the back-drop of their lives and the people in their worlds. Wrennie, Ashoke, Dennis, Ciara, Kumari, Mr Basai, the triplets, Dadiji, Derry. Here, it seemed these people were part of both of them, all cares of a piece, but soon they would take their separate share. Separate responsibilities.

Nora blew her nose.

"You are not leaving dearling," Maya said, "you are just going on. And I am going with you. Also, you remain with me. We will be together always. Always meeting, always parting, and who knows? Who is ever knowing what will come? Everything is the way it is supposed to be."

R.D.'s roar was heard in other rooms, and in the street outside. He stood among the smashed furniture with scrambled thoughts pounding through his head. The preparation for the wedding, the wreckage when it was cancelled. Sarla's state because of it, the struggle to pick up the pieces and now the journey to Bombay to break the glad news to Nina. He breathed in the smell of kerosene, oblivious even to the figure of the unconcious girl before him. "She is the bride I wish for my son," he heard Singh say. And as the flames caught hold of his clothes his mind still swore at her. Bitch, bitch, bitch.

The women sitting in the street below scattered as the blazing figure appeared on the wooden verandah and crashed down towards them, knocking the charpoi over as it crashed into the soft drink stall. Then it lay still.

An old woman took the blanket from her shoulders and smothered the still smoking legs. Clara's place emptied into the street as the man from the boiled egg stand ran with a basin of water, but the fire was out. The body lay blackened, its neck twisted. R.D. was dead.

At first Clara did not give any information. What did she know? So many men. Naturally, there was kerosene in the room. For the lamp and the stove. How could she know how it had got splashed about? Yes, there were matches. People had heard noise, shouting, furniture falling, screams. And in a while she told them R. D.'s name. She did not know that the dead girl was his daughter. It took the police a couple of days to discover that.

Maya rang R.D.'s house while Nora was having her hair done. At least he must come to say goodbye to his guest. The phone was answered by Sarla's brother, Dharma. Sitting on the bed, Maya clutched the sari across her heart and struggled to cope with what was being said.

"Yes," she replied in Hindi, "I am here, but I cannot believe ... yes, I'll put her on the plane and then come. And no one knows what happened? No, it is better if she is not knowing. She would wish to stay. I will write this news. Better let her reach home. By then we may know what happened. No, no need to send car, I will take a taxi. I cannot believe. How could such a thing ...? Very well, send car. But do not come into the airport." She put down the telephone and hugged herself tight to smother the beginning of a cry. It came silently on her breath. As she breathed in again she folded her body onto her lap.

Nora felt the atmosphere even before she saw Maya rocking almost imperceptibly in dry eyed grief. She hurried to her, raising Maya's face with her hands Nora gave sound to the pain she saw there. She grasped Maya in her arms: "Maya? Oh Maya love, don't ..." and she rocked Maya in her arms. "Please don't or you'll start me off," she said, suddenly feeling herself to be the stronger one. "Maya, you said we'd always be together even when we are apart. I'll be back, and you'll come to Ireland.

"That can be your birthday present, a trip to Europe. We have so much to do. There are some wonders in the Western world you know, not the Taj Mahal, but you'll see."

It was going to be alright, Nora thought, as Maya made no move to free herself, but stayed in her arms for so long.

"Ah yes," Maya said at last, "it is hard to part, and I must also tell you that R.D. has been delayed in Bombay." Her voice was a whisper. "He will not be coming to see you off, after all. It is not to be helped."

It felt right. For now, her dearling needed to be protected from this news.

Nora barely noticed New Delhi shrink away beneath the plane. She had never known such anguish. Nor did she attempt to hold back the tears as she thought that if Maya had not been so distressed she would have been alright. She had been coping until she had found Maya on the bed, rocking like that. And then on the way to the airport she could feel the pain coming from Maya even though she had not shed a tear.

Nora cried for so long that without a word, the air hostess brought her a glass of water and a cup of coffee. She took aspirin with the water and as she drank the coffee which had grown luke warm, Nora remembered how she had put her feelings on hold for her flight to India, and thought that even if she could do that now, she would not wish to. She felt too alive. It was painful, but she was aware of something better within the grief, a growing peace with the truth. This pain was about leaving Maya, a pain she would prefer to the shock over the end of her numb marriage and her anxiety about being alone. It was going to be much easier to be alone with the person she was becoming than the person she had been.

Nora had not gone to India in search of anything, but felt she had found so much. Maya, Wrennie, Herself. Even Dennis. She heard Maya say: "Include, do not destroy." And she knew that she would have to talk to Dennis, but could never return to the way they had been. Above the clouds where she had believed there was no point in trying to think about anything, scenes from their lives replayed, in bed at night arranging themselves like strangers, escaping to the "Other Room" for a respite from the loneliness of each other's company, from a bed in which nothing happened. And she knew that she had dumped all that on Dennis's head, and blamed him for it. And he was probably as unaware as she had been. She had accused him of marrying an alibi, but so had she.

She recalled what had stirred in her when she saw Parvati walking down the hall. What had often stirred in her through the years, and she was able to accept those feelings in gentle waves of relief. Her heart had jumped when she first met Maya; those eyes, her roundness, the sari elephants, the way her voice went husky with emotion.

And Nora knew that Dennis could never have been the kind of husband that she had convinced herself she wanted. That was why she had chosen him. Had she ever wanted a man at all? Not beyond a point, she could admit now. Certainly not with a love that had nothing to do with anything but itself. She had run scared of R.D. in London. She had not merely been afraid of being an Indian wife in New Delhi, but really just afraid of R.D. and his love. His passion. And in Basai's study she had known that. And Leo? The memory made her cringe.

Instinctively, she knew that in this first flush of self-acceptance, she could not deal with Dennis. That decision would have to wait, but now at least she felt incapable of slipping back into the old life.

Kesruji had known about that, an attachment that dried the heart. What could be worse? She had fed her sexual frustration, disguised it and nursed it like an invalid child until it grew to a life of its own. Unrecognisable. Nora regretted that she had wasted so much of her life numbed by play-acting. No more of that. And yet, had she known, there would have been no Ciara, no Wrennie.

While she picked at a meal, Nora remembered the little package Maya had put in her handbag: "Open in flight". It was one of Maya's gold bangles and a note: "Dearling, please give this to my cousin Wrennie."

Nora sat up in her seat. Of course Maya had known. Why had it taken until this time of her life to meet someone like Maya? Woman or man. She smiled at the notion of there being a man like Maya. She had learned so much from Maya, she thought, for as bound as Maya was to tradition she had not allowed herself to be drowned in it, as she, from the liberated West, had almost done. She slipped the bangle on for safe-keeping, and went to the wash-room. The woman who looked at her out of the mirror above the wash-hand basin said: "I am not leaving, I am going on."